"I am not a mouse," she said in a firmer voice, almost managing to meet his gaze.

"They call you Lady Dormouse."

"That's not a very gentlemanly thing to point out."

"Ah, but I'm not much of a gentleman. How poorly we suit each other. It's a shame."

"Back out of our betrothal then," she said through tight lips. "I wish you would."

"I wish I could. I've tried to think of ways to do it, but there are more powerful forces forming this union." He stopped and turned to her, tilting up her chin with one gloved fingertip. "Besides that, I find you too fragile and innocent to humiliate with a broken betrothal. It would weigh on my conscience."

Even now, he mocked her. Everything about him made her cross. "I thought you abhorred my fragility and innocence."

He chuckled. "*Abhorred* is a very strong word. No, Aurelia, fragility and innocence aren't bad qualities in a wife. At least I'll know no one has trespassed before me when I mount you on our wedding night."

She drew in a breath as delicately as she could, when what she really needed to do was gasp for air. Of all the inappropriate and coarse things to say! She moved to pull away from him, to flee, but he grasped her hand.

"Does my forthright speech offend you?"

"You know it does," she said. "You...you impolite blackguard."

"Goodness, is that the best you can do? Lady Dormouse indeed. You ought to call me a bastard instead. A bleeding bastard, if you really want to make a point."

Aurelia looked around in alarm, but no one was near enough to hear this scandalous conversation. "Ladies don't talk that way," she said. "Gentlemen shouldn't either."

"And gentlemen shouldn't speak of mounting their brides. I know. That doesn't change the fact that it shall happen very shortly, my Aurelia."

Training Lady Townsend

by

Annabel Joseph

Other erotic romance by Annabel Joseph

Mercy
Cait and the Devil
Firebird
Deep in the Woods
Fortune
Owning Wednesday
Lily Mine
Comfort Object
Caressa's Knees
Odalisque
Command Performance
Cirque de Minuit
Bound in Blue
Master's Flame
Burn For You
Disciplining the Duchess
The Edge of the Earth (as Molly Joseph)
Waking Kiss
Fever Dream

Erotica by Annabel Joseph

Club Mephisto
Molly's Lips: Club Mephisto Retold

Coming soon

To Tame a Countess
My Naughty Minette
Under A Duke's Hand

For Erica, my Facebook pimper,
and Nina, Rose, and Jess
of the Twitter Fangirl Wars.

You make me smile every day.

Chapter One: The Ball

England, 1792

He would not submit.

Lady Dormouse, they called her. His reclusive bride-to-be, shy and shrinking, and by all accounts, ugly as a shrew. Why else would they have kept her so carefully hidden away? Lady Aurelia happened to be daughter to the Duke of Lansing, which was the only reason she was the *ton*'s most coveted marriage prospect.

But not coveted by him. Hunter didn't care that her father owned half the countryside around London, or that he controlled a vast swath of society's brightest statesmen, or that he was King George's most favored noble companion. Hunter didn't want to wed Lady Dormouse. Hell, he didn't want to marry anyone, but he'd just discovered this damned ball was a betrothal ball, arranged by his own father and mother. One day back from a two-week orgy of dissolution at his country estate, to be confronted with a betrothal?

Damn and blast.

His three partners in crime smirked at him from across the ballroom, bemused by his predicament. They wouldn't find it amusing when he was setting up house with a dull stick of a wife, holding tea parties and formal dinners rather than raunchy routs. Thousands of candles illuminated a sickening swirl of silk gowns, bouncing curls, and sleek-coated men bowing every which way. He'd been instructed to dance with Aurelia at least twice, but he'd be damned if he remembered what she looked like.

He could name every courtesan, actress, and ladybird in London by first and last name, hair and eye color, but he hadn't seen his betrothed in over a decade. He'd had better things to do. Hunter Lionel, Marquess of Townsend, was a man of the world, wealthy and powerful in his own right. He was a man of strong will and stronger appetites, as evidenced by the previous weeks' unprecedented descent into debauchery.

But if he must be betrothed this night, as his father had thundered, he would be betrothed on his own terms, for no one, *no one*, pressed the Marquess of Townsend's hand. If he was to spend a lifetime in marital agony, it would be to a woman of his own choosing, family promises be damned. He hadn't made the blasted promises, but sat silently by when, as a boy of fourteen, he'd been betrothed to the neighboring duke's daughter, a girl of four. Ridiculous.

Why, he barely remembered the formal event or the dinner that followed, except that it was extremely uncomfortable. He recalled two big gray eyes staring at him, and a mop of stringy, indeterminately colored hair. He remembered they'd taken his betrothed away before dinner, for the nursery.

It had seemed as stupid to him then as it seemed now, but they'd both had the misfortune to be born to high-ranking dukes, and thus become pawns in a game of alliances. This marriage, his father insisted, would guarantee a purity of line.

Hunter scanned the room for a different purity of line. Big breasts. That would be a necessity. Shapely waist and large hips to grasp when he plunged into his wife's pussy in the throes of marital duty. Most importantly, a pillowy, delectable bottom to spank and play with as suited his will.

Ah, what a pair of arse cheeks he'd enjoyed the night before last. Some local whore his friend Warren had enticed to the party, or perhaps she'd been a good girl enjoying a forbidden tryst with some of London's most notorious rakehells. Whoever she was, she had squirmed and cooed and squealed with delicious enthusiasm as he'd spanked and molested her backside. Hunter smoothed the hem of his waistcoat over his thickening cock, remembering how yielding the tart had been when he slid inside her. Not just her pussy, but her arsehole too before the night was over.

Gossip of his licentious activities must have finally reached his father's ears, goading him to act in this heavy-handed manner. A betrothal ball, indeed, and not one soul had let him in on the scheme beforehand. Very well. He'd wed, but not to their perfectly pedigreed dormouse. He could very well pick his own shackle. Hunter frowned and scanned the room, searching for a suitably buxom prospect among the sea of slender, stiff-necked virgins on display.

His friends approached, formidable gentlemen in their ballroom black: Lord Warren, whom the ladies all adored for his blond curls, and Lord August, dark and severe like Hunter himself. The three of them had grown up together at Oxford, along with Arlington, a great Viking of a man and a duke in his own right. They were all only sons, dogged from a young age by the specters of "duty" and "responsibility," and so they had formed a friendship, encouraging one another in congenial rebellion.

Until now.

Arlington clapped him on the back in sympathy, while August and Warren, both earls by title, guffawed behind their hands at his beleaguered frown.

"I suppose there's nothing for it now, old boy," said Warren. "Perhaps you shouldn't have hosted such a prolonged and lascivious party at Somerton."

"I'll sack the whole staff at Somerton for their talk," Hunter said. "I'm a grown man. I can bedevil whores and doxies if I like."

"Nonsense. It's time to grow up," said Arlington with mock gravity. "And this betrothal has been on the books for an eternity. The Lady Aurelia Dormouse—er—Dumont must be eager to set up at your side."

"Help me find someone else," he pleaded over their laughter. "Some pretty girl. I'll take her into the study and ruin her. I'll take her out to the gardens and—"

"Tie her to a tree and whip her bottom?" August nodded. "I think that bypasses betrothal and constitutes marriage in certain shires."

"I'll do whatever it takes to escape a life with Lady Dormouse. For God's sake, I don't even know what she looks like. They're hiding her in some corner, no doubt, until just before the announcement."

"Look at that bit of goods." Warren jerked a chin at the corner. A young woman in a pale blue gown with glittering sapphires at her neck stared back at the handsome blond earl. Damn, why must Warren's good looks captivate each and every woman of the *ton*? The young lady in question was practically in a swoon under his friend's regard. Hunter was uncomfortably aware of how rough and inelegant he must look beside him, with his exceptional height, and broad shoulders. The courtesans liked his build, but he'd heard it whispered by the ladies *au salon* that he was oversized and coarse.

He scowled at the young chit, annoyed to see she was everything a man like him desired. Her bosom pressed round and pretty as a peach from the constriction of her fitted bodice, while the skirts of her dress flared out over visible hips. No slim, lithe thing, this one. Her hair was glossy and full, rich honey-gold waves curling over her shoulders, a voluptuous temptation framing her innocent gaze. He would like to touch those curls, run his fingers through them. He'd like to grab her and subdue her with a kiss that would leave her far less innocent than she'd started out.

"She's got her eye on you, chap," said Warren.

"Her eyes are on you," he ground out. "You rotting pretty peacock."

"Go to her." He gave his friend a nudge. "Look at that body. You can see she's got a smashing figure, even with the petticoats."

"Yes, go dance with her, Towns," August prompted. "No time to lose."

"I'm going to dance her right out of her reputation, and that's not going to happen here in front of a thousand eyes," said Hunter. "I'll draw her off somewhere and ruin her so the other betrothal will be off."

"You'll have to marry *her* then," Warren pointed out. "Do you dislike the idea of Lady Dormouse so very much?"

"I loathe the idea of Lady Dormouse, especially being forced into marrying her. It's the principle of the thing." He straightened his coat and nodded toward the woman in blue, who seemed more and more alluring. "This pretty piece of arse will do just as well, if I have to marry."

"Where then?" asked Arlington, stopping him with a hand on his arm. "Where shall we bring everyone so you can be caught in the midst of an illicit embrace?"

Hunter thought a moment. "The path beyond the gardens, the one on the left that leads to the follies. Plenty of moonlight there for discovery. Anyone know who she is?" Several high born gents were paying court to her, ranging around with languid gazes. "Is she betrothed to someone else?"

"Would she be looking at you that way if she was?" Warren murmured.

A flush rose beneath the points of Hunter's cravat. She was staring at him, really, with an arousing, fascinated expression of...dread. So she'd heard about him and his friends, perhaps heard about their famous parties. Most of the young ladies had, as in *Stay away from those dangerous gentlemen*. The four of them were as controversial as they were eligible. It was good that she knew his reputation. She would understand even before they married that he was a certain type of gentleman, namely the type of gentleman who didn't stay quietly at home.

"Your mother's headed this way," said Arlington, interrupting his thoughts. "It's now or never. Lure Miss Pretty Arse out the back door and around to the gardens. Work a little of your dark, seductive magic."

"Tie her to a tree if you have to," August added, chuckling. "Whatever it takes."

"Distract my mother, will you? Just long enough for me to get her away." Hunter turned his back on them and headed toward the young lady. Such a godforsaken crush, this ball. Why had his mother invited the entirety of the *ton*? Now he would shame this girl and her parents, and his own parents, and of course the jilted Lady Dormouse in front of absolutely everyone. He paused in his progress to the young lady's side. Did he really want to do this? Was this woman really the one he wanted? For life?

Her eyes locked on his. He hoped she wouldn't resist when he tried to finesse her out onto the terrace, and then to one of the more private paths. Perhaps dark features and a tall, forbidding stature served his purpose here. He'd entice her with his piratical air. Who wanted to be a pretty man like Warren, with all the fragile flowers falling at his feet? Hunter didn't want fragile flowers. He wanted curves and heaving breasts...and curls...

Blast. Her curls were leaving. She shrank back into the crowds as if to elude him. He followed her past the doors and out to the formal garden,

11

pausing occasionally to greet this guest or that. He looked back for his mother and found her exchanging pleasantries with his friends. Faithful chaps. He would have assisted any of them in a caper like this, and probably would one day.

He felt the slightest twinge of regret for Lady Aurelia. Dormouse or no, it was a cruel thing to be jilted. If she'd made the first attempt to get to know him...but then he'd been so rarely at their parents' estates. *By your choice, not hers.*

He shrugged off any pangs of guilt, drawn instead to the alluring shape of his retreating prey. To his delight, she was retreating to the exact dark, wooded area where he planned to tryst with her. She took the garden stairs at a frantic pace and looked over her shoulder as she crossed the manicured expanse of lawn toward the tree line. He hung back in the shadows so she couldn't see him.

Damn. Unfortunate, that he'd frightened the woman. He had to catch her or she'd disappear in the darkness and foil his plan. He cut around a side path and sprinted to where the two ways merged. As she approached, he melted out of the forest and took her arm.

She opened her mouth to scream.

"No," he said, clapping a hand over her lips. If she screamed now, everyone would come running before he'd had adequate time to debauch her. His other arm snaked around her waist, pulling her close. She didn't have the manners to fall into a swoon, but fought him instead, pushing at his chest.

"Don't scream," he said. "Have I given you any reason to panic?"

She squirmed against him, her breath hissing behind his palm. Her body was every bit as delectable as he'd hoped, firm yet soft, and pleasantly curvy and plump. "Stop, my dearest." His voice held a note of warning as his cock stiffened against her front, aroused by her struggling and straining. "Promise not to scream and I'll let you go."

She stared at him, her eyes wide and frightened. Her fingers curled into fists against his chest.

"Will you be a good girl if I lift my hand away and release you? I mean you no harm, of course."

As soon as he edged the first finger from her lips, she drew a great gust of breath into her lungs and let out a piercing shriek. In his rush to muffle her, he got tangled in her skirts and they went down together in an awkward heap. If Arlington brought the crowds necessary to discover them, he'd be accused of assault, not seduction.

"Shh, please," he begged. "I'm not going to hurt you. I only wanted to speak with you. You look so lovely in your..." He looked down again in the dark to double check. "Your pale blue gown. It is blue, isn't it?"

"Let me go," she said against his hand. She trembled beneath him, in anger, not fear. No, this one wasn't a dormouse, which pleased him. She twisted and nearly caught him with a swift knee between the legs. She managed to rise from beneath him, but he blocked her way to the house.

"I wouldn't storm back and make a fuss. No one will believe I dragged you all the way out here against your will." His gaze swept down the front of her. "And you look as if you've already had a merry roll in the grass."

She grimaced, brushing at her front. Her gown was rumpled and dirty, scattered with bits of leaves. She plucked at her skirts and touched the sapphires at her neckline. Mussed curls fell against her face.

"Come here," he said, picking a leaf from the honey-colored mane. How soft her hair was. He put a hand on her shoulder, wishing to soothe her even as he was in the process of ruining her. She looked up at him in entreaty.

"I didn't come out here to tryst with you. I came out here to escape you." Tears gathered in her eyes. "Please, I don't want this. I never wanted this. Please let me go."

"My lady." He feigned devastation, clutching his heart. He had to soften her, at least enough to secure a kiss when his friends brought the gawking crowds. "Escape me? Why?"

"It's Lord Warren I love. I am deeply, deeply in love with him."

"Are you?" Hunter frowned in irritation. *It's too bad he doesn't know your name.* "Why Lord Warren? Do you find nothing to admire in me?"

She ducked her head at his injured tone. "Lord Warren is so cheerful and handsome and dashing. It's nothing to do with you. It's only that he's so perfectly wonderful."

Perfectly dastardly, he thought to himself. *If only you knew...*

"So you see," she said, "I am very, very sorry that I have no feelings at all for you."

"Is that right?" A bit of the gentleman leached from his tone as he pulled her closer. "I'm sorry to hear it, because I have a great many feelings for you."

"But you don't even know me."

"I know that you're out here, alone, and you should not be. It's as if you were trying to lure me here to have my way with you."

"I wasn't!"

"As if you were trying to tempt me to this private glade for a kiss."

He could see that he terrified her. It wasn't the best footing to begin a marriage, but she was pretty and trembling, and her magnificent bosom heaved against his chest in a very exciting way. He stared down into those alluring pillows. "How beautiful you are."

"Please let me go." It was little more than a whisper. A whimper. "Lord Warren is the one I want. I love him. I adore him."

"But he cares nothing for you, I assure you. So why don't we make the best of things?" He twined fingers into those soft, springy curls, still marveling at the texture. Her hair was the color of autumn maple leaves, or light, burnished gold.

"Please." Perhaps now she would swoon. Her trembling had progressed to shudders. Hunter heard voices on the walk, his mother calling out.

"I'm sorry to force this on you," he said. "But I'm a desperate man, and you could do worse, my pretty dove. I'm the Marquess of Townsend. One day I'll be a duke and you'll be a duchess. I'm not as handsome or dashing as Warren, but I'm still quite a catch."

He tilted her face to his. She looked concerned. Confused.

"Kiss me, would you?" he said. "Let's make it convincing." He drew her close, right against his body. How luscious and feminine she was. His hand rested on the curve of her waist, the other pressed to her back. He could feel her heart galloping against his chest. He touched his lips to hers and her mouth tightened as if she'd never been kissed before. He found the thought arousing.

"I say, there they are." Good old Arlington. His voice was deep and ducal, and appropriately concerned. *Yes, there's the scoundrel and the poor miss in his clutches.* Hunter had just enough time to turn from his lady in blue and look guilty as the crowd drew along the moonlight path. His mother pushed through, the massive emerald on her turban blinking in the dim night.

"Thank goodness," she said, letting out a breath. "Townsend has found her. She's here."

His mother, that regal society maven, made her way to them. She took in his exultant expression and the way he still grasped his young victim's waist. The poor thing shied away from him before all these people, but he grabbed at her elbow, pulling her back. "You've caught us," he said loudly enough for everyone to hear. "We were swept away by passion. I shall make things right."

Amused chuckles rippled through the assembly. Arlington grinned. Warren choked back a laugh.

His mother shook her head, clearly exasperated. "Make things right, indeed. We might have announced the engagement at the ball, with a toast and speeches as is proper, but you will do things your own way. Bring Lady Aurelia back to the hall so we can fete this joyous occasion with everyone in attendance. Really, Townsend," she chided in a softer voice. "Mauling her in the dark to begin the official engagement? Her father looks furious."

Hunter stared at his mother. Over her shoulder, he saw Lansing's scowling visage fixed on him and the woman in his arms...Lady Aurelia. Her cheeks had flushed flame red. *Now*, he thought. *Now she will faint.* But she didn't. She backed away from him, picked up her skirts and trudged over to her father. The Duke of Lansing took her arm none too gently and guided her back toward the house.

As for Hunter, he glowered at his friends, now red-faced with barely restrained laughter. He communicated without words all the vulgar, hateful, abominable curses he wanted to heap upon their traitorous heads.

* * * * *

Aurelia wished the servants had not lit so many candles in the library. She wanted to creep behind the high-backed sofa in the corner and hide. She wanted to kneel before her father and mother and beg for forgiveness, but instead she kept her seat across from the fuming Marquess of Townsend.

He hated her. His words, his glances made that perfectly clear. He lounged back, enduring her father's wrath.

"You shamed my daughter, drawing her off and pawing her in that manner. What did you mean by it? What has she ever done to you?"

"Nothing," Lord Townsend replied tightly. "I don't know her at all." He fixed her with a baleful gaze. "Why didn't you tell me who you were?"

"I thought you knew who I was. I knew who you were."

"Did you know this was to be our betrothal ball?"

"We sent letters to Somerton," his father interjected. "They went unanswered."

"I was busy at Somerton," Lord Townsend said through his teeth.

"Yes, everyone knows you were *busy*," said her father in a scathing tone. "And then you returned here to treat my daughter in the same uncouth and lecherous manner with which you conduct your...your personal life." He turned to the Duke of Lockridge, the marquess's father. "I don't know if I can do it, by God, Neville. I don't know if I can entrust my only daughter to this...this..."

He didn't finish the statement. Aurelia wondered what he was going to say.

"I swear to you, henceforth my son will conduct himself with honor." As Lockridge said it, he smacked Lord Townsend upon the ear with his cane. The son didn't make a sound, only seethed with even greater intensity.

As for Aurelia, she stared down at her lap, hot, ashamed, remembering things she didn't want to. The warmth of his lips, the unfamiliar hardness of his body pressing against hers. She'd been so afraid when he lowered his face to hers. She'd thought Lord Townsend's kiss would feel horrible, damaging, and dangerous because of his poor reputation, but it hadn't felt horrible at all.

Not that she knew what kisses were supposed to feel like. She was a lady, a scion of propriety, always faultless in behavior. While she'd understood for many years that she was supposed to marry the profligate son of her father's friend, she'd imagined when it came down to it, everyone would realize he was too much of a rogue.

She'd assumed the betrothal would be broken, allowing her to marry the man she knew in her heart was her perfect companion—the smiling, polite Earl of Warren. Oh, she'd heard gossip about him also, but it was vile, ridiculous stuff, too outrageous to be believed. When she looked at Lord Warren, she could see he was a kindhearted soul, the type of man she could respect and feel secure with. A man like her father. Her father's admirers called him Laudable Lansing because of his exceptional godliness and rectitude. Some types called him Laughable Lansing, but that was because they lacked moral fiber.

Aurelia's shoulders slumped. She lacked moral fiber because she hadn't been able to resign herself to marrying the man her father had chosen for her. She'd fallen in love with another man. She'd tried to run away from her betrothal ball, for all the good it had done her.

Her father paced back and forth in front of Lord Townsend while his parents frowned from across the room. "You shall wed my daughter as soon as it can be managed," he said, "and then you'll settle down into a model husband. More than a model husband. The most solicitous, respectable pinnacle of a husband that any fellow ever met."

"I'll try my best," Lord Townsend replied in an acerbic tone.

Her father's gaze hardened, his mouth thinned in a line. "Indeed you will, or I may see fit to interfere. My daughter has been very sheltered. Very gently bred. You cannot continue to act as if you have no responsibilities."

"I manage my responsibilities," said the marquess. "I have increased the profitability of my holdings by seventy percent in the last five years, maintained two residences, and contributed to social programs and charities. I manage all the responsibilities that I find important. Forgive me if marriage isn't one of them."

"You will not be so mannerless, Townsend," his father hissed. "You'll not show such disrespect to Lady Aurelia."

She stared between the three angry men. In her agitated state, she was finding it difficult to follow the conversation.

"I'm sorry," she asked, "but are we still going to marry?"

"I might have reconsidered," her father said, "but after this evening's display, there's no other option. Your fiancé has made free with you in front of half the *ton*."

Some part of her understood that she was ruined, the Lord Townsend had caused their marriage to become a necessary thing, but some part of her couldn't grasp the finality of it. "Can I not..." Her voice caught in the tangle of her emotions. "Can I not marry for love?"

Her father's brows rose nearly to his hairline. "Are you in love?"

Her eyes flicked to Lord Townsend's. His eyes darkened with something like pity, or disgust. "Lord Warren?" he said, tracing a finger over the arm of the chair. "Unfortunately, he is not up to snuff. Ducal dynasties are at stake, and he's a mere earl."

Aurelia didn't care if Lord Warren was only an earl. He was still titled, still an aristocrat. She turned pleading eyes on her father but he pretended not to see. He frightened her terribly, he always had. She didn't want to disappoint him. She'd always been her parents' perfect, obedient child, though she'd languished, always, in her older brother's shadow. He was the heir, the next duke. She was the daughter, only good for building alliances.

"Perhaps I don't have to marry. Perhaps..." Her voice thinned to a desperate squeak. "If only I had been a son, like Severin. Then there wouldn't be this business of...of marrying me off."

At that, her mother made a soft, mournful sound and hurried from the room. Aurelia's vision blurred. Through her tears, she saw the marquess watching, his features taut, his hair a blur of black waves over his fathomless dark eyes. To her horror, tears overflowed and coursed down her cheeks. She covered her face, so her fine silk gloves had darker spots where she wiped away the wetness.

"Have done with this unpleasant business," said Lord Townsend's mother, fluttering closer to Aurelia and offering her handkerchief. "The poor child is beside herself. She ought to be home in bed."

"She's not a child anymore." Lord Townsend's eyes raked her, from her plunging bodice to her slippered toes. His voice was rough, hinting of licentious things. It made Aurelia cry harder.

The duchess rapped her son on the shoulder with her fan. "Comfort her, would you? Apologize to her. This is all your fault."

"Don't go near her," Lansing barked before Lord Townsend could comply. "You're not to touch my daughter again, not until you're putting a ring on her finger in the church."

"No courtship then?" Lord Townsend arched a brow. "But why should there be? It's been so businesslike to this point."

Her father bristled. "Oh, you're going to court my daughter. You're going to make amends for the mess you've made of her reputation.

You're going to behave like the most charming, well-mannered, and attentive suitor of all time."

"Without touching her?"

"Yes." He nodded and rapped his cane against the floor. "I don't care how you manage it, but you'll convince the entire *ton* that you're enamored of her. However you handle it, I expect her wed by the end of June."

"The end of June?" The marquess sat straighter in his chair. "It's April now."

"You've enough time to put your affairs in order. Do you comprehend my meaning?"

A look passed between the three men that she didn't understand. The marquess turned away first, toward her. His eyes narrowed. He despised her. The kiss, the feel of his body against hers, none of it could overcome the dread seeping into her bones. She was to marry him? This man who hated her?

He stood so abruptly that she shrank back.

"Since I cannot touch you, dear Lady Aurelia," he said in a falsely solicitous tone, "I fear an official betrothal dance is out of the question. Therefore, I'll excuse myself from this ball and let the remainder of this farce play out without me."

He made a crisp bow and left. Aurelia watched him go, chewing her lip until his broad shoulders cleared the door frame and disappeared into the outer hall.

Chapter Two:
Lovely

The Duke of Arlington's garden rustled with swishing coat tails and embellished and ruched silk gowns. The season's most eligible young ladies clustered in pastel groups with frowning chaperones and hawk-eyed mothers, while toplofty gentlemen sized up the possibilities for consolidating families and power. Fans fluttered and come-hither glances flew, most of them toward the garden party's towering blond host.

"They want you, Arlington," Hunter drawled from his position near the east balustrade. "You'd better pick one of them soon, before things come to a head." He gestured toward young Lady Eleanor, who exchanged viciously polite glances with her rivals on all sides. She looked like a puffball, all white and soft around the edges, although marital ambition sharpened her smile. "Shelbourne's chit thinks she has you in the bag."

"For God's sake, she's the Marquess of Shelbourne's daughter, not 'Shelbourne's chit.' Could you attempt to be even a little polite and sociable? I threw this blasted party for your sake, and for your soon-to-be wife."

Both men turned to where Aurelia sat in her protective social circle. The young ladies perched around a tea tray but none of them touched a thing.

"She looks like she's having fun," said Arlington.

"She looks like she'd like to jump off a cliff, but you've none on your vast property. You call yourself a duke of the realm?"

"I'll have to look into acquiring some cliffs."

At nearly thirty, Arlington was the oldest of their mad little group, as well as the most respectable, having been forced into duty and responsibility at a very young age. Outwardly respectable, anyway. The duke was possessed of long, golden hair he sometimes pulled back in a queue, and pale blue-gray eyes capable of freezing those who risked his displeasure.

"These betrothals are a dull business," the duke said, frowning. "People who aren't suited for one another are forced together to breed so society can proceed in the same lockstep manner."

"It's ghastly," Hunter agreed.

"You'll have a pretty wife anyway." Arlington nodded in Aurelia's direction.

Hunter studied her, her spine stiff and her head tilted just so to her companion. "Pretty dull, you mean."

"You didn't find her dull when we pointed her out at your parents' ball." His friend's mouth twitched with amusement.

"I'll get all of you back for that one day," Hunter huffed. "Mark my words."

"We look forward to your glorious transformation once you've been dragged, kicking and screaming, into the state of matrimony." His hilarity died away, replaced by a gloom of concern. "Really, Towns, we wish you the best. If there's anything we can do..."

"There is something you can do. Especially you, Your Grace. Go to Lansing and make an offer for her hand."

"No point in that. She's yours now. You've seen to it, for better or worse."

Lady Aurelia turned to speak to the simpering young woman at her side. Minette, Warren's amiable younger sister. So prim. So proper, all of them. "You're a duke," Hunter said. "Lansing would at least consider you."

"She's always been promised to you." His friend's voice took on a strange tone. "Funny, if not for the adjoining property, I might have had her."

"Would you have wanted her?"

"I don't know. It doesn't matter. You've known for years this was coming, so buck up and be a man about it." He pursed his lips, staring across the garden. "Your Lady Dormouse does have a magnificent set of breasts. No wonder Lansing kept her hidden away."

Out of principle, Hunter refused to moon at his fiancée in public, although he'd had similar thoughts about her breasts, her hips, her pleasingly round derrière. She was womanly, lush. Ripe, one might say, which made her prim mousiness that much harder to bear.

"She's in love with Warren." The words burst out, apropos of nothing. Arlington looked over in surprise. Hunter stared back, trying to act as if it didn't prick him.

"Ah well," said Arlington. "All the ladies love Warren. He puts on a good show with that fancy hair and that devilish tailor of his. I wouldn't take it personally."

"I don't take it personally," Hunter scoffed with a bit too much conviction. "I don't give a whit if she lusts after every man in Christendom. I'm no pillar of fidelity. I expect I'll continue in my old habits after we're wed."

"Then stumble home to your wife looking—and smelling—as if you just rolled out of whore's bed?"

"Not a whore, my friend. A specialized lady of a fine erotic house."

"I know the 'erotic houses' you frequent," Arlington mused. "I know the names of every one of your 'specialized ladies,' and I tell you, you'll need to be discreet. Laudable Lansing won't tolerate a philandering son-in-law."

Hunter didn't much care what the Duke of Lansing would tolerate. He'd spent a decade training a coterie of women to cater to his sexual tastes, and he wasn't going to throw them all away because of a forced marriage to an uptight prude.

Bounteous bosom or no, he doubted the virginal Lady Aurelia would submit to erotic punishment, or sodomy, or oral copulation. He wouldn't give up these pleasures, for he found them essential to his life's happiness. He'd only have to be more careful in seeking them out. He'd pay a little extra for his partners' silence if he had to, to reduce the gossip after he was married. Once his new wife learned what he was into, she'd probably pay the courtesans herself to keep him out of her bed.

And if she complained about his extramarital activities, he'd explain that it was the way of the *ton*, and that she had no power to control him. He'd be a decent husband, as far as he could, but he had no intention of living like a monk only to protect her sensibilities.

"We ought to arrange a decadent orgy the night before the wedding," said Arlington. He paused, considering. "Two nights before the wedding, perhaps."

"Don't arrange anything of the sort. I'm planning to remain celibate that entire week, so I can muster up enough lust to deflower my bride."

"A week? You'll never manage that."

"I can survive a week with no women. It's the least I can do for Lady Aurelia, to show some stiffening in my affections on our wedding night. How about an orgy the following week? I'll be desperate for pleasure after I take a few trips between those ice-cold thighs."

Arlington grimaced. "We'll have to be awfully careful about such things. Maybe the orgy's not a good idea. Lansing is a stickler for proprieties and he could make your life—and your father's life—a bloody hell if you rub him the wrong way."

"I've already rubbed him the wrong way." Hunter stared morosely at his future bride. "Which is why I have to be here playing the lovelorn fiancé like a damned milksop."

"Go and talk with her, would you?" Arlington nudged him the lady's way. "I threw this party so you could prove to the quality that you've been reformed by this engagement, publicly at least. Why don't you go kiss some hands and smile at some simpering ladies?"

"Bugger you, Arlington."

"Then after, we'll visit some houses of iniquitous congress, where you can reward yourself for your impeccable manners and respectability. Go on. Don't stand here talking to me."

Hunter heaved a sigh. "Very well. I'm off to court the Lady Aurelia, if she doesn't run away from me first."

* * * * *

23

Aurelia's whole body went tense as Lord Townsend ambled across the lush expanse of garden. Her future husband looked well enough in his fine embroidered coat, his black hair neatly tamed. Even his expression gave no cause for offense. His dark brown eyes were soft and his features arranged in a semblance of pleasant greeting, but Aurelia recognized his distaste for her. She felt it in every part of her body whenever he was around. Her companions' idle chatter tapered off as he stopped before their table.

"Will you have some tea, Lord Townsend?" chirped Lady Wilhelmina. "Or one of these delicious confections?"

"There's only one delicious confection I'm hungry for at the moment."

Aurelia flushed hot as his eyes settled on her. The women giggled as though he was charming, but she felt humiliated. Must he profess to be *hungry* for her? How crass, how gauche...how completely made up. She hated that they must playact false affection between them.

"Lady Aurelia," he said brightly. "I couldn't stay from your side a moment longer."

She was obliged to offer her hand, and when she did, he bowed over it, brushing a kiss across the back of her glove. "Lord Townsend," she replied in a voice she hoped sounded equally bright. "It's a lovely party, isn't it? The weather is fine."

"The beauty of the day pales in comparison to your charms."

Mockery. Lies. If only Lord Warren were here, she wouldn't feel so agitated, but since her official engagement to Lord Townsend, the man had made himself scarce. Lord Townsend gave her a desultory smile. She imagined he knew every one of her thoughts and mocked her for it.

"Ladies," he said, looking around at her companions, "would you be so kind as to spare my dear Aurelia? I had hoped to stroll with her about His Grace's picturesque grounds."

By asking her friends for permission, he'd more or less stymied her ability to decline. She sighed and rose to take his arm. He covered her gloved hand with his and guided her past clusters of party guests, along the outer perimeter of the duke's gardens. When she glanced over, she didn't see his face, but rather the outline of his muscular shoulder, encased in his meticulously tailored coat. Must he tower over her? But his father was tall, and his mother too. She supposed she would bear grotesquely tall children unless she could find a way out of this engagement.

"It is a lovely day, isn't it?" she said, because she couldn't think of anything else to say to his daunting shoulder.

"Yes, and a lovely party, as you mentioned some moments ago. You seem to find everything lovely. What a charming quirk."

Aurelia wished she could quirk him right between his eyes with the heel of her slipper. "I only meant to make polite conversation."

"Ah, well. I can do that too if I apply myself. Which facile and boring topics shall we discuss? We've already touched on the weather, but I suppose we can revisit it." He turned his head up to the sky. "What a beautiful day, with the clouds and the breeze, and the flowers blooming so madly."

Aurelia refused to be baited. "I do think it's beautiful. It was kind of His Grace to host this party in our honor."

"His Grace likes to do kind things. He's a very proper chap."

"You call the duke 'His Grace'? I heard you were close friends."

"We're longtime friends, and I've called him many things in the course of our history, but in such a *lovely* setting"—he emphasized her word with exaggerated mockery—"I find myself inclined to adhere to formalities." He gave her a speculative look. "Is that what you and your friends do at your tea table? Gossip about me and Arlington?"

"No, we don't do anything of the sort. It's only that your name comes up in conversation, now that we're engaged."

"That must be a trial for you."

Aurelia decided not to answer. In truth, it was a trial, just like everything else about this engagement. This was the third social event they'd attended in one another's company. The opera had been easy—they'd simply sat beside one another in silence until they could leave. Riding in Hyde Park had been easy too, since the bustle of people and carriages made conversation impossible.

This garden party was far too quiet, and strolling on the Marquess of Townsend's arm felt too intimate for her tastes.

"Out of conversation already? No more *lovely* topics?" he jested. "We'd suit one another better if you weren't such a mouse."

"I am not a mouse."

"Look at me and say that."

To her chagrin, she realized she'd ducked her chin practically to her chest. His closeness unsettled her, no matter how she tried to ignore it. His conspicuous maleness tied her in knots. This great, ungainly man was going to be her *husband*. He was going to live with her and get children on her. She'd been sheltered, but she knew how children were made. Well, for the most part.

"I am not a mouse," she said in a firmer voice, almost managing to meet his gaze.

"They call you Lady Dormouse."

"That's not a very gentlemanly thing to point out."

"Ah, but I'm not much of a gentleman. How poorly we suit each other. It's a shame."

"Back out of our betrothal then," she said through tight lips. "I wish you would."

"I wish I could. I've tried to think of ways to do it, but there are more powerful forces forming this union." He stopped and turned to her, tilting up her chin with one gloved fingertip. "Besides that, I find you too fragile and innocent to humiliate with a broken betrothal. It would weigh on my conscience."

Even now, he mocked her. Everything about him made her cross. "I thought you abhorred my fragility and innocence."

He chuckled. "*Abhorred* is a very strong word. No, Aurelia, fragility and innocence aren't bad qualities in a wife. At least I'll know no one has trespassed before me when I mount you on our wedding night."

She drew in a breath as delicately as she could, when what she really needed to do was gasp for air. Of all the inappropriate and coarse things to say! She moved to pull away from him, to flee, but he grasped her hand.

"Does my forthright speech offend you?"

"You know it does," she said. "You...you impolite blackguard."

"Goodness, is that the best you can do? Lady Dormouse indeed. You ought to call me a bastard instead. A bleeding bastard, if you really want to make a point."

Aurelia looked around in alarm, but no one was near enough to hear this scandalous conversation. "Ladies don't talk that way," she said. "Gentlemen shouldn't either."

"And gentlemen shouldn't speak of mounting their brides. I know. That doesn't change the fact that it shall happen very shortly, my Aurelia."

She considered him with a stricken expression. *My* Aurelia? "I'm not yours yet, Lord Townsend."

"I'll make it good for you, darling. Don't worry."

She wanted to spit at him that she wasn't worried, but the truth was, she was terrified. Her gaze dropped to his neatly tied cravat, then down to his broad shoulders and chest. When she looked back up to meet his eyes, he wore a self-satisfied expression.

"You enjoy this," she said. "You enjoy mocking and taunting me. That's why you lured me into this walk."

"In what way am I taunting you? I'm trying to reassure you."

"By threatening to mount me?"

He made a muted sound of reproach. "It's not a threat. It's what's going to happen in precisely eight days. I've been counting the hours until our wedding night. Such is my hunger to possess you."

Oh, he meant to shock her, this loathsome man. She moved her hand to disengage his fingers. "I want to return to my friends."

"Look at me and smile, then. We must convince people we are happy to marry, not trapped in some unwanted and ill-conceived betrothal."

"But we *are* trapped in an unwanted and ill-conceived betrothal. You've made no secret of your disdain for me. None of this is my fault, you know. You shouldn't blame me."

"I haven't blamed you." He smiled at her with unnatural cheer and affection, and led her around a bed of colorful blooms with the greatest seeming concern.

She felt her face might crack from the effort of smiling back at him. She couldn't believe anyone would be fooled by their playacted sentiments. "If you hadn't bedeviled me in the woods at your parents' ball, we might have found a way to convince them how unsuited we are. They might have allowed us to marry others of our station."

"Like your precious Lord Warren? It never would have happened. Anyway, if it matters to you, I'm much better in bed. His technique is impressive, but not quite up to my—"

"No, please." She pressed her hands over her ears, knocking her bonnet askew. "I beg you, don't speak of such things."

"Why not?"

"Because. You know why." He was impossible. He refused to converse with any modicum of decency or respect. "Can we not reference anything to do with your—your bedroom skills—and what shall happen on our wedding night? Can we not discuss it any more until the hour is at hand?"

He turned her to face him and set her bonnet to rights, biting his lip in concentration. She closed her eyes rather than stare at his mouth, then opened them with a start as he brushed a few strands of hair behind her ear.

"I wonder why you have such a negative regard for the act of sexual congress. It makes me wonder if you haven't already been mounted by some brute who didn't know what he was about."

"I have never been m-mounted before," she protested, flushing hot. "I am perfectly pure."

"Are you? Then you're too pure to realize that being perfectly pure is a very dull state indeed." His fingertips lingered, heating the sensitive skin beneath her lobe. He gazed at her, his lips gently curved. "Do you like the way it feels when I touch your ear?"

She set her teeth and shook her head. "No, I don't like it."

"What if I stroked it instead, like this?"

His fingers moved again, not just touching this time, but caressing. She suppressed a shudder, knowing he watched. She could feel his dark eyes upon her even though she averted her gaze. The strange lilt in his voice, the rasp of his words, the slowness of his caress, the nearness of his body, all of it combined to affect her in some novel, disturbing way.

"I wish you would stop."

"No, you wish I would continue," he said. "Don't tell lies."

She blinked, confused and ashamed, because she *did* wish it. But she also wished for him to stop. "Please, you disturb me so," she whispered.

"Do I?" His hand went still, left her and dropped to his side. "Then perhaps there's hope for us after all."

What do you mean by that? she wanted to ask. But another part of her didn't want to know what he meant. He alarmed her for so many reasons, not least of which was his direct, assessing stare. "If you continue to look at me like that," she said, "people will...believe things."

"People already believe things, Aurelia. I have a reputation to uphold."

28

"Please return me to my friends. Your company exhausts me."

"Then we shall have to build up your stamina." His gaze raked her again, head to toe, in that coarse, appalling way.

She pursed her lips in irritation. She would not say one more word because he'd only turn it into something sordid. Fortunately, they were nearly back to her group of friends. The ladies watched them approach, bemused, whispering to one another. When Aurelia tried to wrest her hand from atop his arm, he held her fast by flattening his palm over her fingers. A subtle show of power, but it had its effect. He was telling her, quite stubbornly, that he was in charge.

Oh, how she wanted to challenge him, but all the *haute ton* were in attendance. Many of them were her father's friends, and a great majority were hopeless gossips. She must be cheerful and play her part. She was only thankful for the layers of gloves and silk and linen that protected her from touching the man. When he delivered her to her table with a bow, she could barely bring a smile of farewell to her lips. She feared even her best effort came off as a grimace.

His smile though, was broad and jovial, his dark features relaxing into arrestingly handsome lines.

She would not find him attractive. She absolutely refused to.

But unfortunately, a little bit, she did.

Chapter Three:
Lessons

Aurelia had always been dutiful. She had always been a very good child, the pride of her mama and papa, so no matter how much she wished to dig in her heels and refuse to walk down the aisle on her wedding day, she did not. She stood beside Lord Townsend at the altar and stammered out the vows that bound her to him for life.

Behind her and to the right, Lord Warren stood with Townsend's other friends. She didn't allow her gaze to drift to his handsome visage, but kept her attention fixed on her husband's cravat, on the black pearl pin that secured its neat folds. She could not look him in the eyes or she'd run away screaming like a madwoman. She had never been allowed to make a fuss, and found herself incapable of doing it at the moment it mattered most.

Still, Lord Warren might have made a fuss on her behalf. He might have stormed the altar, scooped her up and carried her away and professed his true love for her. He might have if he understood how much she admired him, but she had only ever admired him from afar, and now it was too late.

After the ceremony, they proceeded to a wedding breakfast at Lord Townsend's London residence, a great, echoing edifice of Italian marble, breathtaking in design and scale. Aurelia smiled until her face hurt, pretending to be delighted with her new husband and her new role as his marchioness. Lord Townsend presided over the gathering in a sleek, gold-embroidered coat, specially designed to match her ivory and gold wedding gown. The rich warmth of his garments did nothing to soften his cool demeanor. She felt unsettled each time he caught her gaze.

Trapped in this farce of a reception, she accepted the congratulations of countless family friends, including a somber Lord Warren and his impish sister Wilhelmina, whom everyone called Minette. After Minette chattered at her for several minutes about the thrill of attending the wedding, the handsome earl bent over Aurelia's hand with a whisper of a kiss.

"I wish you a long and happy marriage," he said.

She wanted to scream at him for failing her. She wanted to scream about everything this day, but she had never been allowed to scream so she didn't know how. She was in every way a dutiful, well-mannered lady who did as she was told.

She felt like she was dying inside.

"Dearest Aurelia," her mother said as she and papa prepared to take their leave. "How proud we are." She squeezed her daughter's hands. "Your father and I have dreamed of this day, when two great Oxfordshire families would be joined together."

Aurelia tried to reply in some equally happy manner, because that would have been the dutiful thing to do, but she found it impossible. "I'm not certain he'll be a good...a good husband," she whispered.

"Oh, dear, what's this?" Her mother patted her in an awkward way. "The marquess is a fine man. He comes from good stock."

"Good stock? He's not a cow, Mama."

"Don't be cross, dear. He'll be a fine husband as long as you are an obedient wife."

Her father nodded and clasped her hands. "Your mother is right, Aurelia. Be a shining beacon of love and obedience, and your husband will follow suit." He leaned closer. "We are counting on you to rescue this young man. If anyone can do it, you can."

"But...Papa..."

Her father was already moving toward the doors. Her brother swept her into his arms, giving her a hard squeeze. "All will be well," he said in her ear. "Because I'll kill your husband if it isn't, and Papa will give him hell."

She tried not to cry, because Brendan's gaze was telling her not to cry, but these empty, useless reassurances did nothing to calm her. She would be the one left alone with Lord Townsend once all the guests took their leave, and she wasn't sure that being a "beacon of love and obedience" would accomplish anything at all.

"Will you v-visit me sometimes?" she stammered, turning to her sister-in-law Georgina.

"Of course. I'll come calling as soon as you like."

"Tomorrow?"

She stifled a smile. "Newlyweds don't generally take callers for a couple of days. Perhaps next week? Brendan's right, you know. Everything will be fine. You make a beautiful bride, and Townsend is..." She sobered. "Well. Be patient with him. I shall pray for your happiness every day."

Her sister-in-law clasped her in a floral-scented hug, and then Brendan and Georgina joined the other guests on their way out. Her new husband bid the last of them farewell, then turned to her. Oh, for all his faults, for all the threat of him, he was rather handsome. Black hair, and piercing, intense brown eyes. Those beautiful eyes softened the effect of his sharply sculpted features. His footsteps echoed as he crossed the soaring marble foyer. His coat's ornate embroidery caught her gaze, or perhaps she was too overcome to look up at him, now that they were alone.

"I suppose we're married now," she said in the echoing stillness.

"It would seem so, Lady Townsend. Are you counting my buttons? I believe there are forty or so."

"What?" She looked up. "Oh no, I'm just..."

"Feeling shy?"

"I am shy, unfortunately. I always have been. I'll try to be a good wife, but I'm..."

"Shy? And tired and overwhelmed? Weddings are exhausting, aren't they?" He stepped closer and brushed a fingertip down her cheek. She strained to hear a whisper of skirts, the footstep of any servant, but she

32

heard nothing. They might have been utterly alone in the house. He tilted her head up and searched her face with his deep, dark eyes. "You'll want to go rest, won't you?"

"For...what?"

"For later." The husky hitch in his voice unnerved her. "It's our wedding night."

She blinked, her gaze skittering back down to his gold buttons. *One, two, three, four...*

"Must you look so deflated at the prospect?" he asked.

She stared at this man, this stranger who really didn't like her very much. He was her *husband.*

"Mrs. Orban," he said in the echoing silence. A servant materialized at the head of the grand marble stairs and dropped a graceful curtsy. "Will you show Lady Townsend to her rooms?"

* * * * *

Aurelia hid in the window seat of her new bedroom and cried. It was weak and silly of her, and doubtless disturbed the household's disciplined staff, but she couldn't help it. At some point, her life had slipped out of her control. Now she was married, forever, to *him.*

The marquess had provided her with a newly refurbished suite—a sitting room and dressing room, and a luxurious bedroom across the hall from his apartments, with a canopied bed as high as the ceiling, all swathed in lavender embroidered silk. Violets scented the air and a fluffy ivory counterpane beckoned her with promises of softness, but she couldn't bear to go near the place where her husband would join her later on. Where he would *mount* her, as he said. She had no doubt he'd make it as unpleasant as possible, despite his promises to the contrary. She didn't trust the man at all. She didn't believe he was very sensitive or kind.

While she hid and cried, servants bustled in and out with food and wine and trunks of clothes and jewelry, and set about unpacking the necessities of her trousseau. Clement, her staunch, proper lady's maid from home, wheedled her into a wisp of a silk shift and a ruffled ivory dressing gown and then went to turn down the bed.

Aurelia scooted deeper into the soothing darkness of the curtained window seat and gazed through the glass. With the little light left, she could see a well-tended garden, and neighboring rooftops in the distance. The window seat's cushions were plump and soft, and the rich lavender curtains provided privacy. She wished she could hide in the little alcove forever.

"Lord Townsend will retire soon," Clement said briskly. "You must come lie in the bed." She crossed the room to coax Aurelia from the shadows of her newfound retreat. "Come now, there is nothing to fear."

"I like the window seat."

"My lady." Her voice held a note of reproach. "Your new husband will expect to find you there."

A knock interrupted her maid's admonishments. Clement beckoned her wildly and Aurelia skittered across the floor. She'd just managed to climb into the monstrosity of a bed when the door opened. She drew in a deep breath as Lord Townsend entered.

Her husband looked even taller and more threatening in the dim light of the flickering candles. He'd taken off his fine, bright wedding garments and put on a deep bronze dressing gown much more suited to his dark eyes and hair. His gaze moved over her, revealing nothing of his feelings. She clutched the sheets closer to her chest.

His eyes moved to Clement, standing beside her, flushed to her roots. "Leave us," he said.

Clement gave one last motherly twitch to the sheets, dropped a curtsy, and exited as quickly as her old, sturdy bones would allow.

Even after her lady's maid left, Lord Townsend remained still, studying her in a very unnerving way. Then he moved toward the bed, his lips turning up in a half smile. "How beautiful you look," he said. "All golden and shiny, like a princess in a fairy tale. Let me see you."

His words were soft, but the sentiment behind them felt hard and demeaning. She clutched the sheets closer. He put his hands over hers and peeled her fingers away.

"Let me see you," he said again, with a bit more steel. He whisked down the sheets, kicking up a breeze of clean linen scent.

Aurelia tensed, her entire body exposed to his regard. Her filmy night rail, made for a bride, left nothing to the imagination. His eyes roved over the silken thing, and she thought to herself, *he had this made for me. He chose this design.* Her mother would not have ordered such a transparent,

34

indecent garment. She looked down, horrified to see the pink tips of her nipples through the material. She lifted her hands to cover her breasts.

He sat beside her on the bed and pushed them back down again. "Don't hide from me, Aurelia. I would see the woman I've married."

He kept his hands on hers so she had no choice but to bear his scrutiny. He stared down at the outline of her too-ample breasts, then back at her face. "Are you troubled?"

"I'm a b-bit nervous," she stammered out.

"It's all right to be nervous." His hands tightened on hers as she tried to pull them away.

"But...do...do we really need to? Tonight?"

His soft smile didn't quite reach his eyes. "Yes, we really need to. The Lockridge and Lansing dynasties are at stake."

"I mean, can we not delay just a few days, until we know one another better?"

His smile deepened. "Do you think it will change anything between us? I'm sorry, Aurelia, but I intend to have you tonight, our wedding night, as custom dictates. Resign yourself to your fate."

He was practically laughing at her. She tried to summon outrage but found herself too nervous to manage it. His nearness terrified her. She stared at his chest, male and hard beneath his robe. She gawked at defined muscle and dark scattered hair, things she'd never known before in her sheltered existence. He leaned closer, so rough stubble whispered across her cheek.

"It's only that you're practically a stranger to me," she whispered.

He dipped his head lower, released her hands and parted the gathered neckline of her shift. His lips brushed against her neck, the curve of her shoulder. "I won't seem strange to you for long." She shivered as he kissed lower. How soft he felt, and yet how dangerous... He nuzzled against the heaving rise of her bosom, just where the material met skin. "I knew you would look this way," he mused, almost to himself. "I knew you would be lush like this, and soft and sweet. What a beautiful body you have, Lady Townsend."

It was the second time he'd called her Lady Townsend, as if reminding her she had his name now. That she was *his*, by societal custom and law. His voice sounded hoarse and low as he murmured more love talk, compliments and endearments. Some response shuddered to life within her, some scary, elemental sort of pulse. His tongue darted out and touched the tip of her nipple through the fine fabric of her shift. She shied back but his arm came around her and held her, and then he sucked at her nipple, hot, warm pressure right through the fabric.

"My lord," she cried. "What are you doing?"

He didn't answer, only turned his head to lick her other nipple. He sucked it through the material, hard, strong pulls, shocking her. Her face burned. Her body burned too.

"No, please." She shoved at him, trying to twist away.

He caught her hands and she found herself pushed back upon the pillows. "No, Aurelia? You're my wife now. There are certain duties you'll be obliged to perform."

"But I don't want this."

"I'm sorry to hear it. However, my will is law in this house, in this marriage, and in this bed." His face was so close to hers, their noses practically touched. "I won't be a beast. I won't demand unnatural acts. I won't demean or degrade you, but I will require that you make your delectable body available to me. And it is delectable."

His robe had parted wider when he came over her. She lay trapped under his heavy, muscled body, her heart pounding.

"Do you know why it's delectable?" he asked.

She shook her head, eyes fixed on his chest. He loosened her shift, drawing the neckline down until her breasts were exposed, framed by the material. The gathered neckline caused them to be lifted and drawn forward, as if offered on display. He ran fingertips over the puckered, sensitive peaks of her nipples, setting them tingling in the most singular way. His slow caresses made the pulse quicken between her legs. A hot wave spread up into her belly. "These breasts are made to be fondled," he said, squeezing them. "They're the perfect size and shape."

"Please, don't," she whimpered.

He left her breasts and sat back, and pushed the shift downward until it tore with a harsh sound. "Oh," she cried as he ripped it nearly to the hem. The elegant thing had been new, and undoubtedly high in cost.

His hands traced down her naked belly to the curve of her hips. "You're magnificent," he said in that same hoarse voice. "Your hips, your bottom. This body is mine now, all of it. Do you understand?"

She shook her head as forcefully as she dared while pinned by his intense regard. "It's not yours. It's mine."

When his fingers grasped her derrière, she shot up and tried to evade him again. He caught her over his arm with a soft chuckle. "If you knew how much I wanted you, you wouldn't bother trying to get away."

She turned, struggling to escape him. His teeth flashed white in a grim smile as he caught her arms and forced her face-down over his lap. The ripped edges of her shift parted, so she felt the silk of his dressing robe, and his warm, hard thighs beneath her. He caught her wrists and placed his other hand firmly on her back, so no matter how she kicked and flailed, she couldn't right herself.

"Really, Aurelia," he said with a tsk. "Is this proper wifely behavior? I've done nothing to hurt you."

"You ripped my clothing," she said. She wished he would let her up. She felt terribly vulnerable in this position. "You're frightening me. You're molesting me, and putting your lips on my—my breasts."

"Molesting you? I was caressing you, lovely girl. Trying to make you feel good." His fingers tightened around her wrists. "I had hoped it wouldn't come to this, tonight of all nights."

"Come to what?" she asked in a high, thin voice. "Let go of me!"

But he didn't let go. He yanked her shift up and out of the way and raised his arm behind her. His hand landed in a crack of fire across her bottom cheeks.

She was too shocked at first to react. Her husband had *spanked* her. Hard. Before she could draw breath to protest he spanked her again, and again, sharp, smarting strokes. "No," she shrieked when she finally caught her breath. "Stop! Stop it!"

"I'll stop when I believe you've been adequately punished for resisting me," he said in a taut voice. "Your body is mine to caress if I wish it. As I said earlier, my will is law."

His will? What about her rights as a wife, and as a person? Aurelia clung to his legs, the bed sheets, anywhere she could gain purchase, but no matter how she fought him, he overpowered her and bent her back over his lap. She slid on the fabric of his robe, her shift so disarranged that her breasts were exposed along with her smoldering bottom. Each crack of his hand felt like fire.

"Stop. Stop," she begged, kicking her legs out. "Please stop."

"I'm not sure you've learned your lesson yet."

"Help," she screamed, thinking perhaps a footman or maid might come to her rescue. "Lord Townsend is beating me. Please! Please help!"

If anything, the blows rained harder and hotter. "No one is going to rescue you, my dear," he said between spanks. "My will is law for them too. Scream all you like. It won't do any good."

She cried instead, hating him for holding her down across his lap, hating his will and his horrible, punishing hand. She cried great, gusty tears of entreaty that didn't seem to affect him in the least.

"Such dramatics," he said, landing some smacks to the sensitive skin of her upper thighs. She gasped and bucked upon his lap. "Didn't your father ever spank you this way for being a bad girl?"

"No!" she wailed. "I've never been a bad girl."

"I beg to differ."

He gave her three more solid cracks and then righted her, setting her on her feet. When she tried to set her shift in order, he tore the rest of it off her. If he'd ordered the garment, he'd destroyed it too. She stared at him, her bottom throbbing and her knees trembling. When she reached to cover her breasts, he made a sound of denial that stopped her.

"It's my body, Aurelia. It's not yours to cover any more, is it?"

She didn't answer. She couldn't answer. No one had warned her that marriage might be this way. In her wildest nightmares of life with Lord Townsend, she hadn't imagined this. "I want to cover myself up," she said plaintively.

"That may be so, but I get pleasure from looking at you naked, so if I take your clothes off, you'll leave them off. If I want to kiss and suck your breasts, you'll let me kiss and suck your breasts. If I want to push you back and take you, you'll spread your pretty little legs and damn well let me do it."

Each word was delivered with cool, crisp inflection, until the quiver in her knees became a shake.

"Now, apologize for resisting me, on our wedding night of all nights," he said. "Say it prettily, my love. *'I'm sorry, my lord husband, for resisting you.'*"

What else could she do? She couldn't bear to be spanked again, and she knew that's what would happen if she didn't comply with his command. She wiped the tears from her face. "I'm sorry, my lord husband, for resisting you."

"Look at me, Aurelia." He waited until she managed to drag her gaze to his. "Let's be clear about things from the start. If you resist me in this again, you'll be punished. If you whine, if you disobey, if you act disrespectfully, you'll be punished. If you annoy me, you'll be punished. Fair warning, my darling. Do you understand?"

She stared into his dark eyes. She was so unsettled, so frightened, so *traumatized*, she couldn't think for a moment. "I don't want that to happen again."

"Then you must behave, mustn't you?" His gaze softened the slightest bit. "It was silly of you to resist when I was only trying to give you pleasure. Husbands and wives do these things. They kiss and caress. They make love. How do you think I felt when you pushed me away?"

"Angry," she managed, when it became clear he wanted an answer.

"Yes, angry. Frustrated. Rejected. Now you have a sore bottom because of it. Turn around."

She did, aching with shame. For long seconds he made her stand there and endure his scrutiny. She flinched as his cool hands traveled over each throbbing bottom cheek. "You'll sit prettily for a couple of days. A helpful reminder for you." He turned her back around. "Lie on the bed and spread your legs now, and try to behave as a good wife should."

She swallowed hard. She had been taught her whole life to keep her legs closed, to be pure and prim. Didn't he understand how difficult this was?

At her hesitation, he gave her a warning look. "I'll get a whip next, and you won't sit for a week."

"I'm so afraid." The words burst out of her, weak and humiliating.

"You're afraid because you're resisting. If you'd let it happen, you'd find it's not as bad as your maiden's fears." He let out a sigh. "Has no one educated you about sexual intimacies in marriage?"

"I was educated," she said, sniffling. But that education didn't mention tearing clothes, and spankings, and whips.

"What would your parents think about the way you've conducted yourself this evening?" he asked. "You're here in my beautiful home, my own lawful wife, and you had to be spanked like a naughty child for refusing my touch. I'm nearing the end of my patience." He pointed to the bed.

Aurelia crawled onto the counterpane, certain he was staring at her hot, aching bottom. When she tried to slip under the sheets, his sharp voice stopped her.

"No. Lie on top. Spread your legs as I told you."

She looked over at him. He'd taken off his robe and turned to drape it over the back of a chair. His buttocks were sleek and tight. His entire back looked powerful, bunched muscles radiating strength. Then he turned.

Aurelia's breath hitched in her chest. From her mother's vague description of the aroused male anatomy, she'd expected something more of the size of a finger. Lord Townsend's member looked the size of all her fingers put together, and then some.

She looked away, feeling panicked. Trapped. She'd been taught the mechanics of sex but never imagined the relative size of things. Lord Townsend would tear her asunder with that thick shaft, and he wouldn't care. That was the worst of it. He didn't care about her, he only cared that she respected and obeyed him. She could not, *could not*, make her legs part. They seemed to draw together of their own accord.

He stood beside the bed, tall and threatening, with that great, thrusting sex organ bobbing obscenely toward her.

"I'm waiting," he said.

She thought he could wait until he died. She couldn't open her legs and offer herself to be plundered.

"You prefer the whip then?" he asked in a patient voice. "Either way, this marriage shall be consummated."

She didn't want the whip. She flinched at the threat in his stare and inched her legs apart. She supposed it was enough to mollify him, for he came to the bed and pressed them the rest of the way open, one palm braced on the inside of each thigh. He knelt between her legs, coming over her so his own body weight and breadth kept her spread open. She could feel the broad, hot tip of him against her most private place.

I'm afraid. Don't hurt me. Please don't make me do this. She didn't say any of the thoughts spinning in her mind because she knew he would disregard her pleas. She tried to think of Lord Warren. Surely he wouldn't have been like this, heavy and rough, and impatient, and demanding. He never would have spanked her for resisting...but she wouldn't have resisted him. She looked up into the face of her husband, guiltily. He'd spank her again if he knew she was thinking about his friend.

And she didn't want to think of Lord Warren right now. He was too lovely to attach to this moment. "Please, just do it," she whispered. "Don't make me wait."

"Oh, but I think I'll make you wait." As he said it, his mouth dipped again to her breasts. She felt disgusted and powerless, being pawed and stared at and slavered over like some East End prostitute. She closed her eyes and laid her head back on the pillow, determined to endure whatever he did to her. He tongued her pebbled nipples, circling them, then he nibbled the sensitive skin surrounding them.

She wanted to disappear. She wanted to feel nothing. But he wanted her to feel.

He continued to tease and suck her breasts until some simmering heaviness developed in response. She didn't feel the heaviness in her breasts, but lower, in her belly and between her legs. Now and again he'd stop and caress her neck and shoulders, pressing kisses along her skin. He kissed her cheeks and her ears, using his fingertips to tease behind them the way he had in Arlington's garden. She wanted to be a proper lady, a good wife, but she felt so lost. The more he touched her, the more the hot heaviness within her grew.

He shifted his pelvis closer, so his rod cradled within the folds of her quim. She tried to lift away from him, but then he contacted some part of her that ached in a completely novel manner. Now each time he touched her nipples with his tongue, she felt a longing *there* that had her shifting her hips.

"You see, my little innocent? It's not all bad, is it?" His fingertips whispered down her cheek, brushing at lingering tears.

But it was bad. It was horrible, because she didn't love him. Even more horrible—her body betrayed her, warming to his caresses. He shifted again, probing at her with his thick member, and she realized that she was wet down there, as if welcoming him to press inside. He moved his hips, tensed them in a sinuous way and slid back.

He meant to enter her now. Panic overwhelmed her. "No," she pleaded. She pushed at him, not even meaning to do it. He caught her hands and pulled them hard over her head.

"Yes," he whispered back, pressing them to the upholstered headboard. He gritted his teeth, his expression intent. He surged forward with a firm, abrupt thrust.

Aurelia cried out, straining at the shock of his entry. He persisted, holding her hands hard, sliding his body over hers as he seated himself deep inside her. It *hurt*. It stung terribly as he stretched her. She arched her hips but it accomplished nothing, only wrested from him a guttural groan.

"Be still a moment," he gasped. "Lie still, Aurelia."

She lay still as a corpse. She never wanted to move again. Any movement only reminded her of the stretching ache, and her vulnerability, and his coarse domination. He touched her deep inside with that thrusting part of him. He was joined to her, within her, and it seemed to cause him as much anguish as it caused her.

"Is that all?" she whispered. "Will you please get it out of me?"

"No," he answered roughly. He drew back and then moved forward again, filling her, invading her, causing that frightening stretch and ache.

"Don't hurt me."

"I won't hurt you, for God's sake. It's supposed to feel good."

His voice sounded tight. She breathed in small pants. Good? It was the most outrageous, intrusive activity imaginable. *This* was what men loved to do, so much that they seduced women, and kept mistresses and whores? She couldn't understand.

"Aurelia," he moaned, as he withdrew and surged forward again. There was no denying it—he found pleasure in this. He gripped both her hands in one of his and used the other to tilt back her head. He kissed her, a strong, insistent play of lips and tongue that forced her mouth open. He pressed his tongue inside her the same way he pressed his—his—thing inside her. Her wrists ached where he held them. She felt an uncomfortable pressure in her pelvis above and beyond his presence there. She squirmed against him, not knowing her part in this bizarre exchange.

"If you do that, this will be quickly over," he said through clenched teeth.

Oh, she wanted it over. She squirmed again and squeezed around him, as if she might be able to force him out of her. He gasped out indecent oaths that blistered her ears. She'd never heard such coarse language. Would he pull away and punish her? What would be worse, enduring more of this "lovemaking" or having her backside blistered again?

Her bottom felt sensitive and sore as his thrusts pushed her against the mattress. She didn't know if she could bear another spanking. Better to be still and let him finish whatever on earth he was trying to accomplish. He kissed her jaw, her forehead, her temple, moving into her, deeper, deeper, deeper. It was fast and slow, hard and soft, long and shallow and then so forceful she slid across the bed. She couldn't get her bearings and she couldn't understand the nagging urgency she felt, that she should be *doing something*. But whenever she moved her hips he looked harried and displeased, and cursed again.

"My hands hurt," she said against his ear. "My wrists."

He let go of them. "Put your arms around my shoulders. Hold on to me," he ordered in a voice so vehement she didn't dare disobey.

Gingerly, she encircled her husband's broad shoulders and let her hands rest on his back. She could feel his muscles work as he moved in her, could feel all the leashed power beneath his dampened skin. He didn't hurt her so much anymore. Her body had finally come to accept his length and girth, but there was still that uneasy feeling of being joined to him. She couldn't close her legs. She couldn't escape him. She felt breathless and anxious to be finished.

With a shuddering gasp, he pressed his cheek to hers and went still. His hips ground against hers, lifting her from the bed. All the muscles in his back tensed as he jerked, and he made a noise that wasn't words, only sounds, like he was dying.

He has had some kind of attack, she thought. *He has died here in my bed and everyone will blame me for it.*

She gave a small, whimpering cry, imagining her father's disapproval, but then he lifted his head and looked at her. He was definitely alive. His gaze burned her, it was so intense.

"What's wrong?" he asked.

"Is it...finished?"

"Yes, damn you. It's finished." He shook his head when her face crumpled. "No, don't. Don't cry. I shouldn't have said that." He dropped his chin. "Damn it to hell."

43

She bit her wobbling lip, not wishing to risk his wrath. A tear squeezed out anyway. "I'm sorry. I'm sorry if I did that wrong."

He made a frustrated sound and pulled away from her, and sat on the edge of the bed. After a moment, he raked a hand through his hair, so that when he turned back to her, the black wavy locks stood on end.

"It's not that you did it wrong," he said. He reached and touched her hair, and rested his palm a moment against her cheek. He kissed her forehead, then drew away, his lips pursed.

She waited for him to say something else, to explain, to calm her confused agitation. But he said nothing. He stood and walked over to retrieve his dressing gown. His organ didn't look so frightening now, having somehow shrunk to half its previous bulk. It wouldn't have been so bad, she thought, if it had remained that size.

"I suppose you'll be more comfortable if I sleep away from you," he said gruffly. "If I stayed in my own rooms."

"Oh. Yes." She would prefer that a thousand times over what had just transpired. "If that's possible, I would prefer it."

He looked away from her, toward the ceiling, then toward the door. "Very well. Good night."

"Good night."

He didn't even put on his dressing gown, only stalked across the room and opened the door, and stepped into the hall. A moment later, she heard his door slam with a bang. Well, my goodness, he was strange. His servants might have seen him in that state of undress. She thought it very reckless of him, even if his room was just across the hall.

She lay shivering in bed, trying to collect her scattered thoughts, trying to understand what had just happened. Her mother said this act could result in affection between a couple, as well as a baby. She put her hand over her womb, wondering how fast these things took place. As for affection, she felt nothing of that. The look he had given her as he quit her company...

She supposed men didn't like being forced to marry, but she'd been forced, too. All in all, it had been a horrible day, even more horrible than she had imagined.

She wept as quietly as she could. She didn't want him to hear.

Chapter Four:
A Bloody Damn Waste

"My, my, what have we here? Observe, my friends. The married specimen." Warren's voice rang out in the dim, smoke-filled confines of their gentlemen's club. A hand flattened atop Hunter's news sheet as another lifted his half-empty glass.

"What are we drinking, Lord Townsend?" asked August in a mocking tone. He took a sip as he slid into one of the seats at the table. "Ah. A big, golden, whiskey-flavored glass of regret."

"Don't say such things," Warren scolded. He knocked off August's hat and made room for Arlington to set a chair beside him. "A married man doesn't feel regret, only the lofty ecstasies of love."

At those words, all three men stared at Hunter.

"Do you feel in love?" Warren prompted.

Hunter couldn't profess to be in love, no. In fact, he'd languished in a most uncomfortable state of self-loathing since he'd left his wife's bedchamber the night before. Aurelia had been beautiful, lush, nubile, innocent—and icy as her glacier-gray eyes. He'd enjoyed himself anyway, availing himself of her hot, tight pussy because it was his right, and because he'd gone without sex the entire week before.

That had been a mistake, of course. He hadn't been as controlled as he ought to have been for her first time. He hadn't been patient, at least not patient enough to overcome her deeply ingrained fears. He'd spanked her, to correct her in the notion that she might ever refuse his attentions, yes, but he'd done it selfishly too. He'd done it because it excited him, pervert that he was. The memory of her round, spankable arse still roused a rigid response in him. Had Warren asked him a question? He couldn't remember.

"He's rendered speechless by the blissful state of matrimony," Arlington said, signaling for more libations. "Let's hope Lady Dormouse flourishes in an equally blissful mood."

"I wouldn't think so, since he's here at the club the day after his wedding," Warren said glumly.

Hunter shrugged. "My wife's in hiding. I hope the servants took her breakfast. Otherwise she's starving to death in her bridal bower."

"You'd best keep her alive, or you'll have to answer to Laudable Lansing," August said. "And he's not one to be crossed. Then there's Little Lansing to worry about. The Marquess of Whatever."

"Severin," said Hunter. "The Marquess of Severin."

"The brother," Warren nodded, still glumly.

They looked around. The Duke of Lansing never showed his face at the gentlemen's clubs but his son—Aurelia's brother—sometimes did. The Marquess of Severin did not appear to be in attendance but a bottle of whiskey was delivered to the table with a note.

"Ah," said August, flipping it open. "With regards from the Earl of Newscombe. Congratulations on your marriage and all that." He flipped the card over to Hunter. "You see, they all want to weasel into our depraved little group, since we're down one member."

"You're not down one member," said Hunter, once he'd turned to thank Newscombe with a nod. "I have no intention of turning into Laudable Lansing and forgoing the sins of the flesh."

"But you've a wife now," said Warren.

"What does that matter?"

"Here, gentlemen," said Arlington, interrupting their spat. "As the first one of us to bed a virgin, I believe Towns deserves some type of commendation." The duke poured for everyone at the table and held up his glass. "To Lord Townsend, who stuck his cock where no cock's been before."

"Stuck is right," said Warren. "How'd you fit it in there without me coming beforehand to loosen her up?"

"All of you are degenerates." Hunter shook his head, refusing to raise his glass. "It's a nasty business, bedding a virgin. Nothing to celebrate, I'll tell you that."

The men drank anyway, and Hunter drank too in the end, because it was easier than dealing with his conscience.

"Wasn't she grateful, then?" August put down his glass with a bang. "If she cried, you didn't do it right."

"She was afraid, damn it. She—" His voice cut off. These were private matters. He leveled a scathing look at his friends and hunched over his drink. Before he married, it was no unusual thing to talk about the women they bedded, since they shared most of them. But now the woman in question was his wife, the mother of his future heirs. "It's none of your goddamn business, but virgins are...skittish."

For long moments there was no sound save the clinking of glasses and the other muted conversations in the room. A gentleman in the corner crowed briefly over a hand of cards.

"You must try to allay her fears then," said August, breaking the heavy silence. "It can't be that difficult. Not for you."

"How not? She doesn't like me. She wanted Warren, you know." He tried to make a joke of it, but his lips twisted and the jibe sounded more like a growl.

"Warren?" August barked out a laugh. "God save her from demons she doesn't know. Did you tell her Warren's a worse deviant than you? An unrepentant hedonist and lover of unnatural sex acts?"

"Well, that could describe any of us," Warren retorted in an injured tone. "It's not my fault Townsey's wife developed a *tendre* for me. I never courted her. She was one of Minette's friends."

Hunter ignored the ensuing bawdy accusations and innuendos. He believed Warren. The man wasn't one to flirt with innocents. Like all of them, he adhered to a code of honor. A morally sketchy one, perhaps, but a code of honor nonetheless. The four of them fulfilled their objectionable desires with experienced, willing women, and by silent agreement, left the innocents alone.

Of course, he'd been tempted to tell Aurelia about Warren the night before, especially when he felt her rejection and revulsion like a weight in his chest. He'd been tempted to pierce her precious, girlish fantasies and tell her just what sort of man she'd fallen in love with, but in the end he couldn't do it. He'd already hurt her so much.

Or had he? Hunter wasn't sure where Aurelia fit into his convoluted code of honor. He hadn't broken any laws, spanking her and bedding her last night. It was a man's right to discipline his wife, and a man's right to enjoy the bit of flesh between her thighs and put a baby in her womb if he wanted to. There were so many more things he could have done to her, sordid, depraved things, but he chose not to. He chose to protect her from that side of him—and from knowing the truth about Warren—and all he'd received in return was her fearful distaste.

"I need to get back to my regular life," said Hunter, and everyone at the table knew what he meant.

"Do you think Lady Townsend will accept your 'regular life'?" August asked.

"She'll accept what I wish her to accept. That's one thing I'll say for my wife. She's easily cowed with the proper methods."

Warren frowned. "Always the disciplinarian. Beaten her already, have you?"

"I would never beat my wife. I may have spanked her, though. She deserved it."

"For shedding virgin's tears? It's going to keep me up tonight, that vision."

"Are you judging me, Warren?"

His friend gave a lurid smile. "I meant, it's going to keep me up in the nicest of ways." He glared at his friend in feigned frustration. "I have to pay Marta or Imogene whenever I want to wallop a delicious arse. You only have to accuse your wife of some breach of behavior and turn her over your lap."

"Marriage has its perks."

"For you, anyway." Arlington grinned. "I don't know how Lady Dormouse feels about those perks."

"She's my little dormouse now, fully and legally. She'll feel what I want her to feel, or she'll be punished for it."

"Poor little dormouse," said Warren, to general laughter.

48

Hunter took a deep drink of whiskey and raked a hand through his hair. It was all very well for them to laugh. He was feeling damn unsettled about Aurelia, and about married life. He would try again tonight to show her some warmth and patience in bed, but he didn't know how long he could hold out before he returned to his bachelor-style pursuits.

* * * * *

Hunter wasn't surprised that Aurelia cried off on dinner, but he felt damned pathetic eating alone the day after his wedding. He ought to have stayed at the club with his friends but that would have caused talk. Here at home, there were only the stone-faced servants to witness the obvious failure of the Lockridge-Lansing alliance.

He sent a message for her to come down and join him, but it went unanswered when the servant was refused entrance to her rooms.

"Has anyone been in her rooms today?" he asked in a fit of temper. The servant informed him that her lady's maid had been admitted for a short time but that the marchioness had not touched any of her luncheon or dinner trays.

"Fix another," he said, pushing his plate away. She could refuse to admit the servants, but she'd not refuse him. He carried the tray himself, mounting the central marble stairway and stalking down the right side corridor to her suite of rooms. A footman materialized, sweeping open the tall, carved door without the least change in his expression, as if it were perfectly normal that his master might carry a dinner tray to his wife. After Hunter entered, the door closed behind him with a barely audible click.

The room was dark. The sheets were turned down on her great, tall bed, but it was empty. He scanned the room, and discovered a faint glow of candlelight shining from within the curtained window seat. He ducked under the pleated silk panels concealing the recessed space. Aurelia curled in the furthermost corner of the right bench, her knees pulled up to her chest. A lace-edged dressing gown pooled around her on the pillows. Its bright, floral-patterned embroidery contrasted with her miserable expression. As she turned to look at him, her gaze communicated dread.

"I see you've found yourself a little mouse hole," he said. He sounded crueler than he meant to.

49

She didn't answer, only drew her arms more tightly around her knees. He sat on the left bench, across from her, the gilt silver dinner tray balanced on his knees. His gaze strayed up to the curtains, then past the flickering candle on the sill to the black night outside.

"I'm happy if you like this place," he said with careful softness, to make up for his earlier tone. "I used to hide in here as a child, when I visited my great-aunt Emma. In the daytime you could see the neighbor's park, with intersecting paths and diamond shaped topiaries. I wonder if they're still there."

"They are," she murmured.

"I've brought you some food. Have you eaten today?"

"I'm not hungry."

"Aurelia."

She seemed to shrink within herself, a miserable, fragile huddle in his window seat. In his house. His wife...and she wouldn't look at him, wouldn't smile or even attempt to make basic conversation.

He deserved it.

"I suppose we'll learn to tolerate one another eventually," he said. "I expected no more from this marriage."

"I don't want to be married at all." She shifted, leaning her forehead against the smooth, leaded glass. "I want to go home."

"This is your home now. You're married to me, and after last night, possibly pregnant with my child. We're bound forever, whether you wish to be or not." He sounded petty, pedantic, like some blasted schoolmaster. So tedious, this being-a-husband nonsense. "I want you to eat something," he said. "And before you say no, pray remember the consequences of disobedience. I won't hesitate to spank you again."

She gave him a look of such burning hatred it might have singed the wool off a sheep, but she unfolded herself from her protective huddle and sat up across from him, pulling her dressing gown tighter across the curve of her breasts. He nudged the tray closer.

"It's only..." She stared down at the artfully arranged dishes on the tray's lace doily. "I'm not well. Perhaps you ought to call a physician."

He felt a frisson of alarm. "A physician? Whatever is the matter?"

"Last night, after you coupled with me, there was...blood."

The anxious pounding in his temples diminished. "There's supposed to be blood. You were a virgin, weren't you? It's an unpleasant business, but I'm told most virgins bleed." He sighed. "Eat something, whether you're hungry or not. Even if you starve yourself to a skeleton, I'll still take you to bed. I have no other choice. There must be an heir."

He sounded like a scold but he didn't know how else to go on. She set him on edge, this listless mouse hiding in his home. She feared him, and he wasn't sure that was a good thing anymore. She began to eat, the tiniest bites that could still qualify as actual consumption of food. Her hair was half up, half down, a disarranged style that made her appear more luscious than she probably wished to.

"*Coupled with you*," he muttered under his breath. "You make it sound so dispassionate. So stiff and cold."

She continued to eat, not glancing up from her plate. He'd spoken low enough that she could pretend she hadn't heard him, but he said the next words loudly enough to be clear.

"I want you to know that if you continue to bar the servants from your rooms, I'll have your doors removed. That would make it interesting when we *coupled*, wouldn't it?"

Her fingers tightened on her silverware. "You wouldn't."

"I would."

"Am I to have no privacy then?"

"If I wish it."

She took another miniscule bite of pheasant, chewing it for so long it must have turned to liquid in her mouth. She had magnificent lips. Fine, straight teeth. He wanted to put something quite a bit larger than a bite of pheasant into her mouth. Eventually, he'd try it.

Of course, she'd fight against him and refuse, and take to her bed in a fit of vapors like any well-bred lady would. Perhaps he wouldn't bother to try. He doubted it would be worth all the outraged whining and crying he'd endure in return. There were a dozen ladies at Pearl's who could perform exotic miracles with their tongues and lips, for a generous enough fee.

He looked away when he realized he'd been staring at her mouth. He was rigid, aching to push her back on the cushions and fuck her right here in her private, velvet-cushioned mouse hole. Perhaps she realized the bent of his thoughts, for she began to eat with greater intent. Pheasant, potatoes, roasted vegetables, and occasionally, a great drink of wine.

Anything to delay the impending bedding, he thought drily. This marriage would kill him within the week.

He had no idea how he'd manage to live with her. He could send her to his country estate, leave her there and go on about life as if she didn't exist, but that wasn't an option until he had at least two sons in the nursery.

"Are you finished?" he asked as she picked at the assortment of cakes. She took a little taste of each, although she appeared to crave more. Why demolish the entire plate of pheasant and vegetables in self-preservation, and then leave the cakes? "You may eat all of them if you like."

She glanced up at him guiltily. "A lady mustn't overindulge in sweets."

"Or she'll be too fat to land a husband? Well, you've got a husband, so you needn't worry about that anymore." He wanted her to eat the cakes because he thought it would make her happy, and she was so unhappy about everything else. But she didn't, and after she wiped her lips and hands, he put the tray aside on the bench.

"Before I take you to bed, Aurelia, I think I'd better inspect your bottom and make sure there's no lingering damage from last night's spanking."

As he expected, she went beet red and pulled her dressing gown more tightly closed. "There's no lingering damage. None at all."

"I wouldn't be a very good husband if I didn't make sure. I doubt you can inspect yourself as closely as I can." He put a hand on her arm and drew her resisting figure over his lap. "Come now. Don't make a fuss or I'll be forced to give you another spanking, and we'll be right back where we began, won't we?"

"It's only—"

"It's only what? That you didn't learn your lesson about resisting me last night?"

She went still across his lap. While she let him draw up her dressing gown to bare her bottom, she vibrated with tension. Fury? Fear? Her reluctance aroused him, as did her ample, porcelain bottom cheeks dappled with two or three scattered bruises from the night before.

"You're not fat, you know," he said as she trembled beneath his fingers. "You're perfect as you are. A man wants curves for pleasure. Nothing worse than a skinny, bony derrière."

Aurelia lay tense and silent over his lap as he ran his palm over the sensitive skin of her bottom. Horrible, to know he stared at her nakedness. He handled her as boldly as he pleased, his full staff straining against his breeches. She could feel it against her hip. Was it true that he found her "perfect"? She'd always imagined herself plump beyond measure, and not attractive at all. She certainly didn't have a bony derrière. If she had, she wouldn't have had any padding at all when he walloped away at her.

Oh, she didn't ever want *that* to happen again.

He kept her splayed over his lap for three minutes or more, groping and fondling her under the pretense of "inspecting for damage." The only thing damaged was her dignity, because her husband had spanked her last night, and now forced her to submit to this lewd inspection. Now and then the edge of his thumb drifted between her bottom cheeks, and she jerked away from him. He only pulled her back and resumed his task.

At last, when her face flamed with humiliation, he released her. "Your bottom looks fine. It's nice to know you can take a decent spanking if the situation warrants. Although I trust we'll not have an encore performance tonight?" He raised an eyebrow as he took up the candle and gestured her to go out. "To the bed, my dear. Heirs don't make themselves."

She preceded him, thinking how terribly awkward and businesslike this was. If she'd wed Lord Warren, she was sure there would have been tenderness, even romance, between them.

But she hadn't wed Lord Warren.

Lord Townsend lit a few more candles as she climbed into the bed. The sheets had been changed, the bloody evidence of their marriage's consummation whisked away by a blushing maid as Clement clucked in a soft, pleased voice about honor and becoming a woman.

There was nothing pleasing about it, although Aurelia tried hard not to do anything tonight that Lord Townsend might interpret as "resisting." He wanted to spank her again. She understood that, even if she couldn't understand the reason. She didn't want to give him any excuse to fulfill his wish.

She stared at the delicate floral pattern on the bed linens as her husband disrobed. What she'd seen of him the night before had thoroughly terrified her. He was made so differently from her. Well, of course he was, but he was even different from other men. He was larger, more physical somehow. She'd felt the hard muscles of his thighs last night as he'd laid her over them. She'd experienced the strength of his arms as he spanked her, and when he'd pushed her back on the bed and...mounted her... Well, then she'd felt an entire array of sensations that set her on edge. She had felt weak and fragile, and overtaken.

Her breath came shorter as he climbed onto the bed beside her. She stared at his face because it was easier than looking at the rest of his body. She felt his hard maleness poke her belly as he nudged her back on the pillows.

"There now, my little mouse," he said. "It won't hurt as much tonight, I promise."

She blinked up at him. "Please don't call me a mouse."

"What shall I call you then?" He dipped his head, pressing his warm lips to her trembling ones. "Something more scandalous? More erotic?"

The way he kissed her...it scrambled her brain. "You may call me Lady Townsend," she whispered.

"I don't think so, little Aurelia." He said her name in a low, breathless rasp. When she turned her face away, he grasped her chin and brought it back again. "I'll call you *ma petite chatte* instead. Do you speak French, my little pussy?"

She startled as his fingers parted the lips of her sex. "I—I don't think I speak the same kind of French you do."

"Undoubtedly."

"And French nicknames seem a bit scandalous."

"How difficult you are to please. I might call you anything and you'd find fault with it." He slid his fingers to a hidden, sensitive place between her legs, a button of flesh that warmed in a very pleasant way and made her jerk against him. He smiled and stroked her again, and again. "My little grasshopper. There."

Her eyes widened. "Grasshopper?"

"Yes, because you're jumpy, and because you chirp when I touch you. A disapproving type of chirp, and very soft, but there you go."

Aurelia didn't think she chirped, but it was possible. The more he fondled her, the less her utterances remained in her control.

"I don't know if I like being called a type of insect," she said, shifting to give him better access to that marvelous bit of flesh.

He chuckled and delved his fingers downward, into the shameful, hot wetness that had developed there. She tried not to resist but he was handling her so freely. "Please...that hurts," she lied.

"It doesn't. It feels wonderful, and your body wants more. Let me bring you pleasure, Aurelia."

He did find the most effective places to touch her. The tips of her breasts, the curve of her neck, and that aching, hot place between her legs. She stared up into his dark eyes, thinking that he smelled very good, like cinnamon and sandalwood, and other things she didn't recognize. An unfamiliar tingling crept up to her breasts and down between her thighs. It wasn't a civilized feeling, but something very uncontrolled and disturbing. The more he touched her, the more the feeling grew. She grasped his arms, struggling to maintain her composure.

"It would be okay for you to...to do things quickly," she said. "You don't need to take the time to p-pleasure me."

His caresses stopped. He looked down at her and sighed. "I do need to take the time. It's difficult to accomplish this properly if I don't."

"If only you understood how uncomfortable this makes me. I don't wish to resist you, but..."

She cringed as he drew away. She expected a slap or a scolding, but he only lay back and rested his head on his arm. He stared at her a long time, his expression impossible to read.

"I'm not like you," she whispered. She sounded cowardly, like the mouse everyone called her.

"You could be like me," he said, moving closer again. "You could be exactly like me, and feel all the pleasure I feel, if you'd only allow yourself to do it. But they've drummed you so full of lessons on primness and propriety, and goddamned ladylike restraint." He added a few more swear words that made her face burn. "They've raised you to be 'good,' to be cold and ashamed, and I'm the one who suffers for it."

"I'm sorry." He was so impassioned, so very angry with her. "Perhaps you could do what you must to get me with child, and then find your necessary pleasures elsewhere. I wouldn't mind."

His expression darkened even further. "Am I that awful? Honestly?"

He looked so irritated, she feared he would spank her again. "I'm trying to be a good wife. Since I can't meet your needs—"

"Since you *won't* meet my needs, you mean."

She rested a hand on his shoulder. It was a pure act of courage, to touch him when he was in this mercurial mood. "I want to bear children for you. I mean to do it, but the rest of it..."

"It's not your fault that you're this way." He sat upright and barked this out in a singularly frightening fashion. "It's not your fault you've been raised to behave like some pure and precious vessel. All your cloying little friends are the same. It's a damned shame, to my mind. A bloody damn waste of everyone's happiness."

"I agree," she said quickly, to mollify him. His cursing disturbed her, but not as much as the thought of another spanking. What did he mean by a pure and precious vessel? She was being a lady, a creditable wife. She was in bed with him, wasn't she?

He made a sound halfway between a mutter and a growl and climbed atop her, nudging open her legs. She felt his heavy, hard thing probing at her entrance and braced for pain, but he didn't thrust inside. He kissed her instead, a soft, tender kiss that stole her breath and made the throbbing start again.

"My lord," she said against his lips. He moved inside her a little bit, and her body tensed to accommodate him. A small plea escaped.

"Remember, I said it won't hurt as much today," he muttered. "And if you truly wish it, I'll be quick about things."

She nodded, her heart and her head full of too many conflicting impulses to form words. As uncomfortable as this act made her, there was something fascinating about it too, something that made her want to pull him close and cling to his shoulders. She supposed it was the very fact that they were joined together in such a close and intimate way. When else did this happen in life?

Her husband entered her, sliding in until their hips met, and then he went still inside her, staring down at her. As he promised, there was no pain like yesterday, only the nagging, stretching ache. She wished she could like this joining, but it was so strange. She held onto his shoulders and lay very still as he moved in her repetitively, in and out, cradling her beneath him. His body seemed a hard, dangerous thing, but his kisses and caresses were so gentle.

As she pondered duty, and marriage, and babies, he tensed above her, and his breathing changed. He let out a ragged gasp and went still, shuddering as he propped himself over her. His organ pressed all the way inside her, holding her pinned to the bed.

Tears formed in her eyes. She was very afraid she would never come to like this. It didn't hurt, and he was careful, but it seemed violent and uncivilized all the same. She was made to be a mother, a pillar of society, not a wanton in the bedroom. She knew it would be best to let him satisfy his needs elsewhere, as much as that offended her sense of decorum. Other husbands did so, in a discreet fashion, although her father disapproved of the practice.

Lord Townsend was nothing like her father.

After a moment her husband drew back, withdrawing from her body. The space inside her felt empty and cold. So did her soul. *I'm sorry*, she wanted to say. *I'm sorry that I'm not warmer to you. This is just the way I am.*

He pressed his cheek against hers and the threatening tears nearly overflowed. Then he rose without a word, gathered up his clothes, and crossed to the door. He turned back to her before he left. "Good night, grasshopper," he said. "Sleep well."

Chapter Five:
Hemmed In

Aurelia tried to act as if everything was perfectly fine as she took tea in Townsend House's parlor. Her mother and sister-in-law had come to call, and her mother's friend, the Dowager Countess Overbrook, who happened to be the aunt of the man she loved. Lord Warren's sister Minette had come too.

But not Lord Warren.

Aurelia had learned months ago, through Minette, that the Earl of Warren's given name was Idylwild. His sister called him Wild sometimes, and if Aurelia had been fortunate enough to have him for her husband, she supposed she would have called him Wild too. Instead she had a husband named Hunter. Taken together the names amounted to Wild Hunter, which was rather off-putting when one thought about it. Such savage names for two refined, titled gentlemen. The thought of savagery brought other memories. A spanking. Rasping words. A hard, probing invasion...

"How does married life suit you?" asked Minette brightly, once the older ladies had spoken at length on the grandeur of her new home and the smart china setting. "Have you quite settled in?"

Aurelia didn't know what "quite settling in" signified, but she replied just as brightly, "Yes, I am very settled in." When the ladies looked at her as if she ought to say more, she added, "Marriage is an interesting thing. There is so much to learn about the other person."

Minette made a face. "Don't learn too much about Lord Townsend. You might not like what you—"

"Minette!" her aunt said.

"I was only teasing. Anyway, everyone knows men are—"

"Minette, you are not old enough to know what men are." The dowager scolded in earnest now, and Minette fell silent to take a sip of tea.

"I know exactly what you mean about getting to know the other person," Georgina said kindly. "I've been married to Brendan for a year now and I still learn things that surprise me. Lovely things, of course. Why, just yesterday both of us learned a wonderful surprise." Her sister-in-law went pink and looked at the duchess.

The older women caught on more quickly than Aurelia or Minette. "You are increasing? Do say it's true, Georgina. What does Severin think?"

"Oh, he's ecstatic. We both are," she said, placing a hand over her still-flat waistline. "Our child will arrive around Christmas."

"A blessed gift indeed," said the dowager countess, then her gaze skimmed to Aurelia. "Soon you'll be in the same condition, and you will be a grandmama twice over, Emmeline."

Her mother flushed with pleasure. "I hope so."

Aurelia flushed too, but not with pleasure. More like fear, anxiety, dread.

"Now I've got to get Warren wed and set up in a happy home," the dowager said in a tone of forbearance. "It's difficult to find quality prospects these days. The ladies throw themselves at my nephew, quite blatantly begging for his hand, but few of them are up to snuff."

"He is such a handsome young man, like his father." The duchess clucked in sympathy for her friend and began to list some possible candidates for Lord Warren. Aurelia sat very still, trying not to upend the tea tray in a fury of despair.

"But our matchmaking cannot be interesting to the younger ladies," the dowager said when Aurelia's spoon rattled against her cup.

"Aurelia, why not take your friends for a walk in the garden?" suggested her mother. "And Lady Overbrook and I will plan our social machinations over tea."

"Social machinations sound fun," said Georgina with a grin, "but a walk outside sounds better. What do you think? Minette? Aurelia?"

Aurelia stood and agreed with a sigh of relief. She would lose her mind if she had to sit and listen to Lord Warren being paired with this lady or that. Minette was a ball of energy and had already crossed to the door.

"Minette," the dowager said, wagging a finger. "Do not be a nuisance to Lady Townsend and Lady Severin."

Aurelia envied Minette her mischievous spirit. Lord Warren also laughed often and had a twinkle to his eyes. Aurelia had curried Minette's friendship to try to catch the attention of her brother, and while it had been in vain, she hoped they would stay friends.

And Georgina, soon to make Brendan a father! Her sister-in-law chattered on about pregnancy and babies as they strolled in the gardens. It was warm, but not unpleasantly so. When they came to a shady area with oak benches they agreed that Georgina must rest. As they sat shoulder to shoulder, Georgina turned to her in confidence.

"You must be honest now, Aurelia. How are things with you and the marquess?"

"They're fine," she hedged. "Really, everything is perfectly fine."

Georgina glanced at Minette, then back at Aurelia. "The wedding night was...?"

She could not, *could not*, meet their eyes. "I'm not sure it's proper to discuss it. Minette is unmarried."

"But I won't be for long," she protested. "Please discuss it. How else will I know what goes on?"

"Why don't *you* say what goes on, Georgina?" Aurelia gestured toward the woman's waist. "In your case, things seem to have worked."

"Aren't they working in your case?" Her sister-in-law seemed concerned.

Aurelia forced a smile. "Everything worked. I can certainly tell you that. I'm just not sure that... Well... He... Things are still a bit awkward between us."

"Oh, dear." Georgina rubbed the back of her hand and then squeezed it. "It takes time to become used to it, it's true."

"Used to what?" Minette asked in frustration.

"Used to being in bed with your husband," said Georgina. "You'll see what we mean in a year or two." She turned back to Aurelia with a thoughtful expression. "The marriage bed can seem strange, even frightening at first, but that will change."

"But you loved Brendan," Aurelia blurted out. "You loved him when you married him. Lord Townsend is a stranger to me. It's very disconcerting."

Georgina nodded in sympathy. "I know he wasn't your first choice of husband, but he's been kind, hasn't he?"

Aside from spanking me and forbidding me to resist his attentions...yes.

"I'm sure in a month or two all of it will seem very comfortable," said her sister-in-law. "Everything will be absolutely well."

Aurelia smiled and nodded, because she knew it was expected, and that Georgina and Minette would be put out if she continued to fuss about her marriage. What Aurelia really wanted to do was fall into her mother's arms and beg her to take her home.

Which was probably why the duchess had sent the three of them outside.

"I'm sure everything will be very well a few months from now," Aurelia said with a conviction she didn't feel. "And perhaps your baby will have a cousin on the way. Wouldn't that be wonderful?"

"I would like more tea cakes," said Minette with a pout. "If you're just going to talk in these vague generalities, let's go back."

* * * * *

Hunter struggled with the decision to return to his former erotic haunts. Well, struggled for a minute or so. Honestly, she'd practically begged him to slake his lusts elsewhere. That was what considerate husbands did.

He believed he'd demonstrated admirable patience, waiting an entire week before he stepped out, and he made sure to leave after she had already retired to her rooms. It was his right, of course, to do whatever he wanted, but she was so naive... She might raise questions he didn't want to answer. It had been a week now, a week of bedding her while she shivered and shrank away. He needed to indulge in some raucous, cathartic sex before he lost his mind.

He and his friends gave most of their custom to Pearl's, a well-appointed and well-managed sex parlor catering to a menagerie of tastes. It helped that it was on the right side of town, so gentlemen who went there preserved a certain dignity in the exchange. Hunter approached the brothel's artfully concealed back door and performed the appropriate three-part knock. A bruiser of a working man thrust his head out. "Good evenin', milord. How can I help ye?"

"Good evening, Fletcher. You can help me by letting me in."

"One moment, please." The burly man disappeared, leaving Hunter on the step to twirl his hat in his hands. This was odd. He was normally admitted as soon as he knocked. Perhaps Pearl was cross that he'd stayed away nearly three weeks. He would just explain the situation, his recent betrothal and marriage. Pearl understood married men and how the world worked.

Within a couple of minutes, the portly matron stuck her head out the door and then propped it open upon one of her ample hips. "Oh, milord. Fancy seeing ye here. I thought you got married last week. "

"I did, Pearl. I am being perfectly honest when I say I'm here with my wife's permission. Her urging, even."

The old woman laughed, though he wasn't joking. For some reason, she still didn't let him in.

"See, the thing is, milord, I hate to tell you, but..."

"Tell me."

"The Duke of Lansing says I'm not to admit you anymore. He says you belong at home with yer wife and you're not to come here."

"What?" It took Hunter a moment to realize he was being had. He threw his head back and laughed. "Pearl, you've always had a hellish sense of humor."

"I wish I was jestin' with you, luv. Believe me, I wish it were a joke but it ain't. The duke says yer not to come here."

This was preposterous. Ridiculous. "The duke can't stop me," said Hunter. "I'm a grown man. I can go wherever I like."

She grimaced. "Well...err...about that."

The first poking fingers of panic, or perhaps fury, traveled along his spine. Jolette, Colette, Paulette, Odette, all the most skilled ladies worked here. All of them knew how to arouse and satisfy him beyond his dreams. "Did he pay you to keep me out?" he asked Pearl. "I'll double it. Although I think it's not well done of you, old girl. I've been coming to your establishment for years now."

Her face wrinkled in sadness and regret. "Ye can't pay me to get in. You can't do anything, milord. That man Lansing, he meant business. He came hisself, he did, and sat in my drawing room looking like 'e was smelling rotten eggs. Said if I let you in here, he'd see to it that my parlor closed and that no one who worked for me could ever do business again. He was right specific, milord. He said I wasn't to let you over the door step, that 'e would know and take away me livelihood."

"I don't believe you."

"But sir, why would I make it up? You been one of my best customers. It's breaking my heart to say this to you, but you can't come to Pearl's no more, nor no other place, I reckon. The Duke of Lansing, he doesn't believe in men messing around on their wives. He says to me, *Honor begins at home.* That's just what he said. Made me feel two feet tall, an' I'm trying to run an honest business here. I told Madam Curtis what he done, how he come here and threatened me, and she said his men done the same to her. Then Mrs. Church said the same, and even Mrs. Purefell what runs that horrid place down near the docks. I imagine you could still get some doxy off the streets if you was sneaky enough—"

"I don't want a doxy off the streets," Hunter thundered, then turned away. Some other gentlemen had materialized and he stepped back to let Pearl do her business, feeling like a mockworthy piece. The lucky young bucks were admitted posthaste while he was barred from taking his pleasure because he had married Laudable Lansing's daughter. It hadn't even been his choice!

"Lansing isn't here now," he pleaded with Pearl when the men had gone inside. "Let me in, please. I'll pay you twice what I normally do. Four times."

"Milord, it can't be. I'm scared of that old duke, I am. He has the king's ear and more."

"Then let me set one of the ladies up in a private arrangement. I'll reimburse you for her loss."

"I can't," Pearl said, genuine worry making her voice quake. "And I don't dare stand here talking to you a bit longer. I'm sorry, milord."

With those words, she shut the door on him, and on his dreams of a pleasurable night. Madam Curtis too, and Mrs. Church. All his usual haunts. He'd never heard of this Mrs. Purefell near the docks, but if Lansing had gone to her he must have gone to every establishment Hunter might plausibly attend.

Damn the duke and his godforsaken moral compunction. Not only was he saddled with an ice cold wife, now he had no outlet for his more perverse desires. It was an impossible situation.

No.

There had to be someone who would defy the duke for enough money. London had fifty or more parlors for gentlemen of questionable tastes, as well as numerous actresses and courtesans for hire. If the Duke of Lansing thought he could curb Hunter's habits because he'd married the man's pure-as-snow daughter, he would shortly be proven wrong.

* * * * *

Three nights later, Hunter stumbled up the stairs of his friend Lord Warren's town home. He pounded on the great oak door so violently that Warren himself answered, looking grim.

"Do you have company?" asked Hunter. "Am I interrupting?"

"My company left hours ago, Towns. It's four in the morning."

"I need a drink."

Warren shied away, waving a hand before his nose. "I think you've had a drink. Plenty of them. Come in and tell me where you've been."

"Where I've been?" All his fury exploded out of him as he stumbled into his friend's dimly lit drawing room. He waved his arms about, yelling at the top of his voice. "I haven't been anywhere. I've been denied. Everywhere." He couldn't believe this was happening. "Three nights now I've been slinking around town trying to get into some house of ill repute. Trying to hire girls. Mistresses. Whores. Warren, he's put them all off limits, every single one in London."

"Who has?"

"Lansing, damn you. The Duke of Lansing. My lofty, putrid, godrotting father-in-law has seen to it that I'll never stray in my marriage to his precious daughter."

Warren made a sympathetic sound. "Sit down. You're in a panic, man. You've been on the prowl already, eh? So much for wedded bliss."

"*Wedded bliss* is a romantic figment of poets' imaginations." He threw himself on the divan near the fireplace and stretched out his legs. "Being married is like being in a cage you can't escape. It's torture."

"Come now, torture? Lady Townsend seems a sweet enough girl."

"She's exceedingly sweet. That doesn't help me get my cock sucked. It doesn't help me bugger her arsehole or stripe her bottom with a cane. It doesn't help me stroke myself to climax while she writhes in ropes at my feet."

Warren grinned. "You're a dirty bastard."

"This isn't funny. My wife can barely stand to touch me, you know. She thinks the most standard marital acts are lewd, and suffers through them with the mien of a martyr. I tried for a week to be faithful to her, but she's so cold and distant. I believe she actually hates me. She was the one who suggested I go elsewhere rather than continue to visit her rooms."

"Why does she hate you?" Warren asked. His brows drew together. "Have you terrorized her, you idiot? Her brother wouldn't hesitate to call you out at dawn, and Severin's a crack shot."

Hunter held up a hand. "I haven't done anything at all to her, aside from that spanking on our wedding night."

"Well done of you. Idiot."

"Otherwise, I doubt our marriage would have been consummated," he said, speaking over his friend. "What am I to do? We're absolutely unsuitable for one another. All I want is one night of blessed release, one night of a melting, obedient courtesan who'll allow me to discharge all my pent up frustrations." He dropped his head in his hands, then looked up at Warren. "Can you call one of your doxies over here? We can share her if you like."

"It's four in the morning."

"You can have her first."

"Townsey—"

"We've shared women before, and we like the same things. What would it matter?"

"Lansing's come to see me too, old fellow."

Hunter's mouth fell open. "What?"

Warren sighed, leaning forward in his chair. "He came to see me just before your wedding, and he wasn't very nice. Threatened to do a job on my public reputation, which I miraculously cling to. Threatened to ruin me if I did anything to assist you in committing 'extramarital vices.' He talked about Minette."

"Minette? He threatened your sister?"

"Not in so many words. He only explained how much harm could be done to her marriage prospects with a word from him here and there." He looked at Hunter. "She's my responsibility, and she'll be hard enough to marry off as it is. I can't help you run around anymore, Towns. I wish I could."

Hunter was flabbergasted. He bent over, grasping great handfuls of his hair. "Why didn't you tell me? Warn me? Did he visit all of you?"

"Me. August. Arlington. Yes, all of us."

"None of you said a word to me. None of you warned me that going through with this marriage would mean—"

"It wouldn't have mattered what it meant," Warren interrupted sharply. "You couldn't have gotten out of it at that point. Not without ruining Lady Aurelia and yourself. Now she's your wife and you're stuck with her." His friend's voice rose in frustration. "We haven't always been the most honorable bunch, but the ruination of decent ladies used to be unthinkable. What has changed in you?"

"My situation has changed," he said through gritted teeth. "Reproach me if you like. When you're married, you'll see."

"When I'm married, I won't give up within a week. Any woman can be tamed and taught if you put your mind to it." Warren crossed his arms over his chest. "Aurelia is a very good girl. She's Lansing's daughter. She's a dormouse, for God's sake, who shrinks if someone looks at her meanly. She will do as you like if you demand it. You must insist upon the behaviors you expect."

Hunter looked up at his friend. "Insist upon—what—? What the hell are you suggesting? You're talking about bedroom behaviors?" He laughed.

Warren didn't laugh. His arms remained firmly crossed over his chest.

"Has she made you into a mouse too?" he asked. "When I marry, my wife will obey me in all things. If I want her to perform unconventional sex acts in the course of our bedroom play, she will. This purity of marriage stuff is nonsense. You are the husband, the ruler of the household. You've spanked her once to assert your dominance, and doubtless can do so again."

Hunter pursed his lips. "It's wrong to use force in sexual matters. She'll resist me and start sobbing or something."

"I have more faith in you than that. If you go about things the right way, there won't be much resistance at all."

Hunter rubbed his temples and groaned. "Says the man who's not married to the daughter of Laudable Lansing. I have as much chance of training her into a whore as I have of sprouting wings and flying across the Thames."

"Not a whore, my friend. A wife who obeys. A wife who wishes to please her husband and has been trained how to do so."

Hunter lay back on his friend's divan. *A wife who obeys.* Lansing had drilled obedience into Aurelia from her earliest days. If Hunter could prevail upon her desire to obey, train her to perform these acts, even enjoy them, what a dream their life might be. But she was so unresponsive in bed. She hadn't the first inkling of sensuality or erotic awareness. She was as glacial as a block of ice. The idea of training her to please him was so absurd it was beyond imagining.

"She cannot even tolerate straightforward intercourse," Hunter said. "She hates when I touch her."

"If that's true, then you have a lot of work to do, old boy."

"I can't, Warren. It's a ludicrous idea. It would never work."

His friend stood and brushed at a spot of lint on his rumpled dressing gown. "In the end, you've no other choice. Lansing has got you hemmed in. You can go without the finer bedroom games for the rest of your miserable existence, or you can teach your wife to play them with you. Now, if you please, I am dead tired and you are three-parts drunk. Sleep there on the divan if you want. I'm headed to bed."

Chapter Six: Denial

By the time Hunter woke with a clashing headache, Warren had summoned the other lads to his place. They drank with him and agreed he was in a hell of a situation, and that Lansing was a wretched old blowhard with more rectitude than wit.

It was evening before he made his way home to Townsend House, mostly sober, but no less unsettled than the night before. He had the damn bad luck to run into his wife at the bottom of the grand staircase. If she could have avoided him, he was certain she would have, but she couldn't very well flee back up the steps.

"Good evening," he said, sketching a slight bow. He looked a fright, he knew. Disheveled, puffy eyed, unshaven, not like any sort of gentleman at all.

Miss Perfect Lady Dormouse, on the other hand, was dressed in pristine ivory silk with puffed sleeves, mounds of petticoats, and an ornately splendid bodice that revealed the lovely expanse of her breasts. She blinked at him, a blush spreading over her cheeks. "Good evening, my lord."

"You can call me Townsend, you know. Or Hunter. We're married."

"Good evening, Townsend," she repeated in a level, hollow tone. "You are well?"

"Perfectly well. I've been with my friends."

He saw in her face that she didn't believe him. She believed he had spent the past few nights with dissolute women. *If only...* If he had, he wouldn't feel so roused by her curvaceous figure, her pleasing, upthrust breasts bundled into her lace-trimmed gown. Damn her for such heartless temptation. He'd best get away from her and regain control of his lustful emotions. "I will see you at dinner," he said.

Her gaze flicked down at his dusty, rumpled clothes in a way that made him feel chastened. "I have a bit of a headache," she replied, lifting a hand to her forehead.

He had no patience for theatrics at the moment. "Let me restate, then, Lady Townsend. I expect to see you at dinner, headache or no."

She narrowed her eyes, dropped the briefest of curtsies, then turned from him to continue on her way. Her tightly coiled curls bounced as she fled across the hall and into the southernmost drawing rooms. She did boring, mousy things in there, like reading and embroidery. What a waste of her luscious body. He'd rather fill her hours with training on how to do the perverse acts the women performed at Pearl's...

Hunter shook his head. Warren was a blighted idiot for suggesting such a thing, since there wasn't a chance of it coming true. He stalked to the study off the grand, high-ceilinged foyer, and knocked out a half hour of necessary correspondence, then went to his rooms to bathe and dress for dinner. His valet hung up his wrinkled coat and waistcoat and shaved his overgrown stubble without a murmur of judgment or question. The warm water, the rasp of the razor, the familiar ritual of putting himself in order finally worked to calm his nerves.

By the time he headed to the dining room, tidied and proper in his formal dinner wear, he felt considerably better. He would approach his present life one day at a time. One evening at a time. One dinner at a time because there was nothing else to do. Perhaps in a few months Lansing would relent, and Hunter could take up his previous pursuits. Perhaps when Aurelia was with child, the confounded old man would bugger out of their business.

One dinner at a time.

Hunter looked around the dining room, finding no trace of his wife. He knew Aurelia had no more headache than he had virtue. He sat and waited for ten minutes, then beckoned a footman.

"Find Lady Townsend and tell her that I require her presence in the dining room at once."

The man murmured "Yes, my lord," and bowed out of the room. Not five minutes later he was back, bowing and scraping even lower.

"Where is my wife?" Hunter snapped.

"Her ladyship begs you to excuse her. She is feeling unwell."

Feeling unwell, was she? Not as unwell as she'd feel when he was finished with her. "Where is she?" he asked the footman.

"Her chambers, my lord."

Hunter pushed back his chair. He was not precisely angry, only very disappointed in the direction of his marriage and his life as a whole. He had a luscious and sexually alluring wife he couldn't make proper use of, and a world of needs with no outlet for the foreseeable future. If he must live in such circumstances, the niceties, at least, would be adhered to. His wife would sit with him at dinner in her revealing bodices, goddamn it, and more importantly, she would obey his reasonable commands.

Or he would become much less reasonable, which she wouldn't like at all.

He threw open her door when he arrived. Her hatchet-faced lady's maid was there, fluttering about. Her startled glance toward the window seat told Hunter exactly what he needed to know. "Leave. Now."

When he used that particular tone of voice, an able-bodied man wouldn't dare cross him. The maid opened and shut her mouth, dropped a hasty curtsy, and fled, shutting the door.

"Aurelia." He used the same sharply dangerous tone to draw out the syllables of his wife's name. "I told you—twice—that I required your presence at dinner."

There was silence, then a strained reply from the recesses of the window seat. "I am not well."

"Come here." If she didn't come he would go in and drag her out, but the authority in his voice did the trick. She poked her head from the curtains and took a few steps toward him.

"Come. *Here.*" He pointed to the spot of floor in front of him, his expression promising dire consequences if she didn't comply.

She swallowed hard and crossed to stand before him, all color drained from her cheeks. Let her be afraid. This confrontation was, after all, a result of her very poor choice to ignore his summons. He gave her a stern looking over, from the crown of her glossy, honey-colored curls to the hem of her primrose yellow dress.

"You look well enough, wife. I don't see you languishing in bed."

"I am ill. My digestion—"

"You said on the stairs you had a headache." She fell silent, a flush creeping over her pallid visage. "A headache? Poor digestion? Which is it? Not one lie, but two. I thought you a virtuous woman, Aurelia."

Her gaze met his but then skittered away. "I did not wish to come to dinner," she said. "I tried to decline politely."

"You lied to my face. And I made it clear—twice—that you would not be permitted to decline. When I send a servant to say that I require your presence at dinner, that is exactly what I mean."

She stared at the buttons of his waistcoat, still silently in rebellion. It would not do.

"Come on then," he said, taking her arm.

She resisted, digging her heels into the floor. "Come where?"

"Come and receive your spanking, for lying and being a stubborn pain in the arse."

"I will not," she cried.

Resist as she might, he was stronger than her. When she wouldn't follow him to the chair under her own power, he lifted and carried her, then sat and threw her over his lap. He pinned her kicking legs between his, and caught one of her arms to secure it behind her back.

"Listen to me, Aurelia," he said. "We can do this two ways. You can accept your punishment without fighting me, or you can fight me and receive twice as many blows. Which do you prefer?"

"This is wrong of you," she said, struggling against him. "I will tell my father."

"Your father would agree with my right to discipline you, especially when I told him you'd lied to me and behaved as a disobedient wife. He's such a stickler for proper behavior. Now, will you fight me, or will you submit?"

She struggled even harder. Very well. A lengthy spanking it would be. He jerked up her skirts with his free hand. No traces of her last spanking remained upon her bared buttocks, but that had been a simple introductory spanking. This would be an assertion of dominance, and if he did it correctly, it would leave lingering marks, not just on her bottom but in her memory. He began to punish her rounded globes with sharp, firm spanks.

"Oh! *Oww,*" she cried, jerking her legs in a useless effort to escape him. "You're hurting me."

"Of course I'm hurting you, Aurelia. It's a spanking. Really, this is by your choice."

"I didn't choose this. I didn't want this marriage. I didn't want *you!*" she yelled.

He ignored her frantic protests, concentrating instead on blistering her bottom. He'd honed his technique over the years, so he could spank a female to any range of severity without tiring his hand. Of course he would eventually need to progress to other implements if she persisted in defying him and behaving as an unruly child. He made a mental note to gather some such implements in his bedroom for the future. Based on her comportment at the moment, he was certain they'd be needed before long.

"Oww," she wailed. "It hurts. How long are you going to spank me?"

"Until you've learned your lesson. I'm not doing this for my own amusement, you know." *Well, not entirely...* "I'm doing this to teach you that lying and defying my commands will not be tolerated in this marriage. When I tell you to come to dinner, you'll damn well do so." He captured an unruly leg that had wiggled loose from between his thighs, and resumed his steady assault. "Furthermore, when I tell you you're to be punished, you will learn to submit to me without all this nonsense."

She twisted until she nearly tugged her arm loose, and then pummeled her feet up against his leg. He slid the slipper off one flailing foot and laid it against her bottom. *Whap!*

She bucked across his thigh and let out a scream of such bloodcurdling agony he wondered if one of the staff would come crashing in. "No," she screamed. "Stop! I can't bear this." Wails and pleas spilled from her mouth as he belabored her bottom with her slipper's leather sole.

"Remember, if you had chosen to take your spanking like a remorseful wife, without these struggles and theatrics, I would have already let you up. Instead you've kicked me, screamed at me, and continually tried to evade the blows."

"I'm sorry!"

He paused, running a hand over her heated, scarlet bottom. "Are you truly sorry? Or do you only wish me to stop?"

"I... I..." She shuddered as he caressed her. "I don't like to be punished."

"But you admit you lied to me? That you twice defied my direct and very reasonable order to present yourself at dinner?"

"Yes, my lord. I did those things." She gave a great sniffle and shifted on his lap.

"Do you wish to be released?"

"Yes," she sobbed. "Yes, please."

"*Yes, my lord* will suffice. And if I release you, will you take your spanking properly, and submit to what you deserve?"

She hesitated, then shifted again with a soft little moan. "Yes, my lord."

He dropped the slipper on the floor. As spanking implements went, slippers packed a hefty sting and were always readily available. If he needed it again, it would be there, but Aurelia seemed prepared to dispense with the kicking and screaming.

He made a fuss of arranging her in the more traditional fashion, over both of his thighs, her hands and her feet resting on the floor. "You are not to kick and buck," he said. "You must stay as you are positioned until I let you up."

"Yes, my lord," she said in a chastened whisper.

He resumed the spanking, delivering the same crisp smacks he'd begun with. He would not go easier on her now that he had her cooperation. He was not one to be manipulated by a woman's tantrums and outbursts, although he had to admit she was taking a considerable punishment to her tender cheeks. He paused to massage her bottom, assessing the damage. Without intention, his finger slipped down within the crevice of her sex.

She tensed and pulled away, but not before he encountered a telltale wetness, a gathering of moisture at her private place. "Be still," he said. She obeyed, but she whimpered as he probed there. Just a fingertip at first, then to his knuckle.

She was copiously wet.

"Enjoying this, are you?" he said under his breath. His little mouse, wet and aroused from a spanking. He could hardly believe it.

She ducked her head and he started spanking her again, only this time he stopped every few blows to slide his fingers through the evidence of her arousal. She drew herself up each time he did it.

"Please, my lord. Don't."

"Why not?" He slipped two fingers inside her. "It pleases me to do this. I believe it pleases you too."

"It doesn't. No!"

"What if I touched you here?" He slipped her own moisture down to the thrusting little nubbin of flesh at the apex of her sex.

She groaned in a kind of horror. He spanked her again, *whap, whap, whap*, and then returned to diddling his hapless wife. Perhaps it was cruel to do this, to confront her with this evidence of her own depraved longings, buried beneath years of lessons on virtue. She had cried before. Now she positively wept, but she kept her feet down and her hands in place as he spanked and molested her in turn.

At last, when her bottom was hot to the touch and pleasingly scarlet, he stopped his onslaught and let her up. He made her stand facing him, with her skirts drawn up over her punished arse cheeks.

"Look at me," he said. "Tell me what you've learned."

Her eyes were stormy, tearful gray, her delicate features flushed and damp. "I'm not to lie to you anymore, my lord. I'm to listen to you when you give me orders. I'm to come to dinner when I'm told and...and be good."

"Have you learned anything about taking a proper punishment?"

"Yes." She nodded and sniffled. "I'm not to resist you. I'm to submit to..."

"To your husband's lawful guidance."

"Yes."

"You've been spanked once already for resisting me, haven't you? And now again. If you persist in this behavior, my love, the punishments will worsen with each subsequent offense. I'll use a switch, or a strap, or a cane if necessary to stop you doing it. Do you want that?"

She shook her head. "No, my lord."

"Go stand in the corner by the window for five minutes and think about the things we've discussed. Leave your skirt up over your bottom so you'll feel the air on your punished cheeks as a reminder."

She turned from him in misery and did as he bade her. It created powerful feelings in him, watching his wife walk to the corner and stand there, compliant, head bowed. He'd spanked countless women but never like this, never with real stakes and a real relationship of authority. His cock throbbed, stiff and thick, squeezed uncomfortably beneath the fitted fabric of his breeches.

He could, he realized in that moment, make her do anything. She'd had a frantic, pained reaction to her punishment, yes, but she'd had a sexual reaction too. Did she feel the same visceral arousal in submission that he felt in commanding her? If she did, she would hide it and deny it as long as he permitted her. It would take skill and patience to bring these submissive yearnings to full flower, especially in a timid creature like her.

But he could do it. Warren had been correct after all.

Aurelia shifted in the corner and made an anxious sound, as if, somehow, she'd been able to follow the direction of his thoughts. He loosened his falls and released his aching cock. He stroked it up and down, staring at his wife's bottom framed by the fine yellow silk of her dress. He had to have her. He had to be inside her just as she was, with her skirts up and her face in full blush as she faced the wall.

He crossed to stand behind her. When she made as if to turn, he stopped her with a hand on her shoulder. "Don't move. Stay as you are."

She shuddered as he stroked her bottom, parting the reddened flesh and delving downward to fondle her hot quim. If anything she was wetter than before, even slicker with feminine lust. He ground his swollen organ against her backside.

"You're learning, aren't you?" he whispered against her ear. "You wish to be my obedient, virtuous wife."

"I... I'm..."

He silenced her with a finger over her lips. "Don't talk. Your five minutes aren't up yet."

His other hand probed her pussy, sliding through honeyed folds. He pushed his breeches down to his knees and pressed his cock to her wet opening from behind. She jerked as if startled.

"Hold your dress up," he ordered. "Don't let it go."

He took her hips and pushed inside her. She was so tight, so inexpressibly satisfying to conquer. She gave a light, breathless whine as he stretched her open with his thick length. At the same time, he manipulated her most sensitive flesh, trying to bring her the same pleasure he felt. It wasn't long before she melted against him. He clasped her tight, encircling her in his arms. He tipped her chin back and kissed her, once, twice.

She didn't kiss him back. She seemed altogether lost in the moment, which wasn't a bad thing.

"Does this feel good?" he asked quietly. "Do you like this?"

She shook her head, but it wasn't much of a shake. It was a very weak denial.

"You mustn't lie, remember," he said, sliding a hand down to squeeze her still-heated arse. "If you lie, you'll have to learn your lesson all over again, and I'm sure you wouldn't like that. Answer me. Does this feel good?"

He stroked and teased her little button until she was practically dancing on her toes. "It feels g-good. Yes."

That whispered admission resonated through his straining muscles straight to his balls and cock. He was going to bring her to climax, his glacial little dormouse, whether she wished it or not. He drove up inside her, stroking and urging her, using her breaths and shudders to judge how to touch her to bring her to her peak. Here his experience served him, for she was, like all women, easily manipulated with the right touches and the right words. He was slow and patient, studying her reactions and using everything he learned to drive her pleasure higher.

When she stiffened against his front, gripping his cock and gasping in the throes of satisfaction, he let out a groan and bucked into her, filling her with his seed. She pressed her hands against the wall as her tight sheath milked him of every last drop. He held her close, reveling in her beautiful surrender. Her skirts stayed bunched between them as he thrust into her with one last surge. *Ahh...*

A successful punishment session, this, for more reasons than one.

He stepped away from his wife and let her skirts fall back to her ankles. She stayed facing the wall as he straightened himself and refastened his breeches. That finished, he turned her about, and used a thumb to force her gaze to his.

She looked confused, flustered, and utterly devastated.

"You would have learned how at some point," he said, stroking his thumb across her cheek. "I would have taught you, little grasshopper, whether you wanted to learn or not."

She stared at him a long moment, then turned her face away. "I am not an insect."

"But you are a woman, aren't you? A woman with desires and feelings, as much as you endeavor to deny that fact." He released her and walked toward the door. "I expect you downstairs at the dining table within ten minutes time, Aurelia. I am positively starved."

Chapter Seven: Dinner

Her husband stood from his seat at the head of the table when she arrived. Aurelia crossed to her place at his right, feeling the weight of his dark gaze as if he touched her with his very hands. She wondered if any of the servants had heard her screaming earlier. She felt that all of them must know of her shame, but one person certainly knew, and that was Lord Townsend.

She nodded at him as she took her seat. He murmured a greeting in return and watched her shift helplessly, trying to find a comfortable way to sit. Her bottom ached. There was nothing for it. At least he'd given her time to compose her appearance—and her scattered thoughts—before the meal commenced.

Aurelia was certain her lady's maid had heard her screaming, but the old woman pretended she hadn't, as any experienced servant should. Aurelia was glad. She didn't want to talk to anyone about what had happened, not yet. She was still coming to terms with her husband's actions afterward, and her own body's traitorous display. The things he had made her feel, both good and bad, defied understanding.

As the servants began the choreographed niceties of the dinner service, she slid a glance at him. He watched her with a studious expression, his lips drawn down in a frown. She was grateful for the food set before her, because it gave her something to do besides make conversation.

Because what on earth was there to say?

"Have you found Townsend House a comfortable home?" he asked abruptly in the silence. "I mean to ask, are your rooms all they could be? Do the servants meet your needs?"

She paused, fork in hand. "Admirably, my lord."

He made a soft sound. "Will you call me Hunter, damn you? There's no one else here."

"Will you refrain from cursing at me, Hunter?" she replied with as much heat as she dared. If she angered him again, she wasn't sure her backside could endure the result. She speared a sauced potato and chewed it woodenly.

Her husband wasn't angry. In fact, he seemed amused. "I like when you're not such a mouse. Yes, I'll try to stop cursing at you."

"And using indecent language. It's very lowering. I'm certain you wish to be thought a respectable gentleman."

"Like your father?"

She clamped her lips shut, not wishing to enter into a spat. In her peripheral vision she could see Lord Townsend's mouth curve up in a faint smile. Now and again he made some unobtrusive gesture that brought a footman running to deliver this and that. She sat very straight in her chair and tried to dine as elegantly as he did, but he had some power, some size of presence she lacked. It didn't help that her bottom ached, and that she burned with embarrassment over the way he'd handled her. Those same fingers that beckoned the servants had been thrust up inside her—and her body had welcomed it.

She almost choked, remembering the humiliation. He glanced at her. "Are you all right?"

She nodded, even though she was *not* all right.

"Do you wonder where I've been these past few nights?" he asked.

She pretended not to hear the question as she placed her silverware atop her plate. "I believe I have finished. May I be excused?"

"No."

She drew in a deep breath and let it out. Yes, she had wondered where he was, but she didn't really want to *know*. She didn't want to be taunted with his extramarital adventures. "I'm sure it's none of my business where you were."

"Oh, but it is your business." He put down his silverware too and took a great drink of wine. "You remember that you gave me permission to seek companionship outside our marriage?"

She nodded, swallowing hard.

"I had intended to do it discreetly, for your honor, but your father has denied me such...dalliances."

She stared at him. "Denied you? How?" She imagined her father standing at the door of some house of ill-repute, barring her husband's way.

He drank more wine, tilting his head back before he swallowed it. "He has convinced every madam and courtesan in London that it behooves them to turn me away." He lifted his glass to her, as if in a toast. "I am therefore obliged to be scrupulously faithful, whether I wish it or not."

"It was none of my doing. If my father has done this—"

"Your father did it," he said, cutting her off. "And I don't blame you, my dear, but I find myself in an untenable situation. Thanks to your father's interference, there is only one female available to cater to my vulgar appetite for pleasure, and that female is you."

Aurelia felt hot and cold and...flabbergasted. "Well, I have allowed you to my bed, haven't I? I'll do my wifely duty whenever you insist upon it."

"Ah, your 'wifely duty.' And grudgingly too," he mocked, raising his dark brows. "Any man would feel himself replete. No, I'm speaking of more than wifely duty. Surely you realize there is an entire world of pleasures to be explored outside the banality of the marital act."

She wished she could disappear, she truly did. "I'm afraid I do *not* realize, my lord. I am very sorry that we do not share the same moral inclinations and desire for indecent pleasures. I am very sorry that we are trapped in this marriage, but I don't know what you wish me to do."

He leaned closer, and waited until she dragged her gaze to his. "I wish you to change, Aurelia. I wish you to agree to satisfy me in whatever ways I desire, no matter the state of your 'moral inclinations.' In light of the servants milling about, I'll not describe the finer points of my requirements."

Amidst the outraged shock, a frisson of fear curled in her belly. "What you suggest would be impossible. Even if I agreed to...to satisfy you in whatever 'vulgar' ways you are talking about, I would not know how."

"You can learn." His voice tautened with the straightening of his broad shoulders. "Let me rephrase that. You *will* learn."

The frisson uncoiled into full-blown anxiety. Surely he could not require her to behave as a woman of the night and participate in bizarre, carnal acts for his pleasure? Whatever those women did for their customers, it was nothing a well-bred lady would ever do.

"You ask the impossible."

He steepled his fingers, studying her. "Yes, I thought the same thing. That is, until this evening, upstairs."

"I do not wish to speak about that," she said quickly.

"Oh, we're going to speak about all manner of things going forward, such as the fact that you don't really have the right—or power—to deny me this request."

He called it a request, but it was a demand, one no civilized husband would set forth. There was no room to be a mouse here. She had to stand up to him or sacrifice her long-held virtue. She lifted her chin. "And if I refuse to submit to such outrageous and immoral expectations?"

"Then you shall be spanked nightly until you realize that submission is a far less painful choice."

She stared at her plate. The filigree design blurred as she tried to control her emotions. She couldn't believe they were having this conversation, that he would demand such things of her, *his own wife*. "You're a monster."

"I'm a man. I'm your husband, which gives me certain rights. Whether they are monstrous, well, that is a matter of opinion."

"When my father finds out—"

He gave a sharp bark of laughter. "You'll never tell your father the result of his ill-thought-out meddling. You would expire of shame and embarrassment before you uttered the first word."

"I'll tell my brother then. He's not so lofty as Papa. He'll listen to me and he'll not allow you to shame his sister in this way."

Hunter shrugged. "Of course you can tell Severin, but then he'd be honor bound to call me out. We'd have to meet at dawn with our pistols, and I could very well end up killing him. His wife is pregnant, isn't she? It would not be well done of you, I'm afraid to say."

Aurelia closed her eyes against the image of Brendan lying shot and bleeding in the morning's dim light. "Or my brother might kill you," she said, to chase away the thought. "He might prevail, setting me free from this horrible marriage."

But as she said it, she pictured Lord Townsend lying dead on her behalf and wished she could take the words back. She hated him, but she couldn't wish him dead. In truth, she didn't even hate him. She disliked him. No, she didn't even dislike him, not fully.

She didn't know how to feel about him.

She didn't know how to feel at all.

Oh, why was everything in such a muddle? Her feelings, her marriage, her entire life? Townsend would have let her be if her father hadn't interfered, she was sure of it. Everyone called her father Laudable Lansing because he was so upright, and so was she.

But perhaps it was not the best way to be in a marriage. She had no warmth, no sensual qualities. She knew it, but she didn't know how to develop those qualities for a man she barely knew. She was so sheltered, so hopeless in the ways of the world that she didn't even understand what acts he might want her to do.

What a hopeless situation. No wonder they were both angry, and sad.

"I don't want there to be a duel," she said, covering her face with her hands. "And I don't want you to suffer for marrying me. I know you're disappointed in me, that I've never learned to be exciting and licentious in the way you would like. Take me back to my father if you wish. Marry someone else."

"You know I can't do that. And I don't want anyone else. Aurelia, come here."

She stared at him, at his outstretched arms. His tone and stance had softened, but his eyes looked so sharp, so direct. There was nothing to do but obey his command. She stood and moved to him, accepting his embrace when he gathered her close against his side. She was coming to know the feel of his body, as well as the layers of his scent: shaving soap, leather, and sandalwood. She stared at his lips, mere inches from hers. They were wide and full, and—she was coming to learn—quite expressive of his moods.

"I'm not taking you back to your father," he said with resolute emphasis. "Ever. So you might as well put that idea out of your mind. We must find a way to rub along together."

"But I don't wish you to spank me every night." *Don't cry. Don't cry, Aurelia.* "And I don't want to learn to do...unnatural things."

"Why 'unnatural'? Because you've been taught they're wrong? I find them quite natural, not to mention necessary to my contentment." His dark eyes held hers as his hand traveled up and down her back. "There are many wives who feel the same, although they'd never admit it. There are countless women who find pleasure in having 'unnatural' things done to them. You were one of them, not even an hour ago." His hand stopped upon the curve of her still-sore bottom. "Will you disappoint me by denying it?"

She clung to him, hiding her face against his hair. "You made that happen. You caused me to feel those things. It was your fault."

She thought she might anger him to say so, but instead he chuckled low against her ear. "If it makes you feel better to believe that, I will hold my peace. But we both know the truth." He squeezed her bottom in such a rough, possessive way that she began to feel the same confusing excitement she'd felt up in the room before. He grinned at her as if he knew it. "I'll keep your secrets, if you will keep mine."

"Oh, please," she said, wringing her hands. She was so afraid of everyone knowing, of people seeing the improprieties he forced upon her like some new blush on her skin. He scrutinized her, one dark brow arching up.

"Is that what you fear? That people will discover the peculiarities of our marital bed, and judge you for it? The secrecy of such play is the most delicious part. Imagine meeting my eyes across the length of some dinner party or some ballroom, and seeing writ there the memory of our salacious adventures, our intimate, sweat-slickened hours."

Aurelia cringed. She didn't like to sweat. She didn't believe she'd so much as uttered the word "sweat" her entire life. "We are so different," she said mournfully.

"Yes. And I am selfishly demanding that you make me happy. But it can go both ways, can't it? What can I do for you? What is lacking in your life, in this marriage, that would make you happy?"

Lord Warren, she thought, but she didn't dare say it. "I don't know," she said aloud. "I suppose I would like to live a peaceful, safe existence. I would like a family. Children." She considered her husband, trying to picture him as a doting father. She could not quite accomplish the task.

"I'll give you children, as many as you want," he assured her. "That goes without saying. You'll have a home and safety the rest of your life. But there must be something more, something frivolous you would enjoy."

She thought hard, but for the life of her could think of nothing. "I have never been very interested in frivolities."

"You haven't been interested, or they've been denied you?" His face took on that dark look again. "In all the time I've known you, I've never heard the sound of your laughter. I've never seen a true smile." As he said this, he brought his hand down beside his plate in such a way that his fork launched into the air, landing with a dull *thunk* against his forehead.

A bark of laughter escaped her like a pistol shot. She clapped her hands over her mouth to stifle it as the utensil slid down the front of his embroidered dinner coat to settle in his lap.

He regarded her in mock reproach as he waved away a footman and mopped his forehead. "If that was supposed to be laughter, Aurelia, you're making a very poor show of it. It sounds more like this."

He threw back his head and laughed with such good-natured vigor she couldn't help laughing too, though her giggles sounded soft and weak compared to his. He nodded. "That's a little better."

How strange, the way his face transformed when he smiled, so he looked handsome rather than dire or threatening. In fact, just at this moment, he regarded her the way a loving husband might dote on his wife. It created powerful, alarming feelings inside her.

"What would you like from me, little grasshopper, in exchange for your forced cooperation?" he asked, pulling her right into his lap.

She blinked at the easy, casual way he held her, and primly rearranged her skirts where they'd ridden up. "I don't know what to ask for. I suppose I am very spoiled by anyone's standards. I've always had everything I needed."

"If you think of anything, let me know. You may find this difficult to believe, but I mean you no harm. I would like for both of us to be happy in this marriage, particularly if it's to include just us two. Perhaps if we try, we can find some way to assuage the tensions in our relationship."

She knew he was extending an olive branch. If only she was brave enough to accept it. "I fear you will be disappointed," she said, holding herself stiffly. "I can only be as I am."

He stroked light fingertips across her cheek. "I wonder if there's more to Aurelia, the Marchioness of Townsend, than you yet realize. My darling, don't be afraid of me. I want you to be happy. If you want safety, I swear I'll keep you safe."

She knew how to react to him when he was coarse or autocratic, but she didn't know how to deal with this tenderness. Just as she was trying to sort it all out, he nudged her off his lap and seemed to go all stern again. "We must finish dinner. The hour grows late."

"I think I am already finished."

"You may be excused then. Try to get some sleep. We're traveling tomorrow."

She halted in her retreat. "Traveling where?"

"The season is over, for all intents and purposes. We shall retire to my country estate where we can commence your...training...in a more private and uncrowded setting."

The word "training" made the hairs rise on the back of her neck. Did he really mean to go through with this? His country estate was in Berkshire, she remembered, nowhere near his parents' or her papa's estate. She would be in the country, far from her friends and family, at her husband's mercy.

I swear I'll keep you safe.

She prayed it was true. She was not at all at ease with the idea of being trained for his pleasure, but with him in absolute control of her life now, what choice did she have?

Chapter Eight: That Good

Hunter sat opposite his wife on the journey west to Berkshire. Being a gentleman, he took the backward-facing bench. He might have sat beside her, elbow to elbow, and offered her a shoulder to lean upon, but he could study her more easily while facing her—and he had become rather fascinated with studying her. Every so often she shifted so their knees wouldn't touch in the middle. Then he rearranged his long legs so they touched again.

It wasn't a great distance to Somerton, but it was tedious with the servants and luggage carts coming behind them. He might have escaped the carriage altogether and gone ahead on his horse if he wanted. It was a sunny, temperate day, perfect for galloping neck or nothing, but he had chosen instead to ride with Aurelia in this velvet-lined and cushioned compartment. He'd become unsettlingly preoccupied with his little mouse after their discussion the night before.

He had tried to be authoritative and unmoving when he laid out his sexual ultimatums, but in the end he couldn't help feeling some tender respect for his wife. She had been embarrassed, shocked, dismayed, but ultimately resigned to a situation she could not change.

And he had meant what he said about doing things for her in return. If she had been haughty and condemning, he would have done his best to make her miserable, but when she put her head in her hands and told him to take her back to her father in that pitiful voice, some part of his armor had cracked. When he whacked himself in the forehead with his own fork, her choked, stifled laughter had shattered it further.

The blasted woman literally didn't know how to laugh.

He could tell she had never been allowed to laugh and make merry, not least of all from the way she clapped her hands over her mouth and looked at him with an expression of horror, like she'd performed some great breach of etiquette. His wife had been given everything, had she?

Except for permission to make merry and have fun.

Hunter and his friends searched out fun and merriment in every aspect of their lives, and wallowed in it when they found it. They always had, ever since they were young lads. What had Aurelia been doing while he was tearing around getting into scrapes as a child and sowing wild oats as a young man? Sitting somewhere stitching flowers on some blasted silk pillowcase, he presumed.

It wasn't her fault she was the way she was. He had to remember that. How sober, how proper she looked now, gazing out the carriage window at the sunny day. He wanted to teach her to laugh and have fun, and to find pleasure where she might. At the same time, he wished to retain authority over her. He wished her to continue to be an obedient and appropriately submissive wife, not one of those shrews who led their husbands about by the balls while other gentlemen snickered behind their hands. It would be a delicate balance to manage it.

He moved forward to peer out the carriage window along with her. "It's not far now, my dear. Not so far as traveling to Oxfordshire."

"Why did you set up your country home so far from the Lockridge estates?" she asked.

He shrugged. "I liked the property. It's a good mix of wilderness and civilization, and the manor itself is comfortable and in excellent repair. And of course, it's closer to London, where I have always spent the majority of my days."

She looked back out the window at rolling green fields, and the last of summer's wildflowers. "It's pretty country. As pretty as Oxfordshire, I think."

"Certainly. At Somerton, there are paths for walking, and lakes and follies." My, was he ever trying to impress her. He had never felt such pride in Somerton before. It was merely a country retreat, a place to escape and occasionally hold parties, an additional estate he might some day pass down to a first-born son, or a second-born, if the first set up at Lockridge. For now, it was to be his and Aurelia's home, and he found himself hoping she would admire it. "Do you enjoy riding? There are plenty of places to ride, and a stable of admirable horses, if I do say so. We could ride out and have picnics now and again, if you like that sort of thing."

She looked down at her lap. "I do not ride especially well, I'm afraid. And I've never been on a picnic."

Never been on a picnic? He'd half a mind to ride to Oxfordshire right now and strangle the Duke and Duchess of Lansing for raising their daughter this way. "Why no picnics? Too subversive for an impressionable young lady? Too much dirt? Too many insects?"

"I was never permitted to run about outdoors or lounge on the ground. My mother said it wasn't ladylike."

Your mother was a blasted idiot, he thought to himself. "Will you raise your daughters that way?" he asked aloud.

She looked at him from under her lashes. "You mean our daughters?"

"Yes, our daughters, though you'll have the raising of them, I suppose."

"Well, I will want them to develop into respectable ladies, certainly."

He couldn't suppress a frown. "And I will want them to have picnics sometimes."

Them. He was already picturing more than one daughter, just as he'd pictured more than one son. He was surprised by this, and a little unsettled. He slouched back upon the cushions, so their knees knocked together in earnest and she was obliged to shift hers away. "I think it a crime," he said, "that you were imprisoned inside during your childhood. Your brother certainly had the run of Lansing Grange. The grounds around your father's house, those old forests and meadows, were irresistible to me as a boy. I trespassed upon them all the time, sometimes with Severin, although he thought me a young, paltry fellow."

"I never saw you at Lansing."

"I didn't come there because I didn't want to see you. The few times I encountered you at the house, you seemed a big-eyed, staring sort of creature. Hair hanging down, and some glaze or something dribbling from your mouth."

She glared at him. "I only dribbled as an infant, I'm sure."

"Well, you were an infant then, practically. It was very off-putting to think of you as my future wife. It was not well done of them, to promise us to one another at such a young age."

She unruffled a bit and eased back against the seat. "But you agreed, did you not? You signed the betrothal document. I was too little."

"Yes. It was ridiculous stuff. It was a time in my life when I dearly wished to please my parents. One of the last times, I might add." He staunchly pushed all such memories from his mind. "Ah, here are the gates, and the limits of the property. Welcome to Somerton."

He was torn between watching out the window at his home—which had last housed a fortnight-long orgy—and watching her. Did he see some measure of awe in her gaze? Somerton was newer and more stylish than Lansing Grange. It was Palladian in design, with great columns and porticos, and wings flanking the great central manor. A road curved gracefully to the grand staircases framing the front door. A Roman-style fountain rose in majestic tiers from the center of the paved courtyard. All around, gardens and fields stretched in a sprawling fashion, easily seen from the head road.

"It's beautiful," she said, with what he believed was true admiration.

And it was beautiful, he thought, seeing it through new eyes. Her eyes. The liveried staff, well-trained by his capable steward, arranged themselves in welcoming lines leading down from the landing. Perhaps Lansing was doing Hunter a favor, making him stay dutifully at home to play master of the manor. How singular, this feeling of satisfaction.

"If you are not too tired, perhaps you'll allow me to show you about the place," he said.

To his pleasure, she cordially agreed.

* * * * *

Aurelia wandered amidst her new rooms, noting lovely furnishings and delicate knickknacks, and sweet-smelling flowers. There was even a private bathing room designed in the latest manner of invention, with a tiled tub for soaking. But no matter the beauty and wonders, she kept returning to stare at the window seat.

It was not in the bedroom as in London, but in the adjoining drawing room, and it was not truly a window seat. Rather, benches had been arranged before the window, one on either side, and then draperies fixed on iron rods in the plaster ceiling overhead. The draperies framed the benches on all sides, creating a close approximation of her hideaway at the London household. There was still a bit of dust on one bench from where they'd drilled the plaster, which led to an inevitable conclusion. He had had this hideaway created quite recently—especially for her.

Rather than go within and sit, she stared at it from the middle of the room, plucking at the folds of her evening gown. She had felt rather speechless and awed at dinner, at the beauty of his house and the crisp industriousness of the servants, but now, staring at the window seat that was not quite a window seat, she fell a little bit in love with her husband. But only a very, very little bit.

If only she could despise him, but he made it impossible. He made her feel furious and powerless with his demands, and then followed with actions so kind she felt utterly unbalanced. No, it couldn't be love she felt, but there was something unfamiliar and hot in her chest. Whatever it was, it made it impossible to sit in the window seat in peaceful docility. It made her want to pace, which, unfortunately, was not ladylike.

"Lady Townsend?" Aurelia turned to find a smartly attired maid curtsying her way into the room. "Pardon me, my lady. Lord Townsend wishes you to attend him now. I'll be pleased to show you the way to his chambers."

The last thing Aurelia wanted to do was go to Lord Townsend's chambers and commence this "training" he seemed determined to put her through, but she gathered her courage and followed the maid. Better that than wait here for him to drag her where he wanted her—and he would drag her, she had no doubt.

The maid led her across the hall and tapped at a great, tall door, and pushed it open. Aurelia entered, nerves jarring. The room was dimly lit;

flickering candlelight illuminated a large bed and heavy pieces of furniture. It was a male's bedroom, top to bottom. She couldn't suppress a shiver.

Lord Townsend stood from a chair by the fireplace, and Aurelia turned to him with her hands clasped before her waist. She stared at his broad chest, and the interesting contours of his jaw and neck, dusted with an evening's growth of stubble. *Her husband.* When would she get used to it, the blatant, shocking intimacy of knowing this man?

She could tell nothing from his expression as he regarded her, whether he felt content, or angry, or sad. "Do you find your rooms satisfactory?" he asked.

"Yes. Thank you very much for the..." Her voice caught a moment in her throat. "For the window seat."

"You must have a mouse hole in every home, yes?" At her frown, he approached her. "But I remember you don't like to be called a mouse. Forgive me."

Before she knew what he was about, he'd grasped her face and tilted her head back by the chin. She bit her lip, staring up at him. He looked as if he would say something, but then he lowered his mouth to hers in a warm, exploratory kiss. She stood very still as his tongue caressed and encouraged her, teasing gently at her teeth. Without meaning to, she opened to him. Her arms and hands hung in space with nothing to cling to, for she was afraid to touch him even as he deepened his kiss. The hand behind her head delved up into her hair and massaged her nape, angling her just so for his passionate embrace. He tasted faintly of cinnamon and wine.

Was it normal to kiss like this? Was it normal to feel as if one was floating away in some kind of stupor?

He pressed her body to his, chest to chest, thigh to thigh. Pins clattered to the floor as he brought her hair down, freeing lock after lock, kissing her all the while. She clung to him as if to seek shelter from the very chaos he created in her. Her breasts felt heated, her nipples tight. She was certain she was growing wet in that secret place, and just as certain that he would touch her there and realize it, and thrust his fingers inside and make her feel ashamed before he pressed his hard, thick manhood into her...

She pushed away from him. Not a great push, for she was even now wary of displeasing him. It was more like shying away. She felt cowardly and pitiable as he studied her.

"Are you quite all right?" he asked.

She touched her lips. "I am here as you commanded me."

"You remember why?" He brushed a bit of hair over her shoulder. "You remember our purpose, the one I explained to you last evening?"

His tone was not the least bit romantic, although his kiss seemed to linger on her lips. "Yes, I remember," she said. *Even though I am not entirely willing*, she wanted to add. But it would be pointless to do so. He'd brought her here to his secluded estate for this purpose, and she had no way to get away.

She took a step back. That, at least, he permitted. He unbuttoned his coat and shrugged out of it, tossing the fine garment over a nearby chair, then turned back to face her. Without his tailored coat pulling him together in the image of a gentleman, he seemed dangerously underdressed.

With a flick of his wrist, he rolled up the first of his linen shirtsleeves, then the other, fixing her with a purposeful look. "I don't want you to become upset when I say this, but I believe it best to begin each evening together with a proper, thorough spanking. I believe it will go a long way in communicating to you the inexorability of your situation. It will focus your attention and render you more eager to perform."

"What?" Her voice cracked, high and shrill. She backed away from him in alarm, her hands splayed protectively over her backside. "I promise you have my attention. I am trying to be good!"

He caught her shoulders before she could flee. "You must trust me, darling. I know what I'm about in such matters."

He turned her with firm hands and began to undo her dress and loosen her stays, removing everything but her sheer, silken shift. She trembled, cross, reluctant, frightened even, but along with all those feelings came another shameful surge of hot tension in her breasts and between her legs, in her body's secret core. It was hopeless to resist him, wasn't it? His power and his will frightened her, but also, curiously, aroused her. She didn't want this, and yet in some sense it felt exciting. Which meant that she was barely more proper than a common trollop, or a whore.

Oh, no. She had thought herself better than this. He sat on a chair and was about to pull her over his lap when he noticed her tears.

"Why are you crying, Aurelia?"

She sniffled. "I'm crying because I feel terribly confused."

He made a soft tsk, wiping gently at her cheeks. "Your confusion is only your mind warring with your body. Let me guide you. Don't resist me, grasshopper, and we'll see where we end up. Answer me. '*As you wish, my lord.*'"

She forced the words out, though her voice trembled. "As you wish, my lord."

"Ah, that sounds very nice. Those are the proper sort of words to say when I give you instructions. Above all, you must be brave and willing to try anything I request. I won't hurt you, I swear. In fact, you'll enjoy great pleasure if you get into the spirit of things."

The spirit of things? What on earth did he mean by that? She found herself guided, for the third time in her short marriage, over her husband's lap. She felt the whisper of fabric against her skin as he pushed her shift up to her waist, baring her bottom.

"Feet on the floor, yes, that's a good girl." His palms brushed lazily for a moment over her naked cheeks, then stroked lower to caress the skin just above her stockings. "And keep those hands out of the way, or I'll use one of your garters to tie them together and keep them still."

"Yes, my lord," she said, though she could barely imagine such a thing.

He made a low, pleased sound and landed the first spank. Oh, mercy, she would never get used to such treatment, and he intended to do this each evening, on a formally regimented basis? It defied belief, and yet her bottom stung with the reality of his intent. He spanked her twice on each cheek, pausing in between so she felt his palm rub across her skin. *Oh, God help me.* After that, he settled into a constant, painful rhythm of measured spanks.

Right away, it was difficult to keep her feet in the position he wanted. Little kicks and cries escaped her, high and shrill in the silence of his room. She wanted him to stop, but she also felt the most confusing sensation of arousal. The heat in her bottom seemed to spread between her thighs, and collect there in a tingly, heavy way. She prayed not to be molested, but her prayers were in vain. He paused in his onslaught and pressed his fingers to her quim. She flushed hot at the slickness gathered there. If he had commented on it, she would have died of humiliation, but he only resumed the spanking, delivering firm, crisp blows in a steady rhythm to her posterior.

"Perhaps you fear these spankings will become repetitive over time," he said as his palm rained down. "But it will not be so. Very soon I'll introduce you to other disciplinary implements. A paddle perhaps. A strap. A birch rod or switch, most definitely. A cane can be highly effective but perhaps best left for moments when you are very, very rebellious."

Aurelia silently vowed to never be very, very rebellious, because the idea of being caned on her bottom terrified her. His palm alone caused her considerable pain. If he was trying to frighten her with threats of more severe implements, his plan worked.

He stopped and pressed the tip of a finger into her damp channel, so that she squirmed upon his lap. Then he pressed the same moistened finger against her bottom hole. She gasped at the shocking contact and tried to pull away, but his arm tightened around her waist to hold her still. She shuddered as his finger caressed and probed there. He forced her to endure these scandalous attentions as her cheeks throbbed from the spanking.

"Please," she whimpered. "It is so improper."

"Nothing is improper between us, now that we're married. You must remember that, my love. I'm only thinking about the time when I shall introduce you to the pleasures of a ginger fig in your bottom. I've an exquisite crop of ginger grown here just for that purpose."

"You will put ginger...inside my bottom?" she asked in a mixture of horror and disgust.

He laughed. "That, and other things. You'll come to love it as I do."

"I won't," she cried, tears gathering again in her eyes. It seemed too monstrous to think about. It was almost a relief when he began to spank her again, the steady, sharp whacks of pain a distraction from all the anxiety roiling in her brain. He spanked her for quite a while, but it wasn't like the first two spankings, where he'd been angry and rough in his discipline. This was more of a controlled endeavor, and when her entire bottom was hot and throbbing uniformly, he stopped.

"There," he said, "I think that will do. Stand now, and take off your shift for me, darling."

She held back the tears, relieved that the spanking was over, at least for today. She fumbled with the ties of her shift as her husband regarded her with frank attention. It embarrassed her to disrobe while he remained dressed, but she did as he asked and inched the garment up over her head.

"No," he said. "Not like that. Not as if you are reluctant and ashamed." He pulled it back down to her hips. "Try again. Take it off as if you're excited to reveal your body to me."

She stared at him. How on earth was she to do that?

"Or, if you feel you need more spanking first..."

"No," she said quickly. "I shall try again. It's only that—"

"No excuses. Do as I ask, Aurelia. Take off your shift without any reluctance or shame. Your body is beautiful, you know. Your curves, your femininity. You should present it as such, with none of this shrinking and blushing."

No reluctance or shame. What a novel idea, and how impossible. She tried again to do what he asked, lifting the shift more gracefully this time, letting the fabric linger over her hips and breasts before she pulled it off and dropped it, with feigned indifference, to the floor. She tried not to...what had he said? Shrink? She stood straight and tall, and attempted to smile at him. She couldn't quite manage it. She could barely hold his gaze, intense as it was.

After a moment, he smiled. "Not perfectly done, but better. We'll practice every day, won't we? Now turn around and show me your red, spanked bottom, my love."

Why did he keep calling her his "love"? The only thing he seemed to love was humiliating her, but it was pointless to balk at his instructions. She turned and presented her back to him, wringing her hands at her waist.

"Now bend down very prettily and remove your garters and stockings."

Aurelia sucked in a breath. Something in his voice, perhaps the low steadiness of it, had the unwilling arousal beating again in that spot between her legs. Dear God, if she bent forward, he might be able to see it, that naughty, throbbing, heated, secret spot that ached for something she couldn't understand.

"No," he said sharply when she tried to crouch down instead. "Bend forward at the waist. Roll them all the way down and then hand them back to me."

Well, there was nothing for it. He was going to insist on her behaving like a lewd woman. She bent forward, fully aware that he would stare at her bottom and nether lips in all their exposed glory. From the approving sound he made, he enjoyed this. She bent forward—twice—to remove her stockings and hand them back to him. When she finished, he made her turn around.

"Let's see if you can undress me with equal sensuality and grace. Go slowly. Start by unbuttoning my waistcoat."

Bother. There were two dozen or more buttons, exquisite and small. She fumbled with them, wondering how one unbuttoned one's waistcoat with sensuality. But then she finished and, with a little of his help, pushed it back off his shoulders. She got the first inkling that undressing a man could indeed be a sensual task. Why, the singular breadth of his chest, and the appealing muscularity of his upper arms...

"I like your expression, Aurelia," he said quietly. "As if you like what you see. Do you like it?"

She didn't want to answer. She was embarrassed to answer, but she said, "Yes, my lord."

"My neckcloth now." His voice had grown huskier still.

She reached to remove the pearl pin at its center. "Where shall I put this?" she asked.

He regarded her through half-closed lids. "Between your lips."

He watched as she put the pin in her mouth, pursing her lips around it. His voice, his expression made it seem that she did something erotic. She applied herself to the folds of his cravat for the sake of distraction, but she could feel his gaze on her. Her fingers brushed of necessity against the strong column of his neck, shaded with a hint of stubble. His jaw moved. Tensed. It looked very...masculine.

She hurriedly untied the rest of the knot and drew the linen from his collar. She set to the buttons of his shirt, nearly overwhelmed by the pure, appealing scent of him. When she reached the last button she realized she must untuck his shirt from his breeches to get it off him. He grinned at her.

"You must undo my breeches too, Aurelia."

96

Her lips tightened around the pin in her mouth. She bent down to pluck at the buttons of his breeches, unable to avoid the obvious evidence of his arousal pressing against the fabric. She stopped when the waistline was loose enough to untuck his shirt, and tried to push the linen garment up over his head. It became a close type of exertion, because he was so tall, and his arms so long. At last he was obliged to help her do it, whipping it up so she fell against his front.

How solid he was. She knew that, had felt the evidence of it over and above her in their marital bed, but now her hands rested on his chest, and she could see every muscle composing his torso, as well as the rough, curling hair that neatened at his waist into a line that disappeared down to...there.

He stood back and she could see his man's part bobbing, fully hard, from his opened breeches. He took the pin from her lips and attached it to the collar of his shirt, laying both aside.

"My valet will attend to that later. Kneel down now and remove my boots," he said.

If he had not used that firm, commanding voice she wasn't sure she could have done it. Kneeling before him put her in quite close proximity to his outrageously formed sex organs. She bowed her head and pulled at his boots, which were the very devil to get off. When she'd finally accomplished it with his help, she tried to rise.

"No. My breeches."

With a faint sigh, she tugged them down. There was very little sensuality in her technique, she feared. She tried to slow down. As she drew them lower she contrived to caress her palms against his muscled thighs. That was sensual, wasn't it? She believed so, because his heavy male member seemed to jerk in response. He stepped out of the breeches. She pushed down his stockings, her face on fire. She thought it must be as scarlet red as her still-warm bottom. That finished, she tried again to stand up.

Again, he stopped her with a hand on her shoulder. "Stay where you are."

She went still, staring up at him. At *it*. It was impossible to ignore his maleness, thrust as it was before her face. What was he going to do to her down here? It was so very hard to hold his gaze.

"Do you see how you've aroused me?" he asked in a strained voice. "By merely removing my clothes?"

She wanted to ask how she could very well *not* see, but it seemed pert to do so. Oh, what did he want? This was all so very strange.

"Look at it," he said. "You'll become intimately familiar with my manhood in the coming days and weeks. Touch me."

"T-touch you," she stammered. "How?"

"Sensually, of course. Stroke me. Explore how it feels."

How it felt? She knew how it felt from having it inside her body, thrusting and probing and stretching her open. But she obeyed him, reaching out gingerly to stroke his rigid flesh. She ran a fingertip from the base to the oddly shaped, purpling crown.

"What do you think of it?" His voice sounded ever more taut.

She regarded its angry red and purple color, and marveled at the veins throbbing just beneath the surface. "It looks as if it hurts."

"It doesn't hurt. Well, only in the most delightful way. Would you like to kiss it?"

She would *not* like to. She looked up at him with pleading eyes but she knew he wasn't really asking.

"Kiss it," he said in a firmer voice. "Kiss my cock."

She had never heard it called a *cock* before. She had never imagined something so depraved as putting her lips on the swollen, grotesque thing. But if she said no, he would only force her to do it in some painful and ignoble way. If this was what ladies of the night did for gentlemen, kissed their hard, thick organs, then she supposed it wouldn't kill her to do it. But she would not pretend to like it.

She inched forward and pressed her mouth to the tip. A warm, salty drop of liquid escaped, and she hurriedly swiped it from her lips.

For some reason, he found this funny. He chuckled and patted her on the head. "That's another thing that happens when you arouse me. It's not dangerous to ingest it. You needn't react as if it's poison."

"May I stand up now?" she asked. She feared she might soon lose her composure.

"No. Not yet." He reached down and rearranged himself. His cock, as he called it. She knew so little of the male anatomy, but there was more to see, more pieces and parts hanging down. She hoped he didn't want her to kiss those too. "Kiss it once more, all around the head. The top part."

His voice sounded curiously shaky. Could this be affecting him as much as all that? He gripped his shaft at the base and thrust it out toward her. She grimaced and did as he had asked, kissing around the ridge at the top of his length. He sighed in a raspy sort of way. She felt his fingers trembling—*trembling*—against the top of her head. They opened and closed in her loose hair.

"Enough," he said. "That is...enough for one day. You did very well."

His voice sounded quite rough now, but his features were pleased. She stared up at him from the floor with some relief. This whole encounter had been terribly awkward and uncomfortable.

And it was only the first day of her training.

"Lie back on the bed," he commanded. "Quickly. You did your job too well and now I've got to be inside you."

She had aroused him with these things she'd done, as awkward as they seemed. He felt great excitement and pleasure, that was obvious, and it made her rather proud. It made her feel...powerful.

As soon as she climbed on the bed, he turned her onto her back and pinned her arms above her head. Their gazes locked from inches away as he eased inside her with a groan. She didn't know why he wanted her to do something so bizarre as kiss his cock, but it had made him very, very pleased. His lips sought hers, dealing a kiss as warm as any he'd given her since he'd taken her as his wife.

"I can barely hold back," he said, thrusting hard and deep inside her. "Will you be able to come, my love?"

"Come where?" she asked.

He made a strangled sort of sound and kissed her again. "I'll teach you how to do it, I promise. Just...not...today." He growled low in his throat and shuddered against her, driving so deep he lifted her hips from the bed.

When his muscles uncoiled, when his body relaxed from its heightened tenor, she stared up at him. "Was that coming? What you just did?"

"Yes." He sighed, catching his breath. "You have done it before too. You remember?"

She nodded. How could she forget the encounter with her body pressed into a corner, her skirts held up about her waist?

He eased off her, onto his side. He traced her lips with a fingertip, such a soft hint of a caress. "You will again, I promise. There is so much to teach you, Aurelia. But I don't think I can bear any more of your innocence tonight."

"Was I that bad?" He had hurt her feelings with that comment.

But then he shook his head and said, "No, my love. Oh, my innocent darling. You were that good."

Chapter Nine:
Confined

Aurelia sat close to the window, looking down upon the U-shaped front courtyard and the glittering white marble fountain which added such grandeur to her husband's home. She held a letter in her hand, written on fine paper, sealed and franked by the Lansing ducal crest.

Dearest daughter, it read.

Your father and I have been thinking of you often in the blessing of your new marriage. We hope the marquess is proving a kind and attentive husband. The house seems empty with both our children gone, although we look forward to the arrival of Severin's child at the holidays. Perhaps a Lockridge heir is not long off. How delightful to imagine it, my daughter. You have always been such a dutiful child, and in this too I am certain you shall make everyone proud.

Aurelia bit her lip. Her mother believed a woman's first purpose, her only purpose really, was to provide her husband with heirs. It had been so difficult for the duchess when she only managed to provide the Duke of Lansing one son and one daughter. Aurelia was certainly doing her duty. If she didn't produce a child soon enough to suit her mother, it wouldn't be through her fault. She traced the outer edge of the letter, thinking she might already be with child. She wasn't sure if the prospect pleased her or not.

101

Remember that marriage is based on mutual respect and great amounts of patience, the letter continued. *Lust is an abomination, and passion is a fleeting, flighty thing, but respect can persevere forever and bring great dignity to both partners. I pray you will respect the marquess, dearest Aurelia, and that you will both find peace in honoring one another.*

With great fondness,

Mama

Peace, thought Aurelia with a sniff. He gave her about as much peace as a stallion gave a mare in heat. She wondered what her mother would say if she wrote back such a thing to her. *I am not certain of honor, Mama. Is it honorable for a husband to spank his wife each day for his own perversion? Can one cling to dignity while being made to do unnatural and lustful things?*

One could not, she was afraid, and she didn't need her mother to tell her so. Aurelia set away the tea tray the maid had brought up, and curled into the corner of the window seat in a little ball. Thoughts of her husband crowded her brain, as they always did when she was idle. She ought to read, or sew, or meet with the steward and housekeeper to learn more about her husband's manor, but instead she sat and puzzled over the dark, mysterious man she had married.

Was he cruel? Or kind? Did he respect her?

Did she respect him?

She pressed her forehead against the glass, her thoughts in a tangle, and then she saw Lord Townsend outside in the front courtyard, strong and broad shouldered upon his black horse. He reined the creature sideways as he spoke to another man, the head groundskeeper, she believed, although it was difficult to tell from a distance.

She watched him point here and there, and wished she could hear what he was saying. He took great pride in Somerton, that was sure, and the servants all seemed to revere their master. The neighbors had great regard for Lord Townsend too. Since they'd come to Berkshire, several of the local gentry had been by to call and pay their respects to her, the new marchioness. They'd spoken with admiration of her husband's generosity, his fairness to his tenants, and his support of the less fortunate in the village. Apparently, one of Aurelia's maids had a very sick mother whom Lord Townsend saw to "in all his kindness." The girl had confided this to Aurelia with a tremor of adoration in her voice.

And so Aurelia didn't know what to believe, except that she was the only one who realized what a perverse miscreant Lord Townsend was, and the only one made to suffer his vile whims.

Vile, Aurelia? In truth, she did not find them entirely so. Sometimes she even feared she was committing the abomination of lust. Was it abominable to look out the window and study the arresting figure of her husband, his strong thighs gripping and guiding his horse, his muscled arms rippling in the close-fitting confines of his tailored coat? Was it abominable to recognize, and appreciate, his obvious virility and the power hinted at therein?

Now he leaned closer to the groundskeeper to show him some sort of rectangular parcel. He must have gone shopping in town. He told her she might go shopping if she wished, but she wanted for nothing, and when she went among people she was forced to smile and pretend to be happily married, which was not such an easy thing.

Lord Townsend swung down from his horse, parcel and all, and handed the reins to a stable boy before striding toward the house. The groundskeeper went off to do whatever his master had ordered. Of course, it had been so in her own home as a child. The Duke of Lansing's word was law at Lansing Grange, just as Townsend's word was law here. It ought to comfort her to know her husband was a capable peer and not a helpless gadabout, as so many of them were. But she didn't find it very comforting when his power and authority were exerted over her.

There was a knock, and then the sound of boots crossing her sitting room. Lord Townsend must have come directly from downstairs. She could hide here or go out to welcome him. If she hid here, he'd only come in to get her, so she decided to present herself to him instead.

"My lord," she said in greeting.

"Aurelia." He looked fresh and bright-eyed, his hair a bit windblown from being outdoors. He smelled faintly of horse, but more of his gentlemanly sandalwood scent. "I've been out to make some calls, and then into the village," he said. "I brought you something. A gift."

The rectangular parcel was for her, then. It was rather wonderful that he'd thought to bring her something, and the way he smiled...broadly and with pure delight. Before she could look more closely at her gift, he hid it behind his back.

"I should ask first if you are a squeamish sort. Do you like insects?"

Aurelia gaped at him. "No. Not very much."

"But this one is special. Come and look." He held it out, and she noted it wasn't a box exactly, but a fine-mesh covered frame of polished wood. At first she thought it was empty inside, but then she saw a flutter of movement and discovered a sleek, very large grasshopper in one corner of the box.

"Oh," she said, shocked. "It's a cage for a bug."

"A cage?" Her husband frowned. "It's a habitat, not a cage. You see, the creature can move about and breathe through the mesh. You can put vegetation inside, such as wheat or barley. The shopkeeper assured me they love alfalfa. It's meant to be a pet."

"A grasshopper for a pet?" She peered in at the poor trapped creature. "Who would think of such a thing?"

He didn't answer at first, only gave her a devilish look. "I keep a grasshopper for a pet. I find her rather diverting."

Did he mean her? She felt laughter bubble up in her throat. She clamped her lips shut so the merriment wouldn't escape, but one small giggle did anyway.

"I am not a grasshopper," she said, trying to be sober, "at least not a real grasshopper like this one." He had brought her a grasshopper as a gift! She wasn't entirely sure how she felt about it. She took the cage and carried it closer to the window in the east corner of the room. They peered through the mesh together. She'd never seen a grasshopper so close up, that was certain. It was larger than she thought a grasshopper would be, with iridescent, patterned markings and delicate wings.

"Oh, they can fly," she said. "I never realized. I thought they only hopped."

Lord Townsend looked closer. "I'm not sure they can fly."

"But it has wings, you see? And look at how strong the legs are fashioned. I suppose this one could hop quite far without using its wings at all. Oh, it's a lovely thought, Townsend, but it shouldn't be kept in a cage."

His eyes widened above the mesh. "I believe that's the first time you haven't lorded me, Aurelia."

She flushed. "Well, it's the first time you've gotten me a gift."

"I ought to have done it sooner then. If you don't take care, you'll be calling me Hunter soon, and acting like a fond wife."

They stared at one another. When he smiled, how handsome he was! She didn't know if she could ever bring herself to call him Hunter, and be so casual and intimate. As she considered the possibility, a green blur launched itself from the mesh enclosure.

Aurelia gasped. "Oh, look, the clasp's fallen open. The grasshopper's escaped the cage."

"It's not a cage," he insisted, turning to look for the thing. "It's a *habitat*."

Then both of them dispensed arguing and set about to locate the creature. "Be careful where you step," she said. "It would be horrible to crush it."

"Where has it gone?"

"I don't know. I'm sure it can jump great distances," said Aurelia, remembering its thick legs. "And it has wings. What if it flies out of the room?"

"They can't fly, for God's sake. They're called grasshoppers, not grassflyers."

The escaped insect chose that moment to fly with a great buzzing racket across the length of the room. Lord Townsend ran after it, waving his arms.

"It's going to go in my bed," Aurelia shrieked. She and Townsend collided in their efforts to ward off the thing. Both of them fell, her husband guiding her atop him with a quick twist of his frame, so she was rescued from a hard crash to the floor.

"Are you all right?" she asked.

He raised and lowered his head. "I'm fine, but the grasshopper's gone silent. I fear I may have landed on our new friend."

"Oh, no." Aurelia hoped it wasn't so. "It's terrible luck to kill a grasshopper in your home."

"I'm going to turn over and you must look beneath me for the guts, my dear."

She was about to protest that she couldn't possibly do such a thing. To locate a smashed grasshopper beneath her husband? But then she realized he was laughing. He tumbled her up and over so he was in the superior position over her.

"You were teasing about smashing it," she said, blushing.

"I haven't smashed it, I'm sure. It's too quick for us."

"What will become of it, loose in the house?"

His laughing gaze turned tender. "Are you afraid for it, my love? How quickly you grow attached. We shall have to get you a proper pet. A kitten or puppy would be more cuddly than a grasshopper."

She blinked, remembering long ago scolding and reprimands. "We always had pets at home, but I was never permitted to cuddle with them."

"Nor sprawl about on the ground having picnics. I remember. But you are sprawled on the ground now, or on the floor anyway. What a naughty girl you are." Her eyes widened as much at his tone as his provocative expression. "Speaking of naughty, how is your bottom today?"

"It's very well," she assured him, to no avail. He was already pushing her onto her stomach, right there on the floor, and pulling her skirts up. She tried in vain to resist him and push them back down. "What if a servant walks in?"

"Then they shall also see how your bottom is." He put a hand on the small of her back to stop her squirming. "Let me look. You know where resistance will get you."

Yes, she did know. She stopped fighting him and lay still. His fingers caressed her bottom cheeks while her stomach flip-flopped and her breasts pressed against the floor. She would not become aroused by this ignominious treatment. She *would not*.

After a few moments of lazy inspection, he made an approving sound. "No bruises, really. Nothing. You can take a good spanking, my dear, and barely show it the next day. Perhaps I'll have to take advantage of that."

"I wish you wouldn't." Her voice felt curiously tight in her throat.

"I'll take your wishes into consideration," he said, turning her back over. "But you know I'll always do what I feel is best."

"My mama wrote me today. She said respect within marriage can bring great dignity to both partners."

"Ah, I agree with your mother." A grin teased the corners of his mouth. "A respectful wife is a treasure indeed."

Very well for him to be amused by her mother's platitudes. She stuck her chin out. "I believe she meant that husbands too must show respect to their wives."

"I'll show you respect. After I show you a lot of other things."

Her eyes widened as he moved his hips against her front. Why, he was blatantly aroused, the scoundrel, here, on the floor, in the middle of the day!

"Dignity between partners is no laughing matter," she said in her most severe and prudent tone.

"Is it not?" And then her grinning husband commenced tickling her, running his fingers over her midsection and up to the sensitive underside of her arms. She couldn't remember the last time such a thing had happened to her. She didn't know whether to beg for mercy or laugh until she couldn't breathe. In the end she did both, flailing and pushing at him, and even kicking once or twice, but laughing and shrieking too, as loud as her lungs could manage. She heard him laughing too, deep chuckles teasing her ear.

"Please, stop," she gasped when she could draw in air.

"I don't want to stop. I enjoy the sound of your laughter, prim Lady Dormouse."

The name had hurt her so many times, but now he was calling her that in good humor, with a twinkle in his eye. It was altogether different, and really, she wasn't a mouse, not anymore. She'd been laughing as loudly as any street urchin, and yes, sprawling about on the floor, even kicking in a most unladylike fashion. The tickling had stopped. He stared down now with a look she recognized, the intent look that always preceded a very thorough kiss.

But as he bowed his head, the shrill *chirp-chirp* of a grasshopper sounded not a few feet from where they lay.

They both froze and looked over toward the sound. Her husband drew a soft breath. "I see it. I think I can trap it in the corner under the table."

"You won't hurt it, will you?"

"I'll try not to. You go fetch the box, or habitat, or whatever the bother it is. Go quietly so it doesn't fly again."

He let her slide from under him. By the time she'd crept over to get the mesh cage and return, Townsend had the grasshopper handily cornered beneath a low table. By slow degrees, he corralled it into the box and latched the door shut.

Aurelia clapped and smiled at him. "Oh, well done. You were ever so patient and you got it back into the box where it can be perfectly safe."

107

He turned to her and she noted an almost shy pleasure written across his face. "I have prevailed, yes. But I thought you didn't want it in the box."

"I don't, really. May we take it outside and let it go? It was a lovely gift, but..."

He stood, looking rumpled and strikingly handsome for all his disarrangement. "Yes, let's take it outside."

He let her carry it. They walked somberly down the halls on their mission of mercy. She knew the grasshopper would be much happier out in the woods where it could be free, and she was grateful that Lord Townsend agreed with her.

He led her across the side lawns to a more wooded area and stopped on the edge. He took the box from Aurelia and peered into it. "I hope this contrary creature doesn't upset the delicate balance of the manor's vegetation and start some blasted plague or something."

A peal of laughter escaped before she realized she ought to chide him for cursing yet again. He smiled back at her.

"It's nice to hear you laugh sometimes, Aurelia. I know you think it's crude or uncultured or some such nonsense, but it isn't. It sounds like angels singing, to me anyway. Not that I'll ever know how angels sing if I don't straighten up."

His beleaguered expression wrested more laughter from her. Now that he'd taught her how to laugh so easily, it seemed she couldn't stop.

He held out the cage with the grasshopper fluttering inside it. It went still and seemed to look at her, although she didn't know where its eyes were. But if it was looking at her, she hoped it would not remember her with too much unkindness. "Would you like to do the honors?" Townsend asked.

She handed it back to him. "I'm afraid it will jump on me if I do."

"I think it shall want nothing further to do with either of us, but I'll release it if you like."

He opened the door and set down the cage. The two of them backed away, and within a few moments the grasshopper had availed itself of its glorious freedom and taken a great hop into the nearby foliage.

"It's better for it to be free, isn't it?" she said with some satisfaction.

"Until a bird eats it for dinner. Yes."

She tried to look cross at him, but she couldn't quite manage it. He looked back at her, feigning irritation.

"So much for my gift. I hope you don't make a practice of casting off everything I bring you, ungrateful chit."

"I am not ungrateful, nor a chit. I only believe that insects must be free."

"You are ungrateful. You have not thanked me yet, not once, for giving you our grasshopper friend." His arms came around her, pulling her close. She felt frightened and thrilled at the same time. His lips came very close to hers. "You ought to be taught some manners, young lady, and I know precisely how to do it."

She felt that hot, tingling sensation in her middle as he pinned her with his gaze. "Thank you," she said through suddenly dry lips. "Thank you for the grasshopper, my lord."

"Back to 'my lording' me, I see. Very pretty sentiments, if a bit late." His hand moved up and down her arm in a mesmerizing trail. "Perhaps we shall have a lesson tonight on how one shows gratitude, my lady? What do you think?"

He teased her, and yet he didn't tease. There was some steel beneath his words that left no question what type of "lesson" this would be.

"As you wish, my lord," she said. *And as I wish...*

His gaze intensified. He pulled her closer and kissed the side of her neck, then lower, over the tops of her breasts to the plunging neckline of her gown. Again she could feel the hard heat of him against her, even through both their clothes.

"I should return to the house," she said, stiffening in his embrace.

At first he didn't let her go, but finally, to her relief, he did. "Yes," he sighed, smoothing a hand over the bulge in his buff-colored breeches. "I suppose the pillowcases won't embroider themselves."

She gave him a questioning look. He took off his coat and handed it to her.

"Take this and deliver it to the butler on your way. I am going to stay outdoors yet awhile. I need to cut some branches for a birch rod which I shall make use of this evening."

She stared at him a moment, then turned and walked away as fast as her shaky knees could carry her. She thought she heard a chuckle behind her but it might have been the whisper of the leaves. No, it was a chuckle.

109

Back upstairs in her sitting room, she slid her parents' letter under some other papers on her desk and tried to calm the erratic pounding of her heart.

Chapter Ten: Gratitude

Hunter awaited his wife with a sense of great contentment. Today had been a good day, not least because he had heard her laugh merrily not once but three or four times. She was changing already, growing more at ease in their home and in their marriage, although she still regarded him with an occasionally wary air.

Of course, she had good reason to be wary. The birch rod lay on the bed, the branches freshly cut and bound. It was not of great weight or length, but similar to a nursery birch. He didn't want to injure his wife or make it difficult for her to compose herself afterward, for that would not advance his plans at all.

At the appointed hour, the door to his room cracked open and his wife slipped shyly inside. He had instructed her to report in nothing but her dressing gown and shift, and she had obeyed. How lovely she looked with her skin flushed just so, everything in her bearing communicating reluctance and no small amount of anxiety. It ought not to arouse him, but it did.

If he was honest, it was much more thrilling to spank and molest his gently reared wife than to pay a jaded professional to cater to his needs. It made him wonder why he'd resisted the marital state for so long.

Her gaze focused nearly at once on the newly made birch rod.

"Must we begin with a spanking every night?" she asked plaintively. "I have not been bad."

"Ah, but these spankings have very little to do with whether you've been good or bad."

"What are they to do with, then? Besides your pleasure?" she asked a bit tartly.

"They are to do with making you feel obedient and compliant to my wishes, as any good wife should be. Remove your dressing gown, and your night shift. I enjoy having every inch of your lovely body exposed to me."

She looked for a moment as if she might argue, but then she stared down at the floor and unknotted the silk tie of her gown, laying it neatly over a chair.

"Remember how I told you to undress," he said in the silence of the room. "Slowly, with sensuality. Undress as if you take pleasure in revealing yourself to me."

He thought this was the most difficult task of all in her esteem. She had not been reared to play the temptress, or seduce randy gentlemen. Her slow moves were clumsier than those of a practiced courtesan, and her expression not exactly one of excited pleasure. If she showed any desire, it was the desire to please him, probably in hopes of avoiding a birching.

But she was not to avoid that fate.

When she was naked and trying very hard to stand tall and not cower upon herself, he beckoned her toward the bed. "Yes, beautiful wife. There is no shame in the way God made us."

She ran a glance down the length of his body. "You are not as God made you. You are fully dressed."

"Do you wish me to undress?"

She fought with herself a moment; he could tell by the way she shifted and bit her lip. Finally, she looked him over again and answered, "Yes."

He smiled and began to work at the buttons of his coat. "While I comply with your wishes, wife, pray climb onto the bed beside the birch rod and face the headboard, positioning yourself on your hands and knees."

She hesitated, and he allowed her a few moments to collect her courage. By the time he started upon the buttons of his waistcoat, she had managed to take a few steps toward the bed.

"You are not resisting, are you?" he said quietly. "There are a great many degrees of birching a woman might receive, from lightly punitive to horrifyingly painful. I am certain you do not wish to experience the latter one."

That got her moving. She climbed up and knelt where he'd told her to. "Hands and knees," he repeated. "With your back straight and your bottom in the proper position."

"What is the proper position?" she asked in a quivering voice.

"Slightly arched and offered for punishment."

She could not quite accomplish it by the time he finished undressing, at least not to his exacting standards. He went to the bed and made a great to-do of positioning her correctly, stroking and prodding and rearranging her for maximum exposure. He felt a pang of conscience as she trembled under his hands. This must be wretchedly difficult for her, especially with the instrument of her impending torture resting on the bed beside her. Poor thing.

"There," he said when she was posed to his liking. "Stay exactly like that throughout your birching. Try to take it like a very good girl."

She murmured something that sounded negative in tone, but that didn't stop him from lifting his arm and delivering the first, rather mild stroke.

Aurelia collapsed onto her stomach with a great wail of pain. Her hands flew behind her. "Oh, that hurts! It hurts far too much."

He tsked and raised her up, forcing her into position again.

"I know it hurts, Aurelia. I remember exactly what it feels like. It might not surprise you to learn that I was birched quite frequently as a child."

"Well, I have never been birched and I don't believe I deserve to be."

She was already close to tears. The birch was indeed a daunting implement, as each stroke imparted a fiery explosion of pain. If she could have felt a stroke from one of his tutor's stout birches, or his father's...

"I am going to continue now," he said. But as soon as he raised his arm, she broke her position, shying away and reaching back to cover her bottom.

He put down the birch.

"You must not reach back, or collapse away from the blows, do you understand me?" he scolded. "You must be still until the end of your spanking."

"I can't be still. It hurts! I am still hurting from the first stroke."

He sighed and sat on the bed beside her, and lifted her into his arms. After a moment she released some of the tension stiffening her limbs. He stroked her hair and held her close against his heart.

"Aurelia, my love. I know the things I do to you seem frightening and strange."

"And painful," she protested. "And unfair."

"Fairness is not at issue here. Your cooperation is. You are not permitted to resist me, as you know."

"I can't help it." She turned her face against his chest. "Please, don't do this to me. Don't make me endure it only for your pleasure."

"You will take this birching," he said. "But if you wish, I'll make it easier for you to submit. Come with me."

He stood her up and marched her over to a lavishly padded and upholstered chaise. He had never spanked a woman here but had imagined, many times, its suitability as a punishment bench.

"Kneel down," he said, making her face the padded back. When she was in position, he went across the room and retrieved the sturdy silk ribbon that cinched closed the waist of her dressing gown. He carried it back to his wide-eyed wife and told her to hold out her hands. When she did, he contrived to thread the ribbon through the back legs of the chair and tie her hands wrist to wrist. When he pulled the bonds taut, she had no choice but to remain bent over the padded chair back. He finished his handiwork with a neat little bow.

She moaned as he stood back to survey her pose. She squirmed, gloriously naked, at his mercy. As he suspected, the seat back was the perfect height to support her hips, and the bonds holding her wrists would prevent her from reaching back to shield her posterior, as well as prevent her from leaving the chaise until he was quite finished with her.

"Perhaps someday you will not need your hands bound, but at the moment I think it best. Now you will have no choice but to submit to your birching, my naughty little miss."

"Please, let me go," she begged.

"Let you go? I've half a mind to keep you there forever. You've no idea the pretty picture you appear." He circled her, like a predator sizing up its prey. "Your full hips and buttocks are thrust in the air, waiting to be spanked." He punctuated the last word with a crisp smack to her behind, then strolled around the front of her. "Your buxom breasts are available to me here in the front, to pinch or tease." He demonstrated just that as she squirmed on her knees and tugged at the ribbon holding her wrists. "And then there is your wiggling, and your anxious chirping sounds. My lovely grasshopper." He forced her head up and sidled closer so his cock reared before her face. It was so tempting to thrust into her half-opened mouth.

"But we've a birching to see to, haven't we? Something about lack of gratitude," he reminded himself out loud. "No more delays."

He took up the birch and flicked her bottom with it. She cried out as if tortured, but he didn't let that divert him from his task. It was much, much easier now that she was properly battened down. Another blow, and another, and then quick, smart flicks to bedevil her. He put a hand on her back to still her when she thrashed her legs about and wailed in protest, but there was not much she could do to avert her fate. After eight stingers, her bottom was red and angry with birch marks. He paused, stroking the punished cheeks.

"It's not so very bad, is it?"

She lifted her head to look at him. "It's terrible. It stings like a thousand spankings. Please, let me go."

"Not yet."

He moved back around to her front and pinched her nipples, reveling in her gasp. "Kiss me with your mouth." He took his cock in his fist and eased the head toward her. "Kiss it as you did the other day."

When she gazed up at him in teary-eyed mutiny, he shrugged and took up a place beside the chaise again.

"No, I'll do it," she screamed, but she was too late. He drew back the birch rod and landed two more stinging blows.

"When you don't obey my requests, I assume you wish your punishment to continue."

"You are awful," she cried.

He birched her again, thinking how very stubborn she was.

"I'm sorry. Please. I'll do as you asked. Please, my lord. I—I'll do it, if only you'll stop."

He returned to his stance in front of her, his cock harder and hotter than ever. "Show me then. Kiss me. Lick around the crown. That's how we begin."

With a whimper, she complied. He threw his head back, overcome by the teasing sensation of her tentative kisses and the hesitant explorations of her tongue. He supposed a very warm bottom was motivation to do just about anything. After a while, he said, "Open your mouth," and she obeyed, staring up at him in dread.

"It won't be awful, my love," he said soothingly. "This is the first skill a courtesan learns, so I'm certain you can master it too. I'm going to move my cock in and out of your mouth. Your job is to suck and caress it as if you were tasting something very, very good. But no biting," he added as an afterthought. "Absolutely no teeth."

She gave him a tragically beleaguered look, but any protests were muffled by the introduction of his very thick and aching rod into her tiny, prim mouth. It really was slow going. This skill wasn't developed overnight, especially when the lady in question obviously had severe misgivings about what she was doing. He wasn't sure if her tears were born of shame, strain, or lack of oxygen.

"Are you breathing?" he asked. "It's important to breathe, Aurelia. If you must, take air through your nose."

After a few forays into her hot, wet mouth he withdrew and stroked back a bit of her hair. "You're doing very well. I know you don't enjoy this...yet...but I assure you I enjoy it very much." Having let her rest, he widened her lips with his thumbs and eased back into her mouth. She swallowed around the tip of him, a delicious suction that almost brought him off. "There are many ribald names for this act," he said to distract himself a while longer. "But I suppose the most official one is oral copulation. It may interest you to know that it can also be done to a woman for her pleasure."

Her expression spoke of disbelief. In his gratitude, perhaps he would show her what she obviously didn't understand. Yes, he was certain he would. Why not? But first he gripped his cock and worked it as he pressed shallowly in and out of her mouth. This was a pathetic display of fellatio, but she was submitting to him in a way he never imagined she would. Each evening, each wicked night, he would make her practice until she was skilled enough to bring him to completion. In the meantime...

He stood back from her and pumped himself to reach his peak. His seed erupted, spurting upward and then pooling down and over the back of his hand. She watched this display, thinking God knew what. That she was trapped in the marriage from hell to a madman, perhaps? He laughed under his breath and went to the basin to wash away the evidence of his climax. That finished, he returned to untie her wrists.

When she was free she jerked away from him. He caught her and stopped her. "Slowly, my dear. Kneel up slowly and take your time."

She wiped a hand over her lip. "I need to wash out my mouth."

"Because my cock was in it? I promise you, I keep every part of my body fastidiously clean. But you may certainly do it later, after I'm done with you."

She regarded him in dismay. "There's more to do? But you have already..." She gestured vaguely toward his softening cock.

"Yes, I have already. But perhaps you would wish to experience oral pleasuring as well?"

"I don't."

"Well, I wish it," he said, steering her firmly toward the bed. He pushed her back, pinning her hands over her head. Her curls lay spread out upon his pillow. Ah, she was lovely. He thought it fifty times a day.

"Leave your hands here," he said, staring at her very intently. "Do not move them or I shall go for the birch and we'll begin our entire evening's activities over again from the start. Would you like that?"

She shook her head violently.

"I didn't think so." Slowly, he released her hands. She shivered atop his thick linen counterpane as he knelt over her to give her a kiss. When her shivers turned to shudders, he drew away.

"Why are you so afraid?" he asked. "I promise this won't hurt."

"But what are you going to do to me?"

"Copulate with you. Orally. Perhaps that sounds too clinical. I am going to kiss and caress your quim and make you feel so good that your hips buck against my mouth."

"But you...you can't," she said, clearly scandalized.

"Can't I?" He arrested her hands before they could push him away, and placed them back over her head.

She swallowed hard, resisting just a little. "I don't think it's at all proper, what you intend to do."

He snorted under his breath. "Nothing proper is any fun. I assure you this is wildly improper, and I shall enjoy every moment of it. So will you."

He began at her shoulders, kissing, licking, tasting, following the alluring path of her curves. With infinite patience he worked his way down to her full, feminine bosom. He drank in her sighs and the soft catches of breath as he toyed with her nipples and the delicate undersides of her breasts. He used his tongue to delineate the majesty of her hips, and then kissed lower as she pleaded *no, no, no*.

He thought to himself, *yes, yes, yes*. He held her gaze as he spread her legs wider with gentle but inexorable pressure, then he kissed the inside of each trembling thigh. Her feminine scent excited him beyond measure. He'd memorized every note of it by now, knew it as well as he knew his own face. He had made it his business to learn the sophisticated pleasuring of women over countless experiences of his youth, and now Aurelia would benefit...if only she would relax. When she tried to close her legs, he pinned them open with his shoulders, then slid his arms beneath her hips to draw her closer to his mouth.

The silly woman actually braced as he pressed his lips to her wet, silken folds—but he knew how to deal with resistance in this quarter. He swirled his tongue around her silken center, teasing and exploring until he found the thrusting bit of flesh that made her moan. He worried the nubbin between his teeth and paid it devoted attention. He opened her with his fingers, probing inside her with infinite patience when she whined and pulled away.

This didn't hurt her. It only hurt her sensibilities, her prim self-identification. "Let go," he whispered. "Think only of pleasure, and your animal needs."

"I'm not an animal," she said.

Yes, he knew that. Not a mouse or a grasshopper, but a woman overwrought with need. He would do this for an hour if that's what it took to fight through her defenses and reduce her to the delectably wanton creature he wished her to be.

But in the end, it took much less time. He didn't scold her when her hands left their ordered place above her head and curled into his hair, and pulled it in an urgent signal of need. He hummed against her heated flesh, spreading her wider, and then lapped delicately at her quim. He learned what made her shudder and what made her groan, and what made her buck against his mouth as he'd told her she would do.

"Please, please," she begged. "Please."

"Yes," was his only reply. *Yes, yes, yes.* When he felt her come off, he slipped his fingers deep inside her to feel her inner muscles contract. He was hard again, hard as steel, hard as granite, and he might have pushed his cock inside instead, but he decided not to. This had been about her pleasure, not his. This had been a lesson in gratitude for them both.

Her fingers loosened in his hair, coming to rest weakly on his shoulders. He kissed back up her belly to the enticing pillow of her breasts, then laid his head there to listen to her wildly beating heart. He lay back and pulled her close, enfolding her in his arms so her head ended up on his shoulder. It was a comfortably pleasing weight.

"Sleep here tonight," he said, nuzzling her shoulder. "There's plenty of room here for the both of us."

She didn't answer for long moments, and he realized his exhausted wife had fallen fast asleep.

Chapter Eleven: Transcendent

Aurelia loved the library at Somerton. Her husband had outfitted a long, soaring room filled with books and huge leather chairs that somehow managed to feel cozy. Thick, deep brown carpets softened the floors. Three great branches of candles lit the space, since dinner had come and gone, and the day's light with it. Townsend sat near the fireplace in a great wingback chair, leafing through some of the London papers as he sipped his port.

Aurelia had staked out a corner of his grand desk for her writing materials and correspondence, and worked now on a letter to her parents. She was careful not to disturb his papers, as she had come to know him as a fastidious landowner who took great care in all his interests.

She understood now that *she* was one of his interests, and that he was doggedly developing her into what he would like, while looking after her with close supervision. As day followed day, she noticed the little things he did to try to make her happy, even as he demanded his own happiness by requiring her to do all manner of licentious things.

Each day, honestly, she minded it a little less.

Oh, she didn't enjoy the spankings. Not the pain part of them, anyway. But there was something in the way he touched her and smiled at her afterward that made the pain and embarrassment seem worth it. His dark looks, which used to repel her, came to seem rather handsome and dashing. His smiles, which used to terrify her, now set up a clamor in her heart. Sometimes she even wondered if he loved her.

But it could not be so. They'd been married less than a month, and they were so very different in manner and temperament. But if love was caring for someone and making them smile ten times a day... She stared across the room at her husband, at his fine long legs, at his strong shoulders, at the faint frown lines between his brows as he concentrated on his papers and occasionally turned a page. His lips arrested her attention, pursed as they were. She noticed them relax into a faint smile, and then realized he was looking back at her.

She glanced quickly down at her letter, as if she hadn't been staring at him, but her pen had long since been put down on the table. She pasted on a thoughtful look as if she had only been considering what to write.

"How is your letter coming?" her husband asked. She could hear the teasing beneath his tone.

"I am nearly finished." She looked down at the rather scattered niceties she'd composed so far.

"I would like to read it before you post it, as usual."

She lost herself a moment in the dark depths of his gaze. "If you wish. But, as usual, I have not written anything negative about you."

His smiled widened. "A difficult task indeed."

She laughed at his teasing expression. Had she ever laughed so much in her life? She was coming to appreciate his dry, often ridiculous humor and enjoy his many jokes.

"Well, there are certain matters I cannot discuss with them," she said, attempting her own joke. "And those would be the matters where I could righteously complain of your faults."

He rewarded her with a great burst of mirth. The sound rang from the high ceilings and she grinned so wide she covered her mouth in a wave of shyness. She didn't know if he really found her jokes funny, or only laughed at them because she'd grown brave enough to make the clumsy attempts.

He looked back at his papers and she bent back over her letter, checking it to be sure she hadn't said anything remiss about Lord Townsend. From the start he had forbidden her to send any letters without his permission, and without them being read first by him. She supposed it was because she had threatened to tell her father and brother what a monster he was, but she'd never do that now.

After composing a few more lines of daughterly news and affection, Aurelia put the last flourishing touches to her signature, then sanded the paper dry.

He looked up as she approached him with the letter, and opened his arms.

She allowed herself to be drawn into his lap. They used to spend this time after dinner in their separate places, in entirely different areas of the house. She used to hide away from him like the mouse everyone assumed her to be, but she enjoyed this better, being close to him. She leaned back against his chest and nestled her head beneath his chin. He assisted in arranging her skirts, murmuring in a gentlemanly fashion about the prettiness of her gown, and then held up the letter before him.

"Let me see." He made a great show of squinting at her handwriting, although she knew it to be perfectly neat and ladylike. "*Dear Mama and Papa...*" He squeezed her lightly. "An estimable beginning."

She giggled at his silliness. "It is a very standard beginning, I believe."

He read on in his deep, rumbling voice. "*I was delighted to receive your letter. Everything continues lovely in Berkshire. You would be impressed indeed with Somerton. There are fields and beautiful gardens turning all the colors of autumn, and a great stately home with windows to the loveliest views. You must come and visit when you may.* Good lord," he muttered. "Let us hope they stay too busy."

"But I would like to see them!"

"So you may return to being their prim, miserable daughter, after all the strides we've made? I think not." He kissed her on the nose, an innocuously tender gesture after the anger in his voice. "You may invite them, of course. But if they come, I'll find some way to be in London on business."

"What if they come for weeks?" she asked.

"Then I'll jump off the north tower," he said with a sigh. "What else have you written in this pinnacle of a letter? *Townsend is well. He stays busy with his duties and takes time to spend with me as well. He is congenial and courteous in all things."* He snorted. "What a bounder, Aurelia. You do not mention here that I spank you nightly, sometimes until you cry."

"I can add it as a post-script," she said, pretending to take the letter.

He made a quelling sound and lifted it out of reach. When she resettled against him, he resumed where he had left off. "Kind and patient in all things. Blah blah blah. *We had pheasant for dinner last night. It was delicious. Townsend's cock came with us from London."*

"Cook," she corrected him.

"Oh, I thought things were finally getting interesting." He pointed to the word in question. "That looks very much like a c."

"It is an o," she said firmly.

He rolled his eyes. "*Townsend's cook came with us from London. It wasn't a very long ride from his city home, only a day's journey. His traveling carriage is much like papa's finest rig, only done in ivory rather than pale blue. I believe the seats are also not quite as wide.* This is gripping stuff, my darling. Your parents will love this letter. But why do you only talk about my cook and my carriage," he asked, peering down at her, "and say nothing about me?"

She pursed her lips and raised her eyebrows. His mouth curved in a smile.

"*Give my love to Brendan and Georgina, and be assured...*" He paused, his gaze lingering on the page. "*Be assured that I am eminently happy here with Townsend. He has proved a respectable sort of husband with a great facility for kindness. He makes me smile every day.*" He looked down at her with a glint of something indefinable in his eyes. A muscle ticked in his firm, strong jaw, and his hand moved a little where it rested on her back.

"Will it do?" she asked, feeling shy.

He looked back at the letter. "Well, I think it very poor that there is no mention whatsoever of the grasshopper, or its churlish attempt at escape, or our valiant struggle to recapture it unharmed. But such subversive activities might well send Duchess Lansing into a swoon, or cause her to come charging over here to rescue you, so perhaps you are a good daughter for omitting that tale."

He lifted her from his lap, and she followed him over to his desk, where he folded the letter and sealed it by imprinting the Townsend crest in wax.

"Very prettily written, my love. Mama and Papa will be in ecstasies when they receive it." He placed it on the pile with his other correspondence. "Perhaps as a reward, we'll postpone tonight's spanking and begin with some fun." He sat back in the upholstered leather desk chair and pulled her closer. "Let's practice what you've been learning. Kneel down."

"Here?" She glanced toward the open door.

"Yes, here. No one will enter unless I summon them."

Aurelia feared she gave him a very ungracious look as she sank to her knees before him.

"No. Stop." He lifted her up again. "You know that was not fetchingly done. Whether or not you agree with my directions, you must obey me in a respectful way. How should you look? How should you reply when I direct you?"

She bit her lip. "I should say, 'As you wish, my lord.'"

"With more docility, if you please, or you will have that spanking first after all."

"As you wish, my lord," she attempted again, with more sweet submissiveness in her tone.

He nodded, and she reached to unbutton the flap of his breeches. She had become somewhat more comfortable around his large, thick rod. Somewhat.

In truth, her husband lay with her every day, sometimes more than once a day, and they did this too now—every day. She might have complained about so much oral copulation if she didn't fear what type of copulation he intended to teach her next. He alluded to it, toying occasionally with her bottom hole, making descriptive promises that sounded more like threats. She hoped if she kept him satisfied enough in this way he might postpone or forget completely about the other things he wanted to do to her.

But another part of her knew that would never happen.

She freed the evidence of his virility and dutifully caressed it with her mouth and lips. Grunts and sighs accompanied softly spoken instructions to lick this or pay more attention to that, or suck harder, or pump him faster. Sometimes he held her head and controlled her movements, but other times he was very still and left her on her own to try to please him.

She wondered how long he would take this night, and whether she'd be able to bring him to completion. The last couple times she had, even though it had taken an interminable amount of time, and then he'd spent inside her mouth, which had appalled her. But when he warned her that she must not spit it out, but swallow it down, she had done so because of the sharp insistence in his voice.

He brushed fingers through her hair, gave a soft moan, then called out, "Landon."

Aurelia froze. Why was he calling one of the footmen? His fingers traced down to cup the back of her neck, preventing her from drawing back the way she wished.

"He won't be able to see you," he said beneath his breath. "Continue, please."

Aurelia felt that she would choke. He held her trapped, his rod nearly to the back of her throat, forcing her to breathe through her nose. But if she choked, surely the servant would hear that. She moved her tongue a little and swallowed, and as she hoped, he loosened his grip.

"Will you deliver this note to the kitchen," she heard him say, "and have the requested items brought back here at once?"

He cannot see me here crouched under the desk, she thought over and over, to keep the panic at bay. But she thought the servant must sense she was there, because her heart beat so loudly. Townsend's fingers massaged her neck, urging her to continue what she was supposed to be doing.

And she did, because she had become so very depraved indeed.

"Good girl," he said once the servant was gone. "Your obedience arouses me, as does your naughty little mouth." His fingers toyed with her curls. "He didn't see you, I promise. And I am very, very close."

As he said it, his cock bucked between her lips. He instructed her to lightly stroke his balls, and when she did, he made such urgent sounds of pleasure that Aurelia strove even harder at her task. When he stiffened, his hands clamped on either side of her head, she prepared herself for his hot liquid seed, and swallowed it without being told.

She looked up at him, blinking. She felt so vulnerable in these moments. She knew she could never live up to the loose women who inhabited his premarital life, but she tried her best. He gazed down at her with a lazy smile and a great sigh of contentment that made her feel like a very talented lady indeed.

"What are you thinking?" she asked as he did up his flap.

His smile widened to a grin. "I'm thinking that a regimen of spanking and sexual training suits you very well. I'm also thinking that you may

125

wish to rise and compose your appearance before the footman returns with the ginger I ordered for your bottom."

She gawked at him as he smoothed her disarranged curls and patted her skirts. "You...you sent a servant for ginger?"

"Did you expect me to go fetch it myself from the hothouse? The cook knows precisely how to prepare it to my specifications. At least, when it is to be sent upstairs, since it's only requested then for one reason. For ladies' bottoms," he specified when she continued to gawk in silence. "For your bottom, tonight."

"I don't understand the point of this activity," she said.

"You'll understand shortly. Ah, here we are." The servant returned, crossing the library with a covered silver tray. "Leave it there, would you?"

Aurelia breathed a sigh of relief that the footman wasn't going to take off the silver lid and present the ignoble item to Townsend as she stood there beside him, the obvious recipient. But of a certainty, the servant knew. A deep blush showed about his ears and neck. The household staff were trained to show no interest, judgment, or emotion in matters, but his blush gave everything away.

Townsend dismissed the man, so she was left alone with her husband in the midst of this very alarming situation. She heard the deep click of the library doors as the servant pulled them closed.

He faced her, wearing a piratical smile. "I would like to reassure you this will not be so bad, little grasshopper, but in truth, the entire point is to unsettle you. Come closer and have a look."

He took the lid off the tray and Aurelia stared down at a very ordinary finger of ginger and a small knife. No, not entirely ordinary. Upon closer inspection she saw the lump of ginger was shaved into a phallic shape with an exaggerated flange at one end. On the whole, it was rather thicker than she would have liked, since he'd already told her where it was going.

"Sometimes I wish I could have married a very boring and continent man," she said, meaning every word. "Is this absolutely necessary? Why do you find pleasure in tormenting me?"

He picked up the small knife and began to carve shallow ridges into the ginger. "It's not the tormenting I enjoy, but your reactions to it. Your moaning, your kicking, your pleas for mercy. It gives me a great, delicious feeling of power and sexual arousal. If you could feel what I feel, you wouldn't question the things I do." He looked up at her from his curious task. "I wonder what you feel. Is it only pain and dread? Or other feelings? Some of the ladies I frequented in London were happily affected by all the things I do to you." His voice lowered a bit. "Sometimes you seem more happily affected than you profess to be."

She could not in a thousand years answer his question, not honestly, at least. Instead, she posed him a question. "What are you doing to that?"

He put down the knife and showed her the bit of ginger, its scent grown stronger in the past few minutes. "I am feathering the flesh, so the effect becomes more potent. Just a bit, you know, since this is your first time. One can employ all sorts of methods to increase the sting."

She swallowed hard. The *sting*? Was this to be a sting like the sting when he used a birch rod or strap on her bottom? But this was to be *inside* her bottom... Her hands crept back to cover her posterior.

"I wonder if my father has perhaps lost interest in monitoring your extramarital peccadillos. If there are ladies who enjoy this, perhaps you would do better going to them. I wouldn't mind."

He gave her a look both affectionate and reproachful. "I have no wish to test your father, not when you have proven such an erotic delight."

An erotic delight. She could hardly fathom it. "You're only saying that so I don't run away screaming."

"If you ran screaming, I would drag you back, as we both know. I am saying it because it's the truth. I've come to prefer tormenting my wife to tormenting hardened working ladies. For one thing, there is some perverse excitement in the way you struggle to comply." His lips pursed, and his expression sobered. "For another, you have grown more than a little dear to me. You are beautiful and compelling to me in a way the others never were."

She took in this brash avowal, not knowing whether to smile or dissolve into tears. There was a time she had believed he hated her. Now they got along in a much more congenial way and she was happy for that, but for him to call her beautiful, and profess that she compelled him? She ducked her head, wringing her hands in her skirts. "I can hardly believe you mean what you say."

"Well, we shall lie that at the Duke and Duchess of Lansing's feet, for never allowing you to learn how very alluring you are."

Those words too, she could barely process, but then her husband was in motion, drawing her over his lap and pushing her skirts up and out of the way. He caught one of her arms and held it tight at the small of her back. With his other hand he caressed her bottom cheeks.

"The first thing you must understand about your arsehole, darling, is that for me to put anything inside it, you must let me have my way. You cannot resist and clench the passage shut."

"I am very sure I can't help doing that," she complained from her defenseless position.

"And yet you must learn how. I shall put things inside it on a more regular basis now, in order to prepare you for eventual copulation."

"Copulation? Who decided copulation there would be a good idea?" Frustration had rather coarse and whining words spilling from her mouth. "Your thing is far too big, and that hole is far too small, and whoever invented this method of sexual congress must have been a dunderhead indeed."

"Perhaps. A lustful dunderhead who enjoyed tight spaces, as many men do. Calm yourself, little one," he said, pausing a moment to massage her tense back. "There shall only be ginger for now, until you grow more used to these earthier pleasures."

Only ginger, she thought. And *earthier pleasures?* More like an abominable act against nature. She felt him reach to the tray, then felt the cold, wet tip of the ginger fig pressed to her bottom. She braced, but so far, it wasn't terribly painful or stinging where it touched her.

"I am going to press it inside you now," he said in the calm, implacable tone he always used for moments like these. "You'll feel pressure and discomfort, but you'll receive no injury. The wider edge will keep it from disappearing inside."

Heavens, she hadn't even thought of such a thing. Then she was unable to think of anything at all as the thick bit of ginger entered her bottom hole. He had told her not to clench but she found it happening instinctively, from alarm or uneasiness. He held her still as he pressed it deeper and deeper. At last the intrusion stopped.

Aurelia lay limp, afraid to even breathe. There was no sharp pain, only a shameful, stretched awareness that the thing was there where it should not be. And then...she felt the sting.

It was bearable at first. Her husband murmured something that might have been "good girl" or "there now" or some other platitude, and Aurelia realized that the burning was intensifying moment by moment. Her bottom hole, which she had always tried very hard to forget existed, now felt alive with a burning, stinging achiness. She twisted her hips, moaning softly.

"Don't fight it," he said. "You shall tolerate this in your bottom for quite some time yet."

"But why?" she wailed. "Why do you want to do this to me?"

"Because it excites me to a magnificent degree." Indeed, she could feel him going hard against her side, although he'd just climaxed in her mouth a short time earlier. "Be still," he chided as her cries of protest mounted and her feet began to kick. "It cannot be that bad."

"It is that bad! I wonder, husband, if you should like to have a piece of ginger shoved in your bottom."

He chuckled, rubbing and playing with her bottom cheeks. "Of course I tried it once to see what it felt like. I discovered that I don't enjoy receiving it very much, but I do so love inflicting it on others, especially kicking, sassy, naughty wives."

"Oh, it hurts terribly! You must take it out."

"I seem to remember you saying something to that effect on our wedding night. But it's not coming out until your spanking is over. In fact, its potency increases over time, which is why a long and arduous spanking is called for when a ginger fig is in place."

"Ohhh," she said, letting her head fall down. It was useless to try to fight him. All the boring, respectable husbands in the world, and she ended up with this one. Precisely her luck.

He did embark upon a long and arduous spanking. At the first crisp smack, she clenched her cheeks and let out a wail of fresh agony. Squeezing upon the ginger increased its potency tenfold. As smacks continued to rain down, she found it impossible to control the clenching of her buttocks, and thus she suffered quite a bit, as each time the ginger delivered more sting.

"I surmise you are discovering why ginger is used in conjunction with corporal punishment," he said. She could hear amusement in his voice, and wanted to slap him for it. "If you do not clench, it will not feel so bad."

But it felt bad even when she didn't clench, and how was she to lay limp and let him punish her hindquarters without squeezing them tight against the blows?

"Please, oh please," she cried. "This is too cruel."

He stopped, allowing her to catch her breath, but of course, the punishing burn in her bottom continued even when his hand was at rest. She believed it was a half hour or more that he stopped and started in a very long and arduous spanking indeed. Somewhere around the middle there were tears. She wiped them away feeling a very pitiable and abused wife, but they were tears of frustration more than anything else.

Nothing about this was unbearable. That was the worst thing. The pain was constant and consistent but eminently bearable, and then...there was so much more. There was the scent of him, and the faint sounds of his exertion, the leather smell of the library and the occasional hiss from the fire. There was the rosy throbbing in her bottom mimicking too well the hot throbbing between her thighs. Oh, why did he do these things to her? And how was she to survive with any dignity? By the end, she wanted him to force her and possess her, and she couldn't imagine why except that she was truly lost to the world of iniquitous sin.

"Please," she said again, and this time it sounded like a completely different sort of plea. His spanking hand paused. The other hand tightened on her arm, then released her.

She was borne up and placed on her feet, and before she could even get her bearings, bent roughly over her husband's desk. She braced herself upon her forearms, staring a bit wonderingly over at the pile of correspondence, and the letter to her papa and mama just atop it. She squeezed her eyes shut and turned her head away. Behind her, Townsend grasped her thighs and plunged his cock all the way inside her, so her hips bumped hard against the edge of the desk.

The ginger was still in her bottom, burning and torturing her, but his thrusting cock brought an entirely new type of torture, because she *wanted* it. She craved it and wished to bend before it just as she was. She arched her hips back to receive him, which brought an appreciative growl to his lips. That a man might ever growl so at her... Her hands made fists as she rested her forehead against the desk.

She felt his fingers curl into her hair. A small tug and he urged her up so her back bumped against the hard muscles of his stomach and chest.

She wished that he was naked, and she was naked, so she could feel the warmth of his skin. He nuzzled his face against her neck, kissing, licking, nibbling. Biting. Her body drew up, preparing to explode. She clutched at him wherever she could, at his thighs, his fingers, the lace at his wrists.

"Come for me now. Do it," he said. "Naughty girl."

"I can't. I can't," she cried. She felt so hot and wild, so ashamed of her uncontrolled behavior. Her lust.

"Yes, you can. You will," he rumbled against her ear.

And she did, crying out as her bottom contracted repeatedly about the ginger, and her spasming channel milked the solid intrusion of his cock. He pushed her forward and pressed hard inside her, hurting her hips on the edge of the desk again, but she was beyond caring. One, two, three crashing thrusts and he went still behind her, whispering oaths and endearments under his breath.

He leaned down over her, his warmth enveloping her. His hands played at either side of her hair, making her feel sleepy and replete. "I will have to think of some better words than *beautiful* and *compelling*," he said after some time. He pressed his cheek against hers, then turned to give her a kiss. "I find they are inadequate to express how truly transcendent you are."

And she thought, *If I am transcendent, you have made me that way.*

Even the ginger couldn't take away the feeling that this marriage, and her burning lust for her husband, was very, very right.

Chapter Twelve: Wilderness Walk

Hunter lounged back on the blanket on the lower south lawn, one leg bent, the other sprawled alongside his discarded coat and hat. He breathed deeply of the fresh scents of autumn leaves and grass. There would not be many more opportunities for picnics before winter was upon them, trapping them inside the house.

Not that being trapped in the house with Aurelia would be a bad thing.

There was a time he might have imagined it so. No longer. Over the past few weeks he'd come to the gradual and lowering realization that he was quite hopelessly in love with his wife.

She sat across from him, the sun playing off her glossy curls, and her ripe, seductive body displayed to stimulating effect by her low-cut gown. The dear thing just had yet another plump finger of ginger fixed into her bottom, which was probably why she squirmed so prettily over tea.

"Some men only fig their women to increase the intensity of a spanking," he said, smiling over at her. "But they are unimaginative, aren't they?"

She looked up at him from beneath her lashes with a harried exasperation that never failed to fire his blood.

"Poor little muffin," he said, handing her a cream-filled cake. "It cannot be easy being married to me."

"A great deal of the time it is not."

He laughed at the barely veiled reproach in her tone. Lady Dormouse was not often in evidence these days, having been replaced by a much more confident—and sometimes downright impertinent—companion and lover. It was considered very gauche among the aristocracy to pant after one's own wife, but with each passing day he wanted her more, admired her more, particularly her courage in fulfilling his unconventional demands.

Many wives would not have put up with him. They would have gone to a father, or brother, and rid themselves of his company if not his name. They would have found a way to live apart from him, and perhaps he would have been content enough easing back into his former life of casual, debauched sex. Instead, Aurelia had decided to submit to him, and slowly unwound from an uptight ice queen to a sensual, alluring bedmate. She had left behind all the virtue and restraint of her youth...for him.

It made him love her with an uncomfortable intensity. Sometimes it seemed his love for her burned through his very veins.

But did she love him? He wasn't sure. Sometimes he thought she did, when she smiled and laughed with him. Sometimes she was still withdrawn, spending lonely hours curled in her window seat.

"Are you happy?" he asked as she licked a bit of cream from her lips.

She looked around the sunny field, and down at the confection in her hand. "Yes. Why shouldn't I be? These cakes are my favorite, and it's a lovely day."

"I don't mean happy just now. I mean, are you happy in general? Are you happy...with me?"

She gave him a long, frank look. "You are very brave to ask that when you've just put ginger in my arse."

"Such language, my dear. You'll have to be punished, won't you?"

She came very near to rolling her eyes. He smothered his own smile and reached for her. "Come and sit with me."

They were finished with tea. He pushed the cakes and cups aside and pulled her against him so they reclined together in the sun. "You smell

like sugar," he murmured. "And other delicious things." He tugged down
her plunging bodice to expose her nipples and the tops of her breasts, and
bent his head to tease the pink tips. They pulled taut into stiff, pointing
buttons he tormented with his teeth.

"Oh," she sighed. "Please, Hunter."

It still gave him a thrill to hear his name on her lips. She'd finally
relaxed into calling him by his given name, in private at least. She
squirmed against him, emitting little gasps no doubt elicited by the ginger.
Still, her hips pressed to his, her head thrown back to give him access to
her breasts. "You like that, do you?" He took one nipple between his
teeth and bit it until she squeaked. Then he held her tight as he licked
away the sting.

"I do like it," she said. "Please...come inside me." Her hands gripped
his shoulders.

"I will, my love. But today we shall try it a new way." His thoughts
wandered to the vial of lubricating oil he'd brought along in his pocket to
accomplish the task. She tensed a bit in his arms but he soothed her with
a kiss. "You shall survive it, I promise." He drew away and stroked her
cheek. "But first things first. It's time to take you to our favorite tree."

"*Your* favorite tree," she said.

She still complained about the rigidity of their spanking regimen.
What lady wouldn't? But she had come to realize that she only got
pleasure if she submitted to a certain amount of pain. And he wasn't
entirely sure she didn't draw some pleasure from the spankings too, as
much as she whined and kicked and pulled faces. She rarely cried in
earnest, which told him a lot.

He stood and reached down to her, stopping her when she would
have adjusted her bodice. "Leave your breasts out, just as they are. I enjoy
looking at them."

She flushed hot, but obeyed. They left the blanket and tea things and
headed out upon the wilderness walk. They strolled at a stately pace, her
arm in his, for there was no rush. The walk consisted of a natural path
wide enough for two, flanked by thick trees and brush. It was shady and
cool, and melodious with birdsong. They maintained an easy silence as
they walked, as comfortable companions were wont to do. Now and again
they heard the rustle of some small woodland creature looking for food or

seeking its nest. After five minutes or so, he paused on the path to twist a slender, low hanging branch from a birch tree.

This done, they continued their walk. Aurelia made no comment as he peeled the leaves from the branch and discarded them, and stripped it into a pliable switch. He'd taught her long ago that pleading or cajoling wouldn't save her from her fate. At length they reached their special tree, a fallen oak nearly four feet in diameter. He put down the switch, and spread his coat over the rough top of the trunk.

He stepped back and nodded to Aurelia. She moved forward with a sigh, her buxom breasts still wantonly exposed, and bent forward over the fallen tree trunk, across his coat so her gown and delicate skin would be protected from the bark. He went instantly hard as he watched her do it. He felt some pleasure wrestling her over his lap or over a spanking bench while she protested and fought him, but he found even greater pleasure when she docilely offered her bottom for chastisement.

He moved behind her and pulled up her skirts, arranging them high on her back so her plump, tensing bottom was on full display. The ginger's flange still peeked obscenely from between her cheeks. He thought of the vial of lubricant; there'd be more than ginger between those luscious cheeks today.

He drew back the switch without further ado, and gave her a few light swats to accustom her to the sting. That accomplished, he laid them on a bit harder, so she danced and fidgeted on her toes. He could see her hands twisting in the fabric of his coat. She had long since learned that throwing her hands back to shield her bottom was a serious offense. He had trained her out of such folly with the types of spankings that did make her cry.

She moaned as the switching continued. The ginger undoubtedly didn't help. He believed he must take it out and let some of the worst of the sting dissipate before he took her arsehole—not just for her sake, but for his. He did so, tossing the fig out into the forest now that it had served its purpose.

"Please, no more," she begged, looking back at him in entreaty. "My bottom feels all hot and used up."

"Shall I switch your thighs instead?"

"Oh, no!"

He did give her a few smarting slices to the backs of her thighs before swatting her bottom again. The quiet, whistling strokes built upon one another, mixed with the yelps and shrieks of his punished victim. He thought he'd better make her quite beside herself before he left off, so she would be docile, perhaps even grateful, for what would come next.

In truth, he felt a bit of a cad to bugger his own wife. It wasn't proper, not in the least, but he enjoyed it and he thought it felt good. Aside from the delicious tightness, there was something about the forbidden nature of sodomy that compelled him, so that he didn't really want to live without it. Aurelia didn't have to like it too—few ladies did. She only had to submit to it. He would happily please her in other ways, but buggery took two and so he at least needed her cooperation.

When her legs started to tremble, and her yelps attenuated into long, pleading cries, he decided she had had enough of the switch. He flung it away and bent to inspect his wife's backside. He rubbed some of the sting-ier looking welts, giving her a few hand spanks for good measure. The red hand prints combined with the neat lines of switch marks to give her arse a well-punished glow. He parted her cheeks, squeezing each one.

"You took that very well, my dear. I know it was a difficult session."

"At least you took the ginger out," she said, her voice still a bit quivery. "It got easier after that."

"But I am going to put something else in." He unbuttoned the flap of his breeches and pushed them down, releasing his rock-hard organ. Just the thought of what he was about to do had him unbearably excited. It had been weeks, after all, weeks of steady preparation in hopes it would go well. "We've discussed this before," he said in a soothing voice as she shuddered upon his coat. "And we've practiced a bit, with the ginger and with my fingers." As he spoke, he availed himself of the little vial of slick oil, dripping some onto the tight bud of her nether opening, and smoothing some onto his fingers. He slipped one finger past the tight ring, massaging gently before proceeding to ease it in and out of her.

She cried out softly. "I'm afraid."

"I know, my love. But there is nothing to be afraid of. It will hurt a little, but you're so brave now when it comes to pain. And if you're a very good girl for me, I promise you shall be rewarded at the end." He added another finger, stretching her tense hole wider, and used the other hand to massage her lower back and her scarlet buttocks. "There now. Two fingers. It's not so bad, is it?"

"But you are much thicker than two fingers."

"Aurelia." He pressed both fingers inside her to the hilt. "Do you trust me?"

She gave a great sigh and finally whispered, "Yes."

Aurelia wanted to trust her husband. He had worked so hard to prepare her to do this outrageous thing he liked, but she was so very scared. He had put so much ginger in her bottom the last few weeks that she had come to think of it as a terribly painful place.

Well, of course it was going to hurt. He'd told her so. She felt cool, slick liquid and then the stretching probe of his fingers, and it felt very uncomfortable. He grasped her left hip with one hand.

"I'm going to go very slowly, all right? You remember your duty is to relax and not to clench."

Oh, that was very easy for him to say, she thought. He was not the one bent over in the middle of a forest with his spanked bottom exposed and about to be invaded by a man's cock.

She whined as he moved forward. She felt the blunt tip of him pressing to her hole, and she knew at once that it was far too big and she wouldn't be able to stretch around him. She knew from her many trips to her knees in his service, how thick and distended the tip of his cock became when he was aroused.

"You can't," she gasped, gritting her teeth. "It won't fit."

"I assure you it will fit if you relax. And, might I remind you, this is like the ginger. The greater you clench upon it, the worse it will hurt." He held her hip harder and nudged another bit deeper inside. "Open. Open," he urged her.

But it didn't feel right at all, nothing like when he made love to her quim. It ached with a terrible burn and she squirmed, trying to evade his forward motion.

"Be still, devil take it," he said. "The tip's inside you. Give your body a moment to adjust to the sensation."

The sensation? It could more aptly be called torment. And once they accomplished this, she feared he would want to do it over and over. Every day perhaps. She had thought she could make a go of this marriage, depravity and all, but now she was not so sure.

"I'm afraid. It hurts so much," she said.

"Aurelia, please." His voice sounded ragged, as tormented as her own. "Please try a bit harder, for me." She could hear him taking slow measured breaths. She felt more of the slippery stuff drizzled down the crack of her behind. He smoothed it around her hole, a touch that felt much more pleasant than the stretching inside. He moved the slightest amount, forward and back.

She braced for more pain but her body, somehow, was relaxing around him. The sharpest, agonizing pain had faded, giving way to a filled-up kind of discomfort.

"What do you think now?" he asked.

"Are you all the way inside? Perhaps it's not so very bad, if you stay still."

He gave a husky laugh. "I won't be able to stay still much longer, and I'm only an inch or so inside." The massaging hand at her back squeezed harder. "Please, Aurelia. We're so close. Relax and let me love you this way."

How strange, to think about this as a type of loving. But she supposed it was. He might hurt her so badly, right now, this second, but instead he tarried and made infinitesimal forays in and out. He was waiting for her to accept him, rather than force his way in and hurt her. She reached back to touch his leg, feeling the strong muscles of his thigh. So much power to hurt her, but she realized that he wouldn't, not in this.

"I...I think it is all right," she said. "But please, go slowly."

"Oh, my beautiful girl," he sighed in reply. He drove forward a little, then a little more. The oil eased the way so there was no painful friction, although she felt terribly full. He pushed in, in, in until she thought she could not feel more impaled. "I'm all the way inside you now," he breathed. "How does it feel? Not so very bad?"

"It feels...uneasy," she whispered. "I am still afraid of being hurt somehow."

"Let me put those fears to rest." He took her hips and began to move, smooth, slow thrusts that found her center and then withdrew, leaving her empty. Distasteful as it seemed in theory, there was something about the act that was connective. He was inside her, *there*, and she was aware of every inch of him at every moment, with every small movement he made.

Once he had driven in and out of her several times, he pressed forward so his front rested against her back, and he embraced her. One of his legs wrapped around hers, bringing them even closer. It was the intimacy, she thought. This was a very intimate act, more intimate than any other she could picture.

His agile fingers delved down the front of her and parted the folds of her cleft, searching out the part of her that tingled and ached to be teased. She sucked in a shocked gust of air, hardly believing he could make her feel so divinely aroused when he was inside her there. Five minutes ago, she had been on the verge of tears from the pain of him breaching her, and now she felt scandalously close to being brought off. He caressed her in time with his deep forays inside her, until her hips moved in rhythm and uncivilized panting replaced her breath.

"You like it," he whispered against her ear. "You naughty, wondrous girl. You like to be fucked in the arse."

His obscenity ought to have disturbed her. Instead, it brought the lustful arousal inside her to a throbbing peak.

"Say that you like it. Tell me. Say that you will wish me to do this again."

"I—I like it," she stammered, not sure if she meant it or if he had only taken over her body and her mind through some unnatural skill.

"Say that you like my cock in your arse. Say it."

"I like your cock in my arse," she whispered. "I like it. Please...please don't stop touching me there. It feels so good."

"Yes, your pussy is hot and wet with wanting. You shall have your reward." The fondness in his voice combined with the dancing of his fingertips, and the very firm buggering of her narrow channel, so that she felt quite transported and outside of herself. She was not Aurelia, proper wife and daughter, but a wild thing like the birds and rustling creatures of the woods. She saw his hand grasp the oak bark beside her, and then he reached forward to pinch her nipples, first one and then the other. He pressed his chin against her hair as he plucked the taut, aroused points.

"I love you. My wife. My beautiful, sensual wife."

She could only sob in surrender as the teasing pain of her nipples released the last of her hold on civility. Her climax built to a roaring peak, and then a shuddering, gasping release. As if from far away, she heard his shout of completion as he drove her hard against the oak trunk, his fingers twisted in her hair. But she was not there beneath him. She was flying free, still shivering in the throes of magnificent bliss.

Slowly, she came back to awareness of the forest. He was stroking her hair and occasionally the crown of her forehead, a steady, soothing touch.

"Do you love me too?" he asked her quietly. "But you must, to surrender to me so completely. Aurelia, how I love you."

She reached to cradle his head beside hers. "Of course I love you. Well, most of the time," she joked. When had she ever joked before she met him? Never.

He laughed so that his still-hard cock bucked inside her. Now that the ecstasy had ebbed away, it was back to feeling rather tender and uneasy there. He pulled away from her carefully, then helped her stand upright and rearrange her dress and her curls where he'd mussed them. He tilted her head back and kissed her for long moments while she readjusted to the reality of her world.

She was a fallen sort of woman, surely, but she didn't think that was so bad anymore. He loved her, and she was very sure she was coming to love him, despite all the reasons she shouldn't. He kissed her with passionate tenderness, his arms holding her safe, his lips caressing and soothing her misgivings away. She loved him for this, for his tenderness and humor, and his wildness. She loved him for the pleasure he'd brought to her life.

She loved him.

All of a sudden, he broke the kiss and turned toward a group of shrubs.

"Do you hear that?" he asked.

Aurelia tilted her head, listening for what he might hear, then a smile spread across her face. A robust *chirp-chirp* repeated amongst the other sounds of the forest, a few yards away at most.

"I believe our pet grasshopper has been a voyeur to our little scene."

She narrowed her eyes in confusion. "What does that mean? A voyeur?"

"Voyeurs take pleasure from watching others' private interactions."

"Sexual interactions?"

"Often, yes." He arched a brow at her. "I am so terribly evil, my dear, that I know all these things, and then teach them to you."

"Have you been a voyeur to other's sexual interactions? Perhaps in your previous adventures?"

He gave her one of his piratical looks and then pretended great interest in searching for the grasshopper. But it had gone quiet, unwilling to be found. They went to a nearby brook to wash up, a practical errand that soon degraded into reckless chasing and splashing. It seemed the perfect conclusion to their bawdy afternoon. He pulled on his breeches and his coat, and ran a hand through his hair, straightening it where she'd tugged upon it.

"I suppose we must go back and gather up our tea things, and return to the house before the servants come looking for us." He turned to her and took her hands in his. "Thank you, my dear, for giving so much to me. It has been a special sort of afternoon."

She could think of nothing to say to that. In fact, the depth of his gaze made her feel raw and vulnerable. She wished she was upstairs in her rooms, near to the window seat so she might hide. Finally she managed to say, "You're welcome," and they set off back down the walk hand in hand, toward servants and manicured lawns and well-appointed rooms, and all the other things that gave a civil veneer to their private depravities.

But when they came out of the wilderness where they had left their blanket and tea, they found three smiling, immaculately attired gentlemen reclining on the lawn, helping themselves, in fact, to some of the cook's cakes.

"Bother," he muttered. "Company."

She looked up at him sharply, but he didn't really seem displeased, only a bit surprised as the three friends noticed them and got to their feet. He dropped her hand and went ahead of her, calling out in greeting to Lord Augustine, and the Duke of Arlington.

And the Earl of Warren, who looked quite as striking and blond and admirable as he ever had been.

Chapter Thirteen: Visitors

Aurelia walked ahead of him on the way back to the house, having quite properly offered her arm to the most distinguished of their guests. Arlington inclined his head to hers, nodding politely to her comments about this and that. Hunter couldn't hear their conversation, but he was sure it was starchily polite and appropriate. His wife had been raised, after all, to show respect to dukes.

Hunter showed no such respect to August and Warren. "You might have sent a message first," he said.

"Sent a message?" August snorted. "Why? Would you have told us not to come?"

No, Hunter wouldn't have. In truth, he was pleased to see his friends, but he wished they hadn't shown up this particular afternoon. He had never before felt self-conscious among these men, his closest friends, but now he did. He worried they might somehow divine the way he and his wife had spent the last hour.

"Did you come into the woods in search of us?" Hunter asked with a carefully casual air.

"No, we were too busy ravishing your tea basket." Warren laughed, then turned a speculative gaze back on him. "Why? What were you getting up to in the woods?"

There was a time in his life when Hunter would have happily related every lurid detail of the past hour's activity to his friends, from the tenor and duration of his victim's screams during the switching, to how long it had taken to work his cock into the lady's arsehole, to the details of how she'd reacted when he did. Warren and August would have had a jolly laugh about it and boasted of their own recent, similar encounters. But now, since the victim in question was his wife, he had absolutely no desire to do so.

"Aurelia and I were taking a walk. We often walk and...and picnic together. She was never allowed to participate in picnics and such when Lansing had a hold of her, so I try to take her on scads of them." He was babbling like an idiot. Warren and August stared at him. "She likes them," he persisted. "And it's good for her to take the fresh air."

August slid a look at Warren. "I don't think I want to know what he was doing to her back in those woods, do you, Warren?"

Warren returned a grimace. "It was obviously something really reprehensible." He turned back to Hunter. "Yes, old chap, it's very good of you to 'take her on picnics' so she can 'have some fresh air.'"

August erupted into laughter. They were joking, both of them. If they only knew... But he didn't want them to know.

He was ashamed of the things he did to his wife.

The thought struck him like a punch to the gut. Yes, he was ashamed to admit that he used his wife in such a fashion, that he demanded sordid acts of her nearly every day. He had been so content with the way they were rubbing along in this marriage that he hadn't even stopped to think about whether he was behaving in a gentlemanly fashion.

He most certainly was not.

It wasn't only his shame that kept his lips pressed in a thin line. There was his wife's honor to protect. He hadn't cared before he'd come to love her, but oh, he cared now. He stared at her back as she walked on the Duke of Arlington's arm, the perfect, proper lady in her perfect, fashionable gown. She would suffer utter annihilation, not to mention public repulsion, if anyone were to discover the nature of their marital dealings. Even his friends, if they knew, would think less of her. They might even believe her a fair target for their amorous wiles.

No, not his friends. They would never disrespect his wife or betray him...would they?

He wondered if these uncomfortable misgivings were related to his newfound feelings of love for Aurelia. All at once there were three more gentlemen in her vicinity, one of whom escorted her upon his arm. Of course, it was Arlington, who was a stick of a stickler when it came to manners around respectable ladies. He wondered how Aurelia felt, if she was fighting the same nervous anxieties he was. He didn't doubt she was, doubly so. He tried to put such troubling thoughts away and exchange pleasantries with Warren and August so they didn't become any more suspicious than they already were.

"How long will you stay?" he asked them.

"As long as you'll have us," said August. "But not so long that we wear out our welcome."

Warren glanced at Aurelia. "We'll try to behave, Towns. We know you're a married chap now, and newly fond of picnics and sitting home by the fire. Lady Townsend looks well."

"She is well. We've both adjusted to our new life, and become close to one another."

There, that was as much as he need say. His friends would take away from it that any disparaging language or behavior toward her would be out of bounds.

"I'm happy to hear you are both happy," said August with typical amiability.

"I'm happy to hear it too," echoed Warren in an even tone that nonetheless pricked him. Hunter pursed his lips. Why did it feel like, in a mere three months' time, a vast chasm had opened between him and his unmarried friends?

"Anyway, I'm not the only one fond of picnics," he said, falling back on the comfortable act of mockery. "I noticed the three of you ate every one of my wife's favorite cakes."

* * * * *

144

Aurelia sat to her husband's right at dinner, with Lord Augustine at her right side, and Arlington and Warren across from her. His friends were the most congenial sort, well-spoken and polite to a fault. They smiled at her often and went to great lengths to include her in sundry conversation, and never made her feel the least bit uncomfortable.

But she felt uncomfortable all the same. She couldn't shake her memories of that afternoon in the forest, when she'd abandoned all sense of decorum and coupled with her husband in a coarsely animalistic way. Even after a long soak in the bath and some quiet time stitching at linens in her sheltered window seat, she felt sullied and not like a lady at all.

She feared Hunter's friends would realize this about her, that she was not a respectable lady. Now and again her husband caught her gaze, even touching her hand beneath the table, as if to reassure her, but he couldn't really understand. Here she was, seated directly across from Lord Warren, a man she once idolized, feeling like the cheapest, most whorish woman in the world.

Did she still idolize Lord Warren? She was afraid to ask herself that question. She tried to behave naturally toward him, as if his comments and questions were no more clever than those of the other men, but she thought perhaps her smiles at him were too wide, her replies to him a touch too high pitched.

She tried not looking at him at all, but then some implacable impulse would draw her gaze his way and she would remember why she had loved him so, why she had called so often on her friend Minette in hopes of catching a glimpse of her brother. He was incredibly handsome.

So is your husband, she reminded herself sternly. She looked over to find Hunter staring back at her with a darkly assessing expression. An unwelcome flush heated her cheeks and spread down the front of her neck. She placed a hand there, as if that might hide her disgrace. Hunter knew she used to have a *tendre* for Lord Warren. She had flung the fact in his face on more than one occasion, and wished now that she hadn't.

"Lady Townsend, have you met many of the neighboring families?" asked Lord Augustine beside her.

"Yes, I have. They came to call soon after we arrived. They don't live nearby so we don't often have callers, but when we do, it's a very pleasant experience. All of them have been particularly welcoming."

"I'm glad to hear it."

"Speaking of callers," said Lord Warren, "Minette sends her warmest regards. She asks that you call on her the very moment you return to London, Lady Townsend. That is a direct quote, by the way," he said, poking his spoon in the air. "The very moment. She said so quite emphatically."

"I shall be happy to call on your sister when we are back in London," Aurelia replied. "I wish you had brought her here with you. It would have given me the greatest pleasure to visit with her."

She saw, or rather sensed, the glances that passed between the gentlemen. Lord Warren nodded. "I'll tell her you said so. She was not able to accompany us this time."

"Oh. But you left her well?"

"Yes, very well," he said quickly. "And very busy. You know how my sister is, always flitting and fluttering about town, and getting into mischief."

Aurelia smiled, remembering many amusing scenes she'd witnessed between Minette and Lord Warren. The past few years, he'd been more like a father than brother to her friend, despairing at her many scrapes while always offering her affection and warmth. It was part of the reason she thought he was so wonderful. Her smile faded as she realized she was gazing at him too long again. She could feel more than see her husband's regard at her left, even though she didn't dare turn to meet it. She looked instead at His Grace the Duke of Arlington, then down at her plate.

"When will Minette make her come out?" asked Lord Augustine, who could always be counted on to fill any awkward silences.

"She's eighteen now," said Lord Warren. "I suppose I must consider her eligible, but she still seems such a child to me." He made a grimace. "Whoever takes her will have his hands full, poor devil. Pardon my language, ma'am," he said to Aurelia.

"Come now," said the duke, his angular face softening into a smile. "Minette is a charming young lady who shall make some lucky gentleman very happy."

After a beat, everyone at the table burst into laughter, even Aurelia, who knew her friend too well.

"I'm glad I had the good sense to only have older sisters," joked Lord Augustine. "All of whom are happily married off."

"Why, you're the only one who hasn't any siblings at all," Aurelia said, turning to her husband. "Were you lonely growing up?"

"Somewhat." He paused, looking around at the other gentlemen. "When I grew older, I had my friends for company. None of us had brothers, you see. All of us are only sons."

She had never realized that either. "I suppose that resulted in a lot of familial pressure for all of you," she said sympathetically.

Arlington was the only one to speak. "I'm sure we all want a handful of sons to our names, eventually. It's what I would prefer, if I had my choice. Being an only son is a dreary thing. But daughters are a blessing too." The men concurred in polite tones.

Aurelia looked sideways at her husband, and then, without meaning to, she looked at Lord Warren, with whom she had always imagined having a houseful of blond, curly-haired sons and daughters. It was a horrible, regrettable lapse of behavior, but it was too late to go back a few seconds in time and not do so. Worse, Lord Warren was looking back at her, so both of them were obliged to guiltily drop their gazes.

"The pudding is so sweet tonight," she said, touching her forehead and putting down her spoon. "I don't know what cook was about. I can hardly think your friends find it pleasing. I'm very sorry."

The gentlemen all insisted that of course they found it delicious and that they were simply too full to eat any more of the graciously appointed fare, and so on and so forth. Aurelia's face burned. She must not remember her old feelings for Lord Warren, or give any sign that she still admired him. She didn't want to.

But she was afraid she did.

Hunter took her hand, and she felt the tension in his grip all the way to her fingertips. "Perhaps you should retire, my dear. No doubt we shall be tedious and linger far too long over our port."

"Of course." The gentlemen would want to drink and relax together, and catch up on their personal news without her hovering about. She stood to take her leave, and all the gentlemen stood along with her. She acknowledged their kind regards and thought she did very well not staring at Lord Warren. In fact, she avoided his gaze altogether, tucked her head down, and went as quickly as she could from the room.

* * * * *

147

As two servants poured wine for the gentlemen, Arlington relaxed back in his seat and nodded to Hunter. "I hope I won't offend you by saying this, but I perceive Lady Townsend has blossomed. She's not so shy and retiring as she once was."

"No more Lady Dormouse," concurred August.

"Yes, she must be quite happy in this marriage," said Warren.

Hunter eyed his rival with something less than a smile. "I'm not offended in the least, as I have noticed the same thing. I've tried to be a positive influence. I've tried to bring some adventure to her previously drab and sheltered life."

"A childhood with Laudable Lansing." August shook his head. "I can't imagine growing up under that man's yoke. You know, Severin is as intolerable as the father, lofty and proper as all get-out."

"Laudable Townsend, I think." Arlington raised his glass to Hunter. "I salute you for making her happy. I admire you for endeavoring to improve her life."

The men all raised their glasses in concert with the duke. Hunter knew he ought to feel flattered, even celebratory, but all he felt was a burning desire to throw a fist at Warren's pretty face.

It wasn't Warren's fault that Aurelia fancied him. The rational part of Hunter's brain acknowledged that. Warren didn't flirt or make eyes at her, or encourage her in any way whatsoever. He had never done so. Which meant that it was Aurelia's fault. It was Aurelia's lingering infatuation with a man who was not at all better than him, a man who was honestly much more of a knave. He wasn't called Wild Warren for nothing. Why did she still have feelings for the blasted man, and what was Hunter to do about it?

To be fair, she had not flirted with Warren either, but she had given him lingering looks that spoke much louder than words. Hunter had a feeling all his friends had noted it. Warren had certainly noted it, for he seemed to be having considerable difficulty meeting Hunter's gaze.

The men drained their glasses and signaled for more, and then August sat straighter in his chair. "Are we going to ask the chap about it?" he said to the others. "Or are we going to wait until we're drunker?"

Hunter frowned. "Ask me about what?"

Arlington traced the rim of his glass with a speculative expression. "Do you know the Wroxham estate, Townsey? Is it hereabouts?"

"An hour's ride or so to the north. Why do you ask?"

"We ask because there's to be a masquerade party there, by special invitation only." August waggled his brows. "It's to be *that* sort of masquerade party, my friend. The very best kind, with the very best women."

Hunter crossed one leg over the other and studied his friends. "Where did you hear this?"

"From young Wroxham in London," said Warren. "His uncle, the former Lord Wroxham, has finally given up the ghost, and Wroxy plans to celebrate his new inheritance and title with a debauched house party to begin tonight, although I imagine things won't get interesting until tomorrow, or even the day after."

Hunter stifled a grin. They must have been bursting at the seams all night to share this with him. "*That* sort of house party, eh? That finally explains why you're out here in Berkshire."

"Yes, and to see you," Arlington said. "You are conveniently on the way and we thought you might wish to come with us."

"You forget I'm under a moral edict from the highest offices to behave myself."

"That's just it," August broke in. "This house party is far enough from London that Lansing won't have his spies tossing you out."

"But if he hears about it—"

"It's a masquerade," Warren drawled. "Meaning you can wear a mask. Plausible deniability, my friend. '*Oh, that wasn't me, but my third cousin, the Lord of Farflungshire, who happens to look almost exactly like me.*' You'll be able to conceal your identity."

Hunter ran a hand through his hair. The crank of it was, the party sounded damn tempting. He'd attended many such routs in his bachelor days, two-week-long orgies of drink and dissolution. He'd been so very good the past few months, staying home, playing the doting husband.

He *was* the doting husband, damn it.

Aurelia had once given him leave to stray, but he wasn't sure she would now, and anyway, he didn't want to. As tempting as Wroxham's masque sounded, some part of him found the idea distasteful. He didn't believe he could consort with the type of women one would find there, not anymore. Not when he compared them to what he had here at home.

"I don't know, gents," he said, shaking his head. "I'm not sure it's worth the risk."

August put down his glass with a bang. "I imagine you'll find it worth the risk when you're rolling about in bed with four pretties who know how to use their mouths."

"There's really no risk," said Arlington, as if reasoning with a child. "Warren is right. With the mask, no one will be able to prove you were there, not even Lansing himself."

"But everyone will know." Hunter threw up his hands. "We recognize every gentleman at these parties, and most of the women. We call each other by name, for God's sake. The masks are nothing more than an affectation, a false symbol of anonymity to make the things we do there more acceptable."

"False symbol or not," said Arlington, "attending in disguise will allow you to dispute any accusations, if in fact any are made. Which I doubt, since this is a country party among a decidedly lowbrow set."

"Blast, Towns," said Warren. "We thought you'd be excited. We thought you'd be half out of your mind to be with a woman. What have you been doing to satisfy yourself?"

"Spending time with my wife."

His friends exchanged glances. Hunter pretended not to notice.

"Listen," said August. "We admire that you're making a go of things here. Really, it's magnificent, but you needn't poker up and try to pass yourself off as the perfect husband for your sake, or Lady Townsend's. It's just us here."

"Yes, and we're in no position to judge," Warren added. "If I'm half the husband you are some day, my wife will count herself lucky. But every husband needs variety, Towns. It's expected that any gentleman of quality will enjoy the pleasures of an erotically accomplished woman now and again."

He wanted to tell them that his wife was more "erotically accomplished" than any courtesan he'd ever paid money to utilize, but of course he couldn't.

"Listen," he said, to put the matter at rest. "I may or may not go. I beg you to proceed with your plans and be off to the party tomorrow if you wish. It's possible you'll see me there, but I can make no promises."

A great deal of grimacing and eye rolling accompanied this announcement.

"I hope I won't become a damned bore when I get a leg shackle," muttered August at a volume certain to be heard.

Warren stared into his glass, grunting in agreement. Arlington smiled at Hunter, but it was the kind of smile that didn't quite reach the eyes.

"We will hope to see you there," he said quietly. "If you decide you wish to come, that is. You may not have such an opportunity again anytime soon."

Chapter Fourteen: Unnatural Things

Hunter left his friends not long after, feeling uneasy in their company, and quite tired. He thought he must have changed a great deal, to feel uncomfortable around men he once considered brothers.

Once?

Was their closeness and camaraderie at an end? Why was he headed straight to his wife's rooms rather than his own?

He supposed in some way he wanted to reclaim her. He'd felt needling jealousy at the way she'd gazed at Warren, and then looked away as if she were doing something illicit. Perhaps she was doing something illicit—lusting after a man who wasn't her husband.

But she had never lusted for Warren, only idolized him as some girlish fantasy that couldn't be farther from the truth. She had loved Warren. She'd told Hunter so on several occasions, although he'd forgotten about it until Warren showed up. Perhaps three months apart wasn't long enough to fall out of love with a person, although it was plenty of time to fall *in* love with a person.

He was going to Aurelia because he was quite certain he loved her, and her arms were the first thing he thought of when he needed reassurance and comfort. Even if the reassurance and comfort was needed because of her.

Perhaps they had only been polite smiles. Perhaps she had looked away so quickly for some other reason. Perhaps the guilty glances they'd exchanged were a figment of his own husbandly jealousy. Perhaps he ought not to visit her after all.

A moment later he was at her door. He cracked it open, peering into the dimly lit room until he located his wife in bed.

"Are you asleep, my dear?"

She sat up straighter within her pillows. "No, I'm not asleep."

Hunter moved toward her, thinking how very provocative she looked in the ruffled, feminine confection of a bed. Since they'd come to Somerton he'd demanded her attendance in his rooms, and even slept beside her on occasion, but he'd never spent time with her here. It seemed a terrible omission because she looked so alluring in her womanly bower. Her light gray eyes bewitched him. Her shift was slightly askew, exposing a fine feminine collar bone, and her honey blonde curls spread wild about her shoulders and down her back. She wore no nightcap as some wives did.

She looked so young. So innocent. That she could remain so after all he'd done to her...

He looked about for any servants, and was pleased to fine none. "May I join you in bed?"

She gave him a wide-eyed look and nodded. He wondered why he asked her permission. He had made it known from the start he would claim his marital rights when it pleased him, in his bed or her bed or wherever else he liked. Perhaps he asked because this seemed so much like her domain. And why did she look so alarmed? If he found Warren here...

But no, he'd just left Warren downstairs with the others, and the man would never stoop to seduce his wife, anyway. None of them would do such a thing, so why was he obsessing like a feather-brained fool?

He needed Aurelia. He slid under the covers beside her and collected her into a comfortable embrace. "How are you?" He glanced at her bedside table. "Reading a book?"

"Yes, a very dry treatise on household management. I thought you would spend more time with your friends."

"No, not tonight. They're to be on their way tomorrow." He saw surprise in her gaze. Or was it disappointment? "Have you recuperated fully from this afternoon?" he asked.

"Have you... Have you come to do it again?"

He threw back his head and laughed at the anxiety in her tone. "What an insatiable monster you must think me. No, I had not thought to do it again tonight."

She watched him expectantly. The poor thing, she was waiting for him to do something horrible to her. Spank her, birch her, demand some lusty sex act. She had perhaps come to see him as something of a one-trick pony. He wanted to prove her wrong. Here in this ruffled and virginal bed, he wanted to make love to her in an utterly civilized way. He wanted to be tender and honorable and gentle.

You want to be Warren, you prize ass. At least the Warren she believes is real.

He silenced the outraged voice in his head and pulled her closer, nuzzling her ear. She smelled faintly of vanilla, a delicious feminine scent that fired his blood. "I want you. I want to make love to you. No spankings, no distasteful demands."

She stared at him in the dim, flickering light. "I don't mind so much anymore, those things you do to me. I no longer find them quite so...distasteful."

"I know. Perhaps that's why I want to be tender to you now." His hand slid lower, cupping her shapely bottom. "Of course, if you really must have the spanking..."

She giggled as he gave her a soft crack, then they smiled at one another as he smoothed his hands over her skin. His fingers traced over the lingering welts from the switching he'd given her earlier. How beautiful and pliant she was, his courageous wife. He wanted to be gentle, so gentle and soft with her, until she ached from wanting. He wanted to reward her. He stroked fingers down the line of her jaw, then turned her head for his kiss. He delved within her lips, stroking and teasing, holding her face cupped in his hands. Did she seem wistful? He heard her sigh.

"What's the matter?" he whispered.

Her fingers closed a bit more tightly on his arms. "Nothing. Please...kiss me again."

He kissed her right out of her delicate shift, tracing his lips across the laces until he'd loosened them enough to ease it up over her head. He removed his own clothes whenever he managed to break from their embrace, and tossed them all onto the floor. His valet would grimace the next morning over the wrinkles, but Hunter didn't care. The woman in his arms was more important than his clothes.

They slid deeper into the sheets, naked and warm. He explored her with languid caresses, taking his time, enjoying her soft sighs. So many times they only unbuttoned flaps and flipped up skirts, and went at it mostly dressed. He resolved to spend more time with her naked, skin to skin. Much more time. He traced over her curves, nestling his cock against the warm, wet entrance to her quim, but he didn't thrust inside her, not yet. He wanted these warm, gentle moments to last. He gazed into her wide, sex-hazy eyes as he slid a hand down to explore her folds. "Are you enjoying this?" he asked. "Or would you still prefer that spanking?"

"No," she breathed. "I think a spanking would be t-totally unnecessary."

He chuckled and buried his face against her hair, so different in color from his. Would they have dark-haired sons and honey-haired daughters, or the opposite? A little of both? He wondered with half his attention why she was not breeding yet. Or perhaps she was. Did she want his children, or had she hoped for the blond, curly-haired cherubs Warren might have given her?

Damn it. He needed Warren out of this bed. He stared into Aurelia's eyes, drinking in her aroused sighs as he manipulated her most sensitive spot. "Do I please you?" he asked in a voice that sounded rather embarrassingly vulnerable. "Is there anyone else you would prefer?"

Was it his imagination, or did she flinch? "Of course there's no one else," she said too quickly. "I prefer you."

"Why?" He pushed her back and came over her, parting her legs with his knees. "Why do you prefer me? You loved someone else once."

She bit her lip, but not before he saw the tremble. "I prefer you," she said stolidly. She reached for him, wrapping her arms around his neck. She tried to pull him close and after a moment he let her, groaning as he sank between her thighs. He felt her clench around him, and wrap her legs about his hips. Why? Why did she prefer him?

He was not completely sure he believed her, which unsettled him very much.

Aurelia clutched at him, steeling her throat against the sob that ached to escape. She blinked back tears. *Why?* he had asked her in an uncharacteristically forlorn voice. *Why?*

She didn't know why. She wasn't even sure she preferred him. That was the part of it that made her want to sob. She wanted to desire her husband above all others, but her ungoverned attraction to Lord Warren remained. She could not control it.

And so she had to lie and pretend to feel differently. She urged him on as he coupled with her, stroking his shoulders and pressing her cheek against the carven profile of his jaw. She had come to love him. She truly believed that part of it and she wanted him to know. She thought if she only tried hard enough, and was disciplined enough, that Lord Warren would fade from her thoughts.

Even in her emotionally fraught state, her husband knew how to bring her pleasure. His closeness and warmth settled inside her, arousing her and comforting her at once. "My love," she whispered as his deep, slow-moving strokes filled her. The blissful splendor brought with it a hollow ache, as Lord Warren's visage rose in her mind. She knew her husband had been speaking of him when he questioned her. If he questioned her any more she wasn't certain she could keep up her act of disinterest. There was too much history to her love for Warren, too many roiling longings that she'd never been able to sort out.

A few tears squeezed from her eyes. *You're a bad wife, Aurelia*, she scolded herself. *A horrible wife.* Her husband chose that moment to draw back from her. She tried to hide the tears but he turned her face back and captured them with a thumb.

"It's all right," he said in a voice so tender it slayed her. "Don't cry."

"I don't know why I'm feeling tearful," she blurted, a liar to the end. "Because you're being so lovely and gentle. It feels like a...surprise."

"Then I shall have to show you this side of me more often. Would you like that?"

"Yes." She nodded. "Yes, sometimes."

He pressed deeply into her, holding her gaze. Through sheer willpower, she returned it, thinking hard about all the things she loved in him, remembering all the pleasure he'd brought her, all the laughter and fun. She remembered the makeshift window seat he'd made for her, and the great, whirring grasshopper in its cage.

He quickened the pace of his thrusts, but still, Aurelia felt each inch of him invading her, making her his. So intently did he possess her that, when she reached a quaking, squeezing sort of climax, she could honestly say she thought of nothing but her own husband, with his dark hair and piercing eyes, and his delicious warmth and scent.

Afterward, there seemed no need for words. He withdrew from her but did not let her go. Instead he pulled her into the curve of his body and rested beside her, so her back was to his front. His arms encircled her, and his chin rested lightly atop her head. She thought he must be asleep, although she felt too guilty and agitated to do the same. But then he spoke in the silence.

"I'm glad they're leaving tomorrow."

Aurelia considered how to respond. She decided to be light and teasing. "I thought they were your friends?"

"They are, but we've grown to seem very different. Marriage has changed me, I suppose. I'm not as comfortable in their company."

"I am not comfortable in their company either. When we came from the woods today and they were sitting on our picnic blanket, I felt intruded upon. I know that's not kind to say."

"I felt the same. We've become used to our privacy." He turned her a bit so she could see the half-smile on his face. "I did ask, and they hadn't ventured into the woods, so they couldn't have seen or heard anything."

"Even so, *I* knew what we'd been doing. I feared they might somehow see it, in my manner or the way I smiled. Do you know what I mean?"

His half-smile faded. "Yes. I would not have made you feel uncomfortable in their company. If I'd known they were coming, I wouldn't have put you in such a situation."

"But even at dinner..." Her voice strained as her throat grew tight. "Even at dinner I worried they would somehow know."

"Know what, my love?"

"Know that I've done such...unnatural things."

Now his face grew positively dark. Not in anger, but some other haggard emotion. "You've done unnatural things at my request, within the confines of our marriage. I don't want you to feel shame over it."

"I don't," she lied again, stroking his forearm to soothe him. "But I don't wish it to become common knowledge either. You know the ways of aristocratic society. If the other ladies came to disapprove of me, I could not be received anywhere. Our daughters might not find husbands."

"Oh, Aurelia, really." He scowled. "I'll be a duke one day, and you a duchess. I have every hope our daughters will succeed upon the marriage mart."

She held her tongue, not wanting him to feel reproached on this night of all nights. "It's only that it must be so secret," she said after a while. "You must agree with that."

"Of course I agree with that. I'm not going to make public conversation about the time I took my wife out to the woods and switched her bottom, and put my cock in her lovely little arsehole. Not least because every peer in London would be after you, trying to seduce you away from me."

He squeezed her as he said it, so she squirmed closer in his arms.

"At any rate," he said when she'd calmed, "my friends have no suspicions about you. They think you an eminently proper wife, and they treated you with respect, didn't they?"

"Yes, of course. I simply fear that every lady and gentleman I meet will see through my polite veneer and think me capable of great perversion."

He laughed. "I am the only one who has managed to pierce through your 'polite veneer,' and I prefer it to stay that way. You mustn't feel secret shame, my love. I would prefer you did not. I don't want you to suffer for my vices."

She gave him an arch look. "One might say being spanked every night is a type of suffering."

"I mean, suffer mentally," he clarified after another bout of laughter. "You are not the only lady of the *ton* who engages in these acts. I promise you there are other men and women of quality who enjoy such things."

"Even so, I should not like to be known as one of them, especially among your friends."

When she said *especially among your friends*, she really meant Lord Warren, and she was afraid, in this intimate moment, that Hunter knew it. He searched her face with far too much acuity. She tried to look blasé.

158

"My friends would never judge you," he said at last. "On that point, you needn't fear." He looked thoughtful for a moment. "I meant to tell you something, Aurelia. There's to be a masquerade at a neighboring estate."

"A masquerade? Like, a ball?"

"Something like a ball. More of a party. Lord Wroxham is having a house party with several...er...masked events."

"How strange for a country party."

"It's not so strange," her husband said. "The thing about a country party is that there isn't nearly as wide a social circle to invite. Often hosts will bring in less toplofty neighbors to fill the ballrooms and salons. When everyone wears masks, it eases social constrictions and allows a duke to comfortably and obliviously rub elbows with a lowly country squire."

"Obliviously?" Aurelia laughed. "How delightful. Do they really not know who the other person is?"

"If they do, it's very poor form to show it." His droll response set her off into more laughter. He waited until she'd settled and then said, "We've been invited, if you would like to go."

Aurelia felt a pang of shocked delight. She hadn't expected this. "I've never been to a masquerade ball."

"I assumed you hadn't. People of your father's ilk find them improper."

"But they are improper, aren't they?" Masquerade balls were considered quite decadent, to her recollection. Her father would never in a thousand years have permitted her to attend one.

Hunter wore a cloaked sort of expression, one she couldn't dissect. "People do behave with rather more frivolity when their identity is masked," he said. "I should warn you that you might see some unseemly behavior there, taking place right out in the open. The guests will sometimes make free with one another. I would insist that you stay at my side."

"Of course." She suppressed a shudder at the idea of some strange, masked duke—or country squire—making free with her. "I would stay right beside you."

He chuckled. "The peril would not be that dire. Do you remember when I spoke in the wilderness walk of voyeurs?"

"Will there be voyeurs there?"

His hooded expression softened. "Yes, little grasshopper. Us. You're no sheltered, innocent lady, thanks to me, and I think it might do you good to see that we're not the only folks in England who enjoy partaking in depraved acts."

She gasped. "Will there be depravity there?"

"When people wear masks, you never know what will happen. Shall we go tomorrow? It is completely up to you."

Oh, she wanted to go, but there were practicalities to consider. "I haven't anything to wear, no costume to disguise my appearance."

"There are several trunks of old clothes upstairs, and I daresay wigs and masks from previous occasions. Unlike your stickler of a father, my parents attended many wild parties in their younger days."

"Is that where you get your wildness?" she asked. "From your parents?"

He didn't answer, only flashed her one of his provoking, piratical grins.

Chapter Fifteen: Masquerade

Hunter knew it was a very bad thing he was doing. No matter how excited Aurelia was, no matter how much he'd lied and cajoled her into delighted expectation about this country masquerade, she would not look back on this night with anything other than sadness.

Still, she deserved to know the truth about her enduring object of adoration.

He had taken all necessary steps to protect her honor, of course. She not only wore a mask, but a blowsy dark-colored wig that would conceal her identity from any friends. He doubted even Severin could recognize her, not that her brother would be at a degenerate party like Wroxham's. As for *his* identity, he was far less concerned. Even if someone recognized him, they would assume the woman on his arm was a courtesan or some cheap country trollop. In his wilder days he'd been known to consort with both, sometimes at the same time.

Everything would be fine, but some part of him quailed at the stratagem he'd undertaken. Part of him wished to rap on the roof of the carriage and tell the driver to turn for home, because it was likely he'd lose Warren's friendship tonight, perhaps August and Arlington's too. All because he wanted Aurelia to leave off worshipping her virtuous ideal of Lord Warren, who did not exist.

She looked across at him, and her lips turned down in concern. "Are you well, Hunter?"

"Very well," he said.

"You look a bit grim. Do you want to sit over here beside me?"

She thought he was queasy from riding backwards. Dear, innocent Aurelia. Still, he accepted her offer and switched benches so they sat shoulder to shoulder as the carriage hurtled through the night.

"You remember that you are not to leave my side tonight," he said in the darkness.

"I remember."

"And that we are only to be voyeurs. If there is dancing or card games, you are not to participate."

"Why not? It's perfectly proper for a married lady to dance or play cards."

"Not the way they'll do it there."

She gave him a harried look that transformed to a smile. "This will be a grand adventure, won't it?" she said, clasping her hands to the front of her low-cut masquerade gown. "I daresay most husbands wouldn't allow their wives such frolics." She grasped his hand in an impulsive, gleeful manner.

He brought it to his lips, feeling like the world's worst blackguard. "Pray don't tell your father I allowed this," he murmured against her palm. "He'll take you away from me and marry you to someone of greater moral character, and all my lessons in licentiousness will have been a waste."

"Oh, you're silly." She tugged at one of the great, outrageous curls crowning her head. "I daresay you'd enjoy starting over with some young virginal miss, perverting her with your debauched curriculum. You are very good at the teaching part, though it's an iniquitous talent indeed."

"You would pine for me, and all my iniquitous talents, as you languished in some decent and austere marriage bed. You would put on a wig and a mask and sneak into my bedroom. And I would spank you for it, you naughty vixen."

She shrieked and burst into laughter as he hauled her over his lap. He spanked her a few times over her skirts, then flipped them up to squeeze her bottom. The steady rattle of the carriage slowed down, and the conveyance turned. He righted her with good-natured words of disappointment and promised to continue the spanking later.

But later, he feared, she wouldn't be laughing and smiling as she was now.

They both looked out the window at Wroxham's courtyard and the impressive manor flanking it on three sides. The entire main house appeared lit from within, and masked guests spilled from the entrance to cluster on the pillared portico. A few guests appeared to be splashing in Wroxham's fountain.

"Are you ready, love?" Hunter asked, lowering his black demi-mask over his face. "Perhaps we shall frolic in the fountain later. For now, let's head inside and congratulate Lord Wroxham on his new title—and his party."

He helped his wife down and checked one last time to be sure no one could possibly guess her identity, then took her arm and led her toward the stately old house.

* * * * *

Aurelia wasn't sure if she ought to be feeling awe or shame. In truth, she felt a little of both. The house was so grand, but the activities inside rather...lowering in nature. Hunter had told her other men and women enjoyed the same acts they did, and this party offered plentiful proof.

At first she was horrified as he led her from room to room, but now she understood that he'd brought her here to show that what they did together wasn't so grotesque in nature. It seemed in every room a masked gentleman had a lady on his lap, his hands at play beneath her skirts. The ladies seemed to enjoy it very much, judging from their moans and cries. Aurelia wondered which ones were in wigs like her, and which ones were daring enough to wear their natural hair. Some of the ladies wore elaborate masks which covered everything, while others wore the thinnest strip of sheer ribbon over their eyes, and the rest of their face fully shown.

"What sort of mask is that?" she asked her husband. "Don't they care if people know who they are?"

"No, they don't." He spoke in her ear so she could hear him in the din of the revelry. "In general, the greater the mask, the greater the

163

personage. The lighter the mask, the more the person wishes to be recognized. That woman"—he pointed to a gorgeous nymph of a lady—"is a famous lady of the night in London. She is here to work, and it behooves her to make her identity known."

"Work at what?"

"Oh, my dear," he sighed with a soft smile. At last Aurelia understood, and an embarrassed flush crept across her cheeks.

"She is here to find customers?"

"Last I heard she was on the hunt for a more permanent sort of protector, which explains her presence here among so many society gentlemen."

"It is difficult to comprehend that these men are all proper aristocrats." She shied away as one of them reached to touch her waist. He was drunk, but not too drunk to perceive her husband's warning glare.

He turned back to their conversation. "Not all of them are proper aristocrats," he said. "Although Wroxham would likely toss out someone of a very low class." He made a face. "The men anyway. Women would doubtless be permitted to remain. Country girls can make enough for their families to live on for a year at a house party such as this one."

"So all these ladies and gentlemen are paying one another?"

"Not all." Hunter craned his head and pointed to a corner of the crowded ballroom. "Although I'm quite certain he is paying that lady."

Aurelia turned and sucked in a breath in surprise. A man, fully and unabashedly naked, stood with his face to the wall while a short, stout woman striped his bottom with a cane. With each stroke, he howled and threw his head back.

"What on earth?" Aurelia cried. "Why is he paying her to hurt him like that?"

Her husband shrugged. "Because he likes it."

"But why? Why does he like it?"

"Why does anyone like anything? The famous Madame Courvesier knows better than to ask. She lives as well as any titled peeress in London, although she's not welcome in proper parlors...in case you are getting any ideas," he said, squeezing her waist.

The dark-haired woman put aside the cane, sat in a chair, and ordered the naked gentleman over her lap. Aurelia could see his hard, red cock bobbing before him as he obeyed her and folded his tall frame across the woman's thighs. Immediately, the woman set about attacking the man's clenching buttocks with a series of sharp spanks. Aurelia watched with some sympathy. She'd been in his position more times that she could remember.

"I don't think I could spank a gentleman for all the gold in Egypt," she said, sidling closer to Hunter. "Look how violently he squirms. And he is so much larger than her."

"And yet she holds him in complete control. It's the reason she's so much in demand at parties like this. Would you like to stay to watch the grand finale, or shall we voyeurs move on?"

"What will the grand finale be?"

His lips quirked at her question. "Never mind." He led her to a quieter corner of the room. "How are you holding up, my dear?" He studied her from behind his dashing mask, stroking a hand down her cheek. "Is there too much wickedness here? Do you wish to go?"

"Only if you want to."

His face seemed to grow harder for a moment, although it was difficult to tell in the light and with his face half-concealed. "I am not quite ready to leave yet. There's still much to be seen."

"Even wilder things than we've already seen?" She wasn't sure she was prepared for that.

He led her from the ballroom down a hallway with door after door, some of them ajar. He stopped outside one, drawing Aurelia forward so she might watch. Five gentlemen stood in a row. All of them, shockingly, had their cocks out and their breeches about their knees. Before them, a woman with a tall, ostrich-plumed wig knelt, licking and sucking each of them in turn.

"Oh my goodness," Aurelia breathed. "Should we be watching?"

"They would not have left the door open if they didn't want an audience. If you like, you may applaud at the end, or even call for an encore."

Aurelia thought she would do no such thing, but she did have some admiration for the woman. She was so graceful as she crawled to and fro, and so practiced in her...technique. The gentlemen groaned and grasped at her shoulders as they thrust into her mouth, although Aurelia noticed that none of them disturbed her fanciful wig. The gentlemen not presently receiving her favors stared at the one who was, pumping their great organs in their hands as they waited their turn. This was depravity, pure licentiousness. Indeed, her husband's favored activities seemed almost innocent in comparison.

"I never imagined such a thing," she said softly.

"I know," her husband replied. "Nor will you ever do such a thing, my dear, although it is a fine amusement to watch."

His teasing comment made Aurelia picture herself on her knees before all the gentlemen, a scandalous, frightening idea which she thrust from her mind right away.

"Shall we leave them to it and move along?" he asked. "I imagine nearly all these rooms are occupied."

They went a bit farther down to another open room. From the door Aurelia saw two ladies kneeling upon a very fancy tufted couch. They were bent over at the waist, their bottoms almost obscenely thrust out. She heard the crack of a riding crop and saw the girls flinch, then heard them giggle.

I would not be giggling, she thought.

Hunter guided her inside, so she saw the gentleman wielding the crop. He was tall and powerful in physique, and wore a half-mask which matched his dark green waistcoat and undone breeches. His hair was blond and mussed, and he wore a positively satanic grin. He turned to them, his thick, meaty erection grasped in his fist, then gave a bark of laughter.

"Ah, you're here after all, Towns, and a gorgeous bit of muffin on your arm. I swear to you, neither Lansing nor Aurelia shall ever hear of it from my lips."

"Enjoying yourself?" her husband asked him. "You look as if you are."

The man turned back and flicked both the reddened female bottoms with his crop. "I'm trying to, believe me. These two beauties polished my cock to a pretty shine but now they say I can't have their arseholes. None of these country whores are willing to take a man's meat up their backside, and it damn well makes a fellow cross." He cropped them again, one and then the other, with lazy, flicking strokes as the two women wagged their bottoms in a lewd display. Aurelia came to realize with slow clarity that this wickedly erect, half-dressed gentleman was Lord Warren. He pushed his mask up over his blond curls to take a closer look at her.

"What about your little trollop there, my friend?" His gaze fastened on her breasts with lascivious intent. "Where did you find her? And more to the point, can I bugger the tasty little tart after you're done running her through?"

She took a step back, closer to her husband. She felt horrified. Sickened. *This* was the man she had idolized as the very pinnacle of kindness and virtue? This man, who leered at her and cavorted in this dissolute state? She turned to her husband but his gaze was locked on the other man's.

She turned back to Lord Warren. He had grown very still as he took a closer look at her, at her gown and her wig. He cursed under his breath, shoving his grotesquely large phallus back into his breeches and doing up the buttons. "Damn you, Hunter," he hissed, putting space between him and his giggling wenches. "What are you about?" He turned to Aurelia with a look of dismay. "My lady, forgive me. I did not realize—" He turned back to Hunter, his hands in fists. "I should blacken both your eyes for this, you filthy bastard. I should bloody well drag you outside."

Aurelia feared they would indeed come to fisticuffs, but she was too overwrought to care. How could she ever look at Lord Warren the same way again? Since entering this chamber, she had seen too much, heard too much, and seen far, far more of her former *tendre* than she could ever hope to forget. She lifted her skirts and turned blindly for the door, running down the stairs, pausing only to push away an inebriated gentleman who groped at her. She flew through the crowded great hall, past laughing, cavorting revelers and out of the house into the cool breezes of a dark autumn night.

* * * * *

His wife stared out the window as the carriage barreled back toward Somerton. She'd torn off her wig as soon as they entered; it rested now in the corner of the bench, along with her mask and his. She hugged herself, blinking rather more than she usually did.

"Forgive me," he said in the darkness. "I'm sorry if you were troubled by what you saw."

"Why would I be troubled?" she asked in a taut voice. "What Lord Warren does is none of my affair."

"I wanted you to see, Aurelia. I wanted you to realize Warren is not the virtuous swain of your dreams."

She turned and stared at him. "You knew he would be there?"

"All of them were there, grasshopper. August and Arlington too."

"But you took me there to see *him*, not them. You took me there to see...that." Her voice rose along with the heated color in her cheeks. "You said we ought to go so I could see the two of us aren't so different. It was all a false premise, a lie."

"No, I wanted to show you that too. Please, don't be angry. I was tired of you being...deceived."

"Deceived by whom?" she snapped.

She pursed her lips and looked back out the window. He rubbed his forehead and thought about joining her on the other seat. He wasn't sure he'd be welcomed.

"I wish you hadn't done this," she said a moment later. "You might have just told me."

"You wouldn't have believed me unless you saw him for yourself."

"And so you took me into that room and humiliated both of us! Honestly, Hunter, how petty and childish. Lord Warren must be furious. I doubt he will remain your friend."

"I don't care about his friendship so much as I care about losing you."

"Losing me? I'm right here," she said, throwing up her hands.

"Losing you to *him*," he barked. "You still care more for him than me."

"I most certainly do not. Don't be ridiculous."

Ridiculous. Petty. Childish. Such flattering words. He didn't care what she thought of his actions tonight. He had done what he must to cure her of her infatuation. He hadn't done any more than any husband might do.

Aurelia stared from the window a long while in silence. "I have been very foolish about the world," she said when she finally spoke again. "I thought most men were like my father, men with honor and good morals. But most men are like those men at the party, I suppose. No one ever told me. I didn't know."

"There are plenty of men with honor and good morals," Hunter said. "But your Lord Warren is not one of them."

"He's not *my* Lord Warren. He never was. And I don't know how you or I should judge him, considering the things we do." She bit her lip hard, plucking fitfully at the edges of her gloves. "I have no room to look down on anyone. I suppose I am no better than those giggling, slatternly women back there."

"Yes, you are," he said sharply. "You're the Marchioness of Townsend. You're my wife, as much as you love another."

"*Loved* another."

"Still, you loved him. Yesterday, the day before, you loved him, before I revealed to you who he truly was."

She glared at him. "What do you mean to say?"

He waved a hand. "Nothing. I mean to say nothing."

"You think I'm a slut. A whore who lusts after other men. Is that it?"

"Aurelia, don't."

"You made me this way," she cried. "You wanted me to be wanton."

"Yes, for me! Only for me. I never meant you to get wet in the quim at the thought of bedding my goddamned friend."

His wife stood with the carriage in full motion and cracked him hard across the face. He grabbed her hand before she could hit him again and pulled her against him. She struggled as he held her by the wrists. "That was foolish."

"You're foolish," she said, her lips inches from his. "You don't understand anything about how I feel. You've never tried to understand."

"I understand everything," he replied in a flinty voice. "I have always understood from the bitter start. I saw the looks you gave Warren across the table last evening. You appeared as besotted as you ever were. Perhaps that's why you're so angry right now. Perhaps that's why you fled the party as if the devil's own hounds were at your heels."

"I fled because he disgusts me, and you disgust me too."

"Ah, my dear." His grip tightened on her wrists. "I'm sorry to learn I disgust you. It didn't seem so last night, or the night before." A raging ache burned inside him, an ache of hurt, an ache of loss. He didn't want to share her affections with any other man, especially a man he called a friend. He didn't want to share her body, her lusts, her desires. She may not love him, but she was his, damn it, and he wouldn't let her forget it. In a blind fit of heat, he gathered up her skirts, holding them beneath the arm he had wrapped about her waist.

"No," she said. "Leave me alone. Don't touch me."

"I will touch you. You are *my* wife, not Warren's nor anyone else's. *Mine*." He drove his fingers within her, and found her copiously wet. "I disgust you, do I?" he mocked as she cried and fought against him. "Even so, you're primed and ready to be fucked."

"No, I'm not. Stop this."

He ignored her, reaching between them to unbutton his breeches. His arm tightened at her waist as she struggled. He tried to kiss her but she turned her head away and instead he tasted tears on his lips.

"You're hurting me," she said as he thrust another finger up inside her. "I don't want you, not like this. Not angry and vengeful."

"Just close your eyes and pretend I'm Warren," he snarled in a voice that didn't sound like his own. She pushed at him as he positioned himself, and then she threw back her head and let out a blood-curdling scream.

That scream at last brought him to his senses. His groom was slowing the carriage, undoubtedly troubled by the noises coming from the passenger compartment. He couldn't have been half as troubled as Hunter.

He released his wife. She backed away from him, pulling down her skirts and smoothing them in a jerkily frantic way. "I said not to touch me." Her voice trembled, rasping and low, as if the scream had taken all the sound out of her. "I don't want you to touch me. I want you to leave me alone."

Hunter stared at her, still half in shock at what he'd done. "I'm sorry, Aurelia. I shouldn't have—"

She held up a hand when he moved to comfort her. "Don't. Please." She huddled in the corner of the coach, trembling, her eyes wide and tearful. It was the same look she'd given him on their wedding night. Were they back to that? The distrust, the loathing?

And it was all his fault.

He banged on the wall above his head to signal the groom to stop. It took only a few seconds for the carriage to roll to a halt but to Hunter it felt like an eternity as Aurelia stared at him in that haunted way.

"I shall comply with your wishes," he said, standing to disembark. "I will leave you alone. I pray you will go home to Somerton and try to forgive me for what just occurred. I was...not myself."

She began to weep again, copious tears he had caused through his jealousy and temper. "You're leaving?" she asked in a wretched voice, peering out the door into the dark countryside. "Where will you go?"

He didn't have an answer for that. He only knew he couldn't bear to stay in the carriage with her after the way he'd frightened her. The way he'd hurt her. He shut the carriage door and called up to his man.

"Take Lady Townsend home. I'll walk the rest of the way."

Whether he would walk home, or walk back to Wroxham's, or wander the countryside in a fog of self-hatred for several more hours, he didn't know. His groom raised a questioning brow but didn't gainsay his master. After a short pause, he flicked the reins and continued on, the carriage lantern bobbing along until Hunter couldn't see it any longer.

He was left with his own torturous thoughts in the middle of Berkshire, under the blanket of a vast, oppressive night.

Chapter Sixteen: Difficulties

Aurelia sat at the window in her room, looking out at the courtyard. Late morning sunlight gleamed off the cobblestones. Now and again one of the manor's servants went out on some errand, as if it were a normal day. She supposed it was, only her husband had hurt her past bearing and then deserted her, so things did not feel normal to her.

She was not within the special window seat he'd made for her, because it reminded her too much of earlier days when they were in harmony with one another. If only Lord Warren had never come to visit. If only Townsend had not thought it necessary to dampen her feelings toward the man. But that was her fault, because she couldn't govern her attraction and be a proper, faithful wife. She had screamed at her husband in the carriage last night, and slapped him, and he...he had tried to take her against her will.

She turned from the window and pressed a handkerchief to her eyes. That part of it had been so ugly and frightening. She had already felt such guilt over his accusations, and then to be grabbed and violated in that way. No matter that he had stopped and released her, and said he was sorry. By then, the emotional damage had been done. How could she trust him now? How could she feel safe?

And for God's sake, where was he? She'd felt nothing but relief when he alighted from their carriage in the middle of nowhere, but now, in day's harsh light, she felt twinges of worry that grew with every hour.

From far off, she saw a rider approach. Hunter had not had a horse, although he might have borrowed one from a neighbor. Or it might be someone else, bearing unfortunate news. Try as she might, she couldn't stop imagining Hunter in a ditch somewhere, or in a flooded culvert, floating face down. If he had come to harm, she couldn't live with herself. But as the rider entered the courtyard she saw it was neither her husband nor a stranger.

It was Lord Warren.

She absolutely could not receive him. She could not. But when the chambermaid tapped at the door to ask if she was at home to the Earl of Warren, she turned from the window and said, woodenly, that she would receive him in the main drawing room, because she understood that if the two of them did not exchange words now, they would never exchange words again.

She went downstairs at once, before she lost the necessary courage to see him. Her eyes were puffy and her clothing rumpled, but it couldn't be helped. When she entered the drawing room, she found him standing beyond the fireplace, in the far corner, as far from her as it was possible to stand. In contrast to her, he looked immaculately turned out, his dark blue coat without a wrinkle, and his pure white linen crisply starched. He held his gloves and hat, as if he expected to be thrown out at any moment.

He made a polite bow, which she acknowledged, but she couldn't move a step closer to him, and she couldn't seem to smile.

"I understand Lord Townsend is not at home," he said when she didn't make any move to welcome him. "Thank you for allowing me to speak with you. I will not impose upon your courtesy for long."

She crossed to sit on a divan in the middle of the room, for fear her legs wouldn't hold her. She did not invite him to sit, and so he didn't.

"Lady Townsend," he began in a tight and rehearsed fashion, "I must offer my deepest regrets for the scene you stumbled upon last night. If I had known—"

"I didn't stumble upon it. Townsend took me there because he wanted me to...to see you." She laced her fingers together in her lap. "It was entirely my own fault."

He didn't speak for a moment, only stood back in his corner looking awfully brittle. "Your own fault? In what way?"

She must not cry. She absolutely *could not* cry. She lowered her head and pressed her palms against her eyes. "It humiliates me to say this. Well, you have been humiliated too, so I suppose I owe you the explanation. As a younger woman, in my naiveté, I conceived an abiding admiration for you. I imagined myself, well...very much in love with you, as silly as that seems."

Somehow she managed to look over at him, her face flaming like a bonfire.

He looked stricken, or perhaps embarrassed on her behalf. "I confess I had heard something to that effect after you and Townsend married."

"And so I suppose my husband wished to weaken my feelings toward you. Although, in truth, I never would have acted on them. Those feelings had lately begun to fade."

It was an excruciating moment. Lord Warren made a low, miserable sound.

"I can only be proud that you esteemed me once, but I'm glad such feelings have faded. You understand now that I was never worthy of your admiration. Perhaps it's best Hunter showed you the truth, even in such a shocking way."

"I don't think it's best," she said. "It's only made me sad." She looked away from him, her emotions in disarray. "I had come to conceive a great affection for my husband, and I would never have been unfaithful. So it matters not what type of man you are to me, not anymore."

He was silent a long while. At some point, he switched his hat from one hand to the other, then gave her an implacable look. "No matter the reason, he shouldn't have taken you there. It was no place for a lady. I grieve for the loss of your innocence."

Aurelia gave a bitter laugh. "My innocence? You know your friend, the man I'm married to. Do you think he's left me with even a shred of my former innocence?"

Lord Warren crossed to stand before her. "You must be straightforward with me," he said in a strained voice. "Do you find your

174

situation here unbearable? It did not seem so when we saw you together. You appeared content with one another."

"We were content with one another. The truth is, I was very happy with my husband until you came to visit." She gazed into Lord Warren's clear blue eyes, the eyes that used to set her aglow. They no longer did. She missed her husband. She was so worried about him. "I've been terribly foolish," she blurted out. "I hurt Townsend's feelings. I hurt his pride by taunting him. I told him plainly so many times that I wanted you instead, that you would have been a better husband. I never realized until last night how much he took my words to heart. Until he..."

His gaze sharpened as she choked back the words. "Until he what? What has happened between you and Townsend?"

She could never tell him what had happened in the carriage, not in a thousand years.

"Your eyes are red from crying," he persisted. "What did Hunter do?"

Every word made it more difficult to keep from bawling again. "We had a row last night after we left the masquerade. But that is not your fault. None of this is your fault."

"Or yours."

She waved a hand. "It doesn't matter whose fault it is."

"What kind of row did you have?" he pressed.

"Please." If he did not leave, she would completely lose her composure. "You have apologized and we have made our peace. I wish you would go."

"You do not appear to be at peace." He crouched down before her, so his knees practically touched hers. "Has he hurt you, Lady Townsend? You must tell me if it's so."

"Why? What does it matter?"

"That's as good as a yes." His vivid eyes narrowed in fury. "What did he do to you? Beat you? Make rough with you?"

"We hurt each other," she cried over his outraged questions. "I hurt him and he hurt me. And it's all because you came here and disrupted everything. I wish you would go away and let both of us be, and let me heal this rift with my husband. Because he's not here and I don't know where he is, and it's been hours now since we quarreled, and I'm very, very afraid."

By the end of this outburst, she had rather fallen apart. Lord Warren moved to sit beside her on the divan, and offered his handkerchief. She took it and wiped her face, feeling miserable, frightened, and helpless. "I have to calm down," she said. "I have to think."

"Think about what?"

"How to fix things. How to make him come back."

"So you want him to come back?" Lord Warren asked.

"Yes, of course. I'm worried for him. I love him." As she said the words, she knew they were true, despite the wretched ways they'd hurt one another. "I want to fix everything that's wrong between us. I can't bear to lose him. Why must this all be so—so difficult?"

"It was difficult," he said in a soothing voice. "It needn't be so anymore."

She shook her head, hiding her face in her hands. "If we can't forgive one another, things will be difficult indeed. I'm afraid the pleasant times between us are over for good."

"They aren't," Lord Warren said firmly, drawing her hands from her face and taking back his handkerchief to wipe her tears. "The pleasant times are just beginning. There's much more to come, anniversaries and children and all the accompanying adventures. Townsend won't give up on this marriage, my lady. I can't think of a more unlikely scenario. I believe he loves you, and only took you to Wroxham's party to vanquish an obstacle to that love."

They both understood Lord Warren was the obstacle he meant.

"Not that I could ever please you as he seems to," the man continued. "Pardon my plain speaking, but all of us expected the worst in this marriage. We expected our friend to drive you out here to Somerton and leave you, and go back to town so he might live the way he used to. But he did not."

"Because my father wouldn't allow it," Aurelia said. "That's the only reason he didn't."

"Even so, if he had the choice now, he wouldn't take it. He could have gone to Wroxham's party last night or even all week without your father knowing. We invited him to come with us, imagining he would be desperate to escape the bonds of marriage even for a short time, but he said no. None of us could fathom it. But then, none of us are in love."

Aurelia frowned. "If you understood about love, you would never have invited him to go in the first place."

"I assure you that I am ashamed of my behavior. I can never atone for the grief I've caused you." He stood and paced across the room, turning his hat about by the brim. "But I'll go looking for your husband and return him to you, I swear it. I have an idea where he might be found."

She stood to join him at the window. "I've been watching all day. What if something happened to him?"

"Nothing's happened. I'll send him right home, and then I'll be off for London." He paused in the act of pocketing his handkerchief, and offered it to her. "Will you need it anymore?"

"I have others." She made herself smile, only because he looked so bereft. "Just please bring my husband back to me. We must endeavor to sort ourselves out."

"I'm certain you'll manage it. Since you've been at Townsend's side, I've seen a strength and steel within you that I never knew existed. Despite the rather distressing history between us, I would be honored to count you as a friend, if you can bear to put our pasts behind us."

Aurelia only thought for a moment before she nodded. "Of course we can be friends. I don't harbor romantic feelings toward you any longer. I have changed, you see."

He gave a small bow, along with a genuine smile. "I admire you for casting your misguided yearnings aside. I'm a devil of a fellow, I assure you, and I pity the woman who'll have to marry me. Pardon my language."

"Perhaps this unpleasant episode will spur you to lead a better life. Perhaps that is how you must atone. You shouldn't continue to dally with your gentlemen friends, and tempt my husband to do bad things. You are far too fine a person to linger at dissolute parties and consort with loose women."

He blinked at her rather cross scolding. "Am I?"

"Yes. I have always believed you are. You're handsome and polite, and very respected in Parliament. You've practically raised Minette from a child, and she's delightful."

"Now you are baldly lying to me, my lady. Minette is a scamp."

"She is delightful," Aurelia repeated stubbornly. "Please tell her I miss her."

"I promise to do so." He began to draw on his gloves. "I hope you'll call on her when you and Townsend return to London. In the meantime, I shall do my best to find your absent husband and send him home. And once I do, dear Lady Townsend"—he took her hands and gave them a light squeeze—"the rest shall be up to you."

* * * * *

Hunter awakened to the not-so-gently prodding toe of a riding boot. He cracked his eyes to the harsh light of day and took in the room around him. Tables and a chaise, a rumpled bed, painted silk wallpaper. Some chamber at Wroxham's? He winced as his head gave a throb. He groaned against his pillow only to find it shifting from under him.

"That's a good girl, Big Bess," said a faraway voice. "Go find some other bed."

"I'll find a more comfortable one than the floor anyway," she said with good natured grumbling. "Will 'is lord be all right then?" She peered down at him. "Done nothing but cry upon me bosom all the night, much as I tried to steer him otherwise." She made a ribald gesture to the area between her generous thighs.

"Don't take offense, Bess." That was Arlington's voice now. "The man is rather enamored of his wife."

"Oh, poor thing."

As the woman moved away, Hunter's head fell back and hit the floor. He barked out a curse, stretched his aching limbs, and blinked up into Warren's hard features.

"If you nudge me again with your boot," Hunter growled, "I'll rip it off and shove it up your arsehole."

"Get up," Warren snapped back. "I want you on your feet before I lay you on your back, you pestilent son of a bitch."

Hunter slung an arm over his eyes. "I'm not getting up if you're only going to deck me. I can't get up anyway. My head's pounding."

"You're getting up, man." Warren put his hands on Hunter's disarranged collar and dragged him to his feet. Then, as promised, he socked him so hard in the face he went down again.

"You fiend," Hunter yelled. "Take yourself off to the devil." He opened one eye to find his assailant still glaring down at him. "I brought Aurelia here because she loves you, goddamn you. I'd do it again too. She's *my* wife. *Mine*."

"We all know that," said Warren in a cool voice. "And that lick wasn't for bringing her here. I'm a big boy and I can handle a bit of well-earned embarrassment. No, that was for hurting her afterward and making her cry."

Hunter turned on his side, probing his cheekbone, inspecting the damage after its run-in with Warren's fist. How pathetic he was, sprawled on the floor in this house of degeneracy. His stomach clenched in self-loathing. "I made Aurelia cry. I know." Then fury washed over him again. "How did *you* know?"

"I've just been to see her," Warren announced. "She's worried about you, so you need to bugger off home."

"You went to see *my wife*?" Despite the pain, despite the threat of Warren's fists, Hunter lurched to his feet ready to do murder. Arlington, the tiresome bastard, got in his way. "She's seen enough of you lately, hasn't she?" Hunter bellowed at Warren.

"Thanks to you, she's seen more of me than she ever should have. Now stop squawking and make yourself presentable, you bleeding arse."

"Why did you go see my wife?" Hunter demanded to know, as Arlington steadied him on his feet.

"I went to apologize."

"You stay away from her. Just stay away. She doesn't care for your apologies."

"Perhaps not," said Warren. "But I rather hoped you and I would stay friends when this little crisis of yours is over, and that means staying on good terms with your wife."

"*Staying on good terms*," Hunter mimicked bitterly. "Is that what you'll call it now? I'm sure she received you eagerly as soon as you showed up on the doorstep." He infused the word "received" with filthy connotation.

"I ought to blacken your other eye for that, but I fear it might cause Aurelia distress." Warren gave him a hard look. "For your wife's honor, I'll tell you that when she received me she did not so much as invite me to sit down. We exchanged words of polite apology and regret, and then she

179

started to cry over you. She's anxious to 'fix things.' She's also worried to death since you haven't come home."

The throb in his head turned to an ache. He collapsed into a nearby chair. "One of you bastards give me some water. Or more whiskey. Either one."

"No more whiskey for you," said Warren. "We'll have no more drunken-man-in-love antics."

Aurelia was worried. She wanted to fix things. She must still love him, at least a little, even after the things he'd done to her the night before. By sheer force of will, Hunter stood under his own power. His head spun for a moment, but a glass of water relieved the hot scratchiness in his throat. "I have to go home and see my wife. I have to make myself presentable. What did I do last night?" he asked, inspecting his person. He was still dressed, and relatively clean. "I only meant to have a drink."

"You had about ten drinks," said August as Hunter crossed to the wash basin. "Then Big Bess sat in your lap and you started crying, and you confessed to a regrettable amount of poor behavior while she patted you and murmured, *'That's all right, me lor', that's all right.'* Finally you passed out and fell from the chair, Bess on top of you. After we had a good laugh about it, we let you lie."

"Bugger the lot of you." Hunter had a horrible thought. During his drunken rambling, had he revealed all the sordid things he'd done to his wife? "Did I talk about Lady Townsend?" he asked.

They exchanged glances. "Only Big Bess knows what you talked about," said August. "And anyone who overheard was probably too drunk to remember."

"Pay attention, man. You're splashing water all over the place." Warren handed him a mostly-clean towel. "Don't worry about Big Bess. Worry about getting yourself home to the woman who loves you."

"Have to shave," Hunter said, scrutinizing his gaunt, scruffy visage in a nearby looking glass. "Arlington, can I borrow your razor?"

The man handed over his shaving things with a skeptical look. "Need any help?"

"I can do it myself," Hunter lathered his stubbled cheeks, then threw back his head and let out a groan. "Why did Aurelia ever agree to marry me? Why hasn't she left me by now? Why am I even here? Why did I come back to Wroxham's instead of staying with her?"

"Because you're a stupid arsehole?" asked August.

"Those were rhetorical questions," snapped Hunter.

"It was a rhetorical answer."

Hunter ignored his friend's mocking tone and applied himself to wielding Arlington's glinting razor. "How often does your man sharpen this thing?" he asked, thrusting his chin forward.

"Every day," said Arlington. "Doesn't yours?"

Hunter hissed as he nearly nicked himself beneath the chin.

"For God's sake. Be careful, would you?" said Warren. "I've promised Lady Townsend I'd get you home alive and in one piece." He wrestled the razor from Hunter and began to flick away his stubble with firm, smooth strokes. Hunter thought that if their situation was reversed, he'd be tempted to slice his friend's throat.

But Warren wasn't that sort of chap.

"I'm sorry," he said gruffly, closing his eyes. "I'm sorry for what I did to you, and her."

"I'm inclined to forgive you, only because I understand. I mean, I don't understand. I don't know this person you've turned into, but I know you make Lady Townsend happy, so I'll restrain myself from beating you to a bloody pulp."

Hunter was rather grateful for that as he regarded his bloodshot eyes in the glass. Warren hadn't left him with any bruises or black eyes to frighten Aurelia. Though he could have—and probably wanted to—his friend hadn't hit him with all his strength. Hunter used the towel to rub away the last of the shaving soap. "Thank you, Warren," he said, and he wasn't only thanking him for the shave.

Across the room, August and Arlington broke into appreciative applause.

"We've had apologies and peaceable grooming. It appears we shall all remain friends," said Arlington.

"Yes. All is forgiven," agreed August. "Right?"

"Wrong," said Hunter, collapsing in a nearby chair. "There's one more person who has to forgive me, and it's the person with the least reason to do so."

"Aw, Towns." August waved a hand. "Big Bess will forgive you. She's a hell of a gal."

Arlington punched the younger man on the arm. "He doesn't mean Big Bess, you idiot. He's talking about Lady Townsend."

"Oh."

A mood of gravity descended on the company. Arlington was the first to speak. "Judging by the way she looked at you when you emerged from the woods together that day, your wife cares for you very much. It was clear for anyone to see."

"That was before," said Hunter. "Last night, I...I was frustrated. She was upset about Warren, and I lost my temper. I said and did unpardonable things. I don't know how I'll face her when I get home."

"Might I suggest facing her on your knees, with apologies spouting from your lips? She's an understanding sort of person," said Warren. "If you had to fall in with the Doting Love-Shackle Brigade, I'm glad it was because of her, because I think she's worthy of all the angst you feel."

August rolled his eyes. "The Doting Love-Shackle Brigade. God save us."

Arlington chuckled, then nudged Hunter on the shoulder. "Go on then, Townsey. The longer you wait, the harder she'll be to face. You can borrow my horse, if Warren will go with you and bring it back again. Then the three of us will probably head back to town before we trouble your marriage any further."

Hunter looked at Warren. "Will you ride with me? I'm sorry for the way I've acted these few days. You've always been a good friend to me, whether I deserved it or not."

Warren clapped him on the back with a grin. "You don't deserve it, you tiresome bastard. But yes, I'll go. I promised to deliver you home to her, and that was almost two hours ago."

Chapter Seventeen: Danger, or Bliss

Aurelia awakened to the softly spoken prompt of her name. She sat up on the window seat to find her husband looking in at her, framed by the draperies. He was in breeches and shirtsleeves, and he looked every bit as woebegone as she felt.

"When I first saw you curled up in the window seat in London," he said in a soft voice, "you seemed too beautiful for words. Certainly too beautiful to belong to me."

"Oh." She remembered that moment. It seemed so long ago. "I was hiding there from you."

The smallest quiver of a smile touched his lips. "I knew you were hiding. I didn't blame you then and I don't blame you now." The smile went away, and he looked so sad. "I need to apologize and explain, and beg for forgiveness, but I don't think I deserve it, so I don't really know what to say. May I come in, Aurelia? Please?"

He had never asked for permission before. She granted it with a small gesture, since her throat felt too tight to speak. He ducked within the space and sat beside her.

"I wasn't hiding here," she said once she regained her voice. "I was watching for you at the window. I suppose I must have fallen asleep."

"I'm so sorry for what happened last night, darling, for the way I hurt and frightened you. How wrought up you must feel."

Tears gathered in her eyes. "A little."

"And then I left you alone. I thought you would want me to go. I didn't know what to do, how to face you. I didn't know how to explain what came over me. I felt angry and jealous, and impassioned by suspicions that weren't true. I'm not making excuses. God knows there's no excuse for treating you so roughly. For making you...cry."

She was very close to crying again. She wanted to break down sobbing, and hide her face in the soft pleats of his sleeve. "I was so worried," she finally managed to say. "I was afraid you'd never come back."

His hand covered hers on the bench between them, tentatively, as if he feared she might pull hers away. "I was afraid you wouldn't want me back. Aurelia, look at me."

She could hardly do it. But they had to speak now, just as she'd had to speak with Lord Warren earlier. She met his gaze with as much directness as she could, and then he spoke in a gentle, somber voice.

"I promise you, I'll never behave in such a way again. My idiotic accusations—how I hate myself for them now. I know you've never encouraged Warren, and that you've resigned yourself completely to our marriage."

She couldn't bear to hear him say it that way. "I haven't resigned myself to anything, Hunter. I came to love you."

"Do you still love me?" His voice roughened with emotion. "Even a little? Please don't cry, my darling girl."

"I don't want to cry." She took her hand from his to press her fingers against her eyes. "I want everything to be sweet again, and comfortable between us, the way it was."

"I want that too. I'll do anything to regain your trust."

"Just don't frighten me so." She reached out to him and buried her tear-dampened face against his neck. His familiar scent and warmth enfolded her. Oh, she had been so afraid he was lost. "Don't leave me again. We have to trust each other, and have discussions about what we're feeling before things turn into a snarl. Don't you think so?"

"Yes. We must be open and honest with one another about everything."

"You should know Lord Warren was here," she said, drawing back from him. "I received him in the drawing room. Nothing untoward happened, I promise."

He brushed away her tears. "I know. I saw him and he told me." He cradled her head in his palm, then took her hand and pressed kisses to each of her knuckles, and then the sensitive underside of her wrist. She shivered, momentarily lost to sensation.

"You saw Lord Warren?" she asked when her thoughts cleared. "Where?"

"At Wroxham's estate." He paused in his tender ministrations and looked up at her. "Nothing untoward happened, I promise. Just an unfortunate amount of drunken self-recrimination. Aurelia, forgive me for the terrible things I said to you last night, and the things I did. For my rude and petty jealousies, and my unconscionable attempt to force you. I know I don't deserve your forgiveness, but I'm asking it anyway. I'm so unworthy of you."

"No, that's not true."

He turned her face to kiss her forehead, and both her eyes. He pressed a kiss to her temple and slid his lips down to her ear. "I'm afraid it is true, little grasshopper. If I were a better man, I wouldn't shame you the way I do. I'd let you go. I'd let you live away from me."

The idea horrified her. "I don't want to live away from you. Please, Hunter, I love you. I love *you*. You must believe I care nothing for Lord Warren or anyone else, not since we have each other."

"I know. I understand that now."

"And I've said that I'll do whatever I must to make you happy."

His hand squeezed more tightly around hers. "But you shouldn't have to. Damn it, I should have more self-control. I want to give you a respectable marriage. I want to treat you like the lady you are, not my erotic concubine."

She pursed her lips, feeling a wave of irritation. "I've spent a lot of time learning how to be your 'erotic concubine' and now you say you want to treat me like a lady?"

He frowned back at her. "My dear, I practiced that speech an entire hour on the way here. I did a great amount of soul searching and decided I must treat you with more respect."

"I don't want more respect," she argued. "I want you." She stared down at his strong thighs, his big hands that had brought her as much pleasure as pain. She looked into his eyes that could be dark and brooding, but also kind and affectionate. She wanted all of him, the darkness and the light.

"When I met you, I was only half a person," she said. "I was prim and distant and so closed up. You might have come to hate me, but instead you tried to make me happier. I know it wasn't easy. I fought you, and I fought my feelings until you gave me no choice but to relent, to play, to smile, to become fully opened to life for the first time." She paused, holding her husband's gaze. "It was important to you to help me be happy. How could I do anything less for you?" She took her hands from his and threw her arms around his neck, insinuating herself against his strong, masculine form. "I didn't love you at first, but now I do. By God, I do. I couldn't live without you, as maddening and perverse as you are."

He relaxed by slow degrees, resting his head against hers. "I believe that is the most lovely thing any person has ever said to me." He massaged her back, her nape, holding her so close her breath crowded her lungs. "Aurelia, I want to be happy, but only if you're happy too. Only if you can forgive me for the ways I've hurt you."

"I forgive you," she said with all the feeling in her heart. "When you left last night, I didn't know what you would do. I thought you might never come back, and I thought about a life without you, and..." She pressed her cheek to his, swallowing back a sob. "I would be happy if you would never, ever leave my side again."

She felt him draw in a sharp breath. "Don't fret anymore, my darling. Please." He wound his fingers in her hair and pulled her closer still. She eased her hips against him, clinging to his broad shoulders. His sharp breath became a gasp. "If you don't take care, this tender moment shall become a much less tender moment and a rather more carnal moment."

She hummed softly, caressing the tense, bunched muscles at his neck. "Somehow you manage to be tender and carnal at once. It's one of the things I love most about you."

"Aurelia, I warn you that you're very much in danger." To clarify, he arched his hips against her. She thrilled at the thickness of his arousal.

"Danger, or bliss?" she whispered to drive him on.

"How naughty you are," he whispered back, "to transform my selfless pledges of respectability into an erotic tryst."

"The first night of our marriage, you were angry at me for resisting. Now you're angry at me for being too eager."

"Not angry. But I spanked you that night for resisting me. Perhaps I should spank you now for not resisting me enough."

Aurelia burst into laughter at his now-familiar piratical expression. "You'd spank me for absolutely any reason, and we both know it. For blinking too many times in a minute. For breathing. For wearing the color blue."

"For mocking your husband," he said, pulling her down over his lap. His hands were gentle but firm as they arranged her, arse up. He spanked her once over her skirts and Aurelia felt an immediate surge of pleasure.

"What a tyrant you are," she said. "It always comes down to another spanking."

"As it should."

"I suppose I should simply wear backless gowns and petticoats so you can spank me all the time, whenever you wish, without battling all that fabric."

He stopped in the act of drawing up her voluminous skirts. "My goodness. What a capital idea. How very provocative that would be, especially when we went out in society."

She let out a scandalized gasp as he landed a bare-bottomed spank. "I meant, of course, that I should wear such an outfit when we were in private, alone together."

"What would be the fun of that?" At her outraged snort he spanked her again. "You could start a trend, my love. All the fine ladies' bottoms exposed for whenever discipline is warranted. As an added bonus, we would all know which wives had recently been chastised, and gossip about the reasons why."

She squirmed as his hand walloped her tender cheeks. "But there isn't always a reason why, as in our case. *Ouch!* Must you be so severe during a playful spanking?"

"Are you trying to tell me how to spank you?" he asked, raising a brow.

"No, my lord," she said quickly, lest severe turn to wretchedly painful. "But I am still tender from that switching."

He paused to trace over the lingering welts, then spanked her directly on top of them so she wriggled over his lap.

"Oww, please... I'm not trying to direct you, but is this degree of spanking entirely necessary?"

"I thought you said I made you happy," he teased. "And yes, it is."

She gave a little moan of terror and happiness, and of all the other things he made her feel. Before she could quite figure out what those things were, he'd pulled her up and drawn her astride his thighs.

"Now you shall have a little ride, my sweet, on a very well-endowed stallion."

"I'm not an exemplary horsewoman, I'm afraid."

He undid the flaps of his breeches in jerky movements, and positioned his swollen cock between her thighs. "No, but you're an exemplary erotic concubine, aren't you?"

She thrilled to the feeling of her husband's thick length pressing within her. Within moments, she was stuffed full of him to the hilt.

"Oh, Hunter," she whispered. "It feels so much better than the spanking."

He chuckled and gripped her buttocks, then smacked each one so hard that she clenched around his cock. "I wonder if you'll like it along with a spanking."

Oh. *Oh.* She clung to his shoulders, bracing for his favored pairing of pleasure with pain. When she tried to move up and down on his cock, he grasped her hips.

"No, naughty girl. I'm going to make you come like this, with me inside you, still."

She gawked at him, thinking such a thing would never be possible, but even as he said it, her walls clamped around him and she became even more aware of his presence inside her body, stretching her wide. He spanked her left cheek and she clamped even harder.

Ohhh...

Next her right, then her left again. Each time he spanked her, she arched against him, contacting his pelvis with her most sensitive place. He paused in the spanking to tug at the back of her gown, loosening it. "Pull down your bodice," he ordered. "Take out your breasts and offer them to me."

She swallowed hard at the sensual authority in his tone and did as he asked. When he lowered his lips to suck at her nipples, she threw her head back and almost fell off his lap. He braced his feet upon the opposite bench, bending his legs so she was forced down into the curve of his hips. His cock delved even deeper as she pulsed around the thick intrusion.

He alternated spanking her and toying with her nipples, drawing them into pebbled peaks. Whenever she tried to reach for him, he spanked her harder and reminded her she was to be offering him her breasts, and so she'd be forced to cup them toward him for more torment.

"You are going to kill me like this," she pleaded, as an aching heat grew within her. "Please move inside me. Please, I want to feel you move."

"No," he said in a kind but inexorable tone. "Feel me inside you. Feel how I fill up your juicy, hot pussy. Feel how I inhabit you. For now, that's all you're getting, naughty girl."

"Tyrant," she whimpered, gazing at him in unfocused lust.

Hunter had every intention of letting her come, but he also had every intention of making her suffer for a while first. Not because he thought she'd been naughty, as he teased, but because he adored her reactions when he made her endure particularly lascivious things, and there was nothing more lascivious than resting inside her, thick and hard, and making her beg for more.

God, how he loved her for putting up with him.

When he had felt her tears against his neck, it was as if they entered his veins and coursed throughout his entire body, healing the last scars of his heart. She was crying for him, emotional for him.

She was happy with him.

It seemed a miracle. He would always value her love, but he thought he valued her happiness more. When she smiled, his entire world was painted in new colors. And when she whimpered...well.

That did something else to him altogether.

He spanked her, biting back gasps as each spank resulted in a tensing jerk at his cock. What a magnificent new activity to add to their repertoire. Between spanks, he teased and laved her nipples with his tongue, biting down now and again so that she squeezed around him even harder. He would have loved to do this for hours, spanking and caressing her and feeling her bear down around his organ, but he wasn't going to last more than a few minutes.

"How does that feel?" he asked, spanking her again. "How do you feel, Aurelia?"

"I feel...at your mercy," she gasped, still holding her luscious breasts. "I feel as if I'm going to explode."

Did she have any idea that he felt the same way? His hips began to move against her in slow, measured increments. Her breath shuddered. She reached for him, but he made a warning sound.

"What are your instructions?"

"Oh please," she cried. "Please let me hold you."

He moved in her a little more. "You are holding me. Quite satisfactorily, I might add." He fastened his lips over each nipple, exploring and sucking until she jerked against him. "Come for me, little grasshopper. My wonderful good luck charm. I want to feel you come."

He caught her moans, drank them up in an encompassing kiss as he gave her a few final spanks and then clasped her against him. She wriggled and squeezed so expertly that he was hard pressed not to shoot inside her at once. He could see the signs of her impending climax, her stuttering pants, her wild gaze.

"Come for me," he ordered, pulling her down harder upon his rod in quick, blunt jerks. "My beautiful love. My naughty wife."

"Ohhh," she cried, her exclamation resounding in the curtained window seat. She shuddered, fondling her breasts, bucking on his cock. Her walls clamped him in a rippling, delicious pressure.

He went off at once with a guttural groan, pressing her down so hard on his cock he worried he might injure her. But she only smiled and laughed with pure pleasure. He would always remember the first time he'd heard her laugh, the short, guilty burst of merriment when he'd flipped his fork into his forehead. To hear her laugh now with such abandon—as he gave her a rough rogering, no less—it made him feel replete.

When she collapsed against him, he held her hard, basking in her scent and her voluptuous femininity. *She loves me*, he thought. *And she accepts me just as I am.*

He pulled her head back, threading his fingers through her hair, and gave her a deep, forceful kiss, communicating all the eager love he felt. "I don't know what I ever did to deserve such happiness," he murmured against her lips.

"Well, that's simple. You gave happiness in return, and taught me how to feel it too." She paused, gazing up at him. "I did make you happy just now, didn't I?"

He burst into his own merry laughter. "I think the answer to that is obvious, you little imp. Quite obvious." He moved his still-hard cock within her sheath.

Her eyes went wide. "Oh my."

"Oh my, indeed. I believe I could go again, if you're up for another ride, Lady Townsend."

Over the sound of her soft giggles, he heard hoof beats in the courtyard. Not one horse, but a team, and the rattle of a coach. "What the devil?"

He shifted without disengaging her from his lap, so they could both look out the window. A grand, gilded traveling carriage wound around the front entryway led by a team of four, with two groomsmen at the front and two at the rear. They wore gleaming white and gold livery and smart red caps that matched the horses' harnesses. He squinted at the ornate coat of arms on the side of the carriage. "Who would be coming to visit us at this hour? Do you recognize the crest?"

"Yes," said Aurelia with a soft moan. "I recognize it well. That's my father's carriage. I think we'd better save the ride for another time."

Hunter thought his wife was probably right about that. "Bloody hell," he said, lifting her from his cock and helping her to her feet. He had the distinct feeling this wasn't going to be a friendly visit.

Apparently the Duke of Lansing's sphere of influence spread to the country shires after all.

Chapter Eighteen: Happiness

A footman tapped at the door a few moments after they'd made themselves presentable, and handed Hunter a note. He flicked it open and scanned the contents.

"My lady, your father the duke awaits us downstairs in the front drawing room." He turned back to his wife, watching the way she threaded her fingers together. "Everything will be fine, my love. You remain here while I meet with your father. Clement can help you compose your appearance, and stay with you until—"

"No," said Aurelia. "I won't let you face him alone."

"But it's undoubtedly my head he wishes to gnaw off."

"He shall have to gnaw my head off too then."

"Really, all this talk of heads being gnawed off," he muttered under his breath.

"I believe you mentioned it first. Ah, here is Clement."

The lady's maid had spent many years in the Lansing household but her loyalties lay solely with her mistress. She moved into the room with brisk efficiency. "We'll have you ready in no time," she assured Aurelia. "And then you can go down on your husband's arm."

Hunter squeezed his wife's hand and took himself off, leaving her in the woman's capable care. He went to his rooms down the hall and had his valet freshen his appearance, and put on a newly pressed waistcoat and coat. His man configured a flawless, starched cravat knot within half a minute, which was one of the reasons Hunter paid him so well. After a quick glance in his looking glass, he met his wife outside her door. She looked pale and tense, the very image of the woman he'd married, the woman who had spent her early life under a tyrant's hand.

"What if he's here to take me away from you?" she asked.

"He won't."

"But what if he tries? He's very powerful."

Hunter placed a finger atop her lips. "No one is powerful enough to take you away from me. I'd never allow it. I'd fight him until my dying breath." He moved his finger and pressed a kiss to her mouth instead. The rough embrace gentled to a tender exploration, and then he pulled away and smiled down at her. "Trust me. Everything will be well."

He truly believed that, but he still proceeded with some trepidation toward the drawing room. The Duke of Lansing sat ramrod straight on a chair in the center of the room, attended by their household butler and his own stone-faced valet.

Aurelia stopped a few steps into the room and dropped a low curtsy as her father rose from his seat. "Papa. You should have said you were coming. What a joy to welcome you to our home."

Her father screwed up a look that was not quite a smile and held out a hand to his daughter. "Come and give me a kiss, dear Aurelia."

It pained Hunter to watch their stilted interaction, to include the air kiss she bestowed upon his jowled cheek. He determined then and there that he would be the exact opposite sort of father, and tumble about with his sons *and* his daughters, and greet them always with smothering hugs.

"Now," the duke said in a commanding tone. "You must run along and leave me alone to talk with your husband."

Aurelia took a couple steps back, but then stopped. "Anything you wish to say to my husband, you can say to me as well. We keep no secrets from one another."

At that, the duke's eyebrows snapped together in an almost comical fashion. Lansing scowled at Aurelia, but she held her ground, much to Hunter's satisfaction. It was time for him to enter the fray. He moved toward Lansing in a manner of exaggerated ease. "Will you have some refreshments, Your Grace? We are not quite to the dinner hour."

"I want no refreshments," he said gruffly, sitting down again. Hunter led Aurelia to a nearby divan and settled beside her. Lansing glared at both of them. "I want a word with you alone, Townsend. Send your wife away."

Your wife. Not his daughter? Hunter took her hand. "As my wife already informed you, anything you have to say can be said in her presence."

"Not this." The duke glowered again at Aurelia. "It is impertinent to remain when you've been asked to leave."

"I wish her to stay." This time, Hunter's reply was edged in steel. "Say what you must say. I assume from your demeanor this is not a friendly call."

"I wish it were a friendly call," the man blustered, "but your continued disgraceful activities preclude it from being so."

"Papa," Aurelia said sharply. "I do not think—"

Hunter held up his free hand, the one not clasped in Aurelia's. "Let him speak, my love."

"You call my daughter your 'love,'" the duke sniffed. "It pains me to see such guile. My dearest Aurelia, I have it on the most confident word that your husband recently attended a debauched event in the company of low companions."

"The masquerade at Lord Wroxham's estate?" she asked. "I know he attended that event, because I was with him."

Lansing's brows snapped even tighter, and a flush spread across his face. Hunter imagined those brows tangling into a squirming knot and almost dissolved in laughter. Instead he squeezed his wife's hand and somehow managed to keep a straight face.

"There is so little to do out here in the country," Hunter said. "You must forgive us the occasional masquerade ball."

"I am very disappointed in you." The duke directed this remark to his daughter. "A masquerade such as the one your husband attended is no place for a well-bred lady."

194

"I assure you I was not the only well-bred lady there."

"That is not my point." The duke banged the tip of his cane against the floor.

Hunter regarded him with warning in his gaze. "I would ask you not to take that tone of reprimand with my wife."

"How about I take it with you then?" the duke barked. "What do you mean, taking my daughter to such a licentious gathering, particularly in the company of your no-good friends?"

"What do I mean?" Hunter repeated the duke's words in an equally hard voice. "Perhaps I'm trying to make up for a decided lack of fun in her childhood. Perhaps I enjoy seeing her smile and make merry. Perhaps she demanded to go."

"Never. Not my Aurelia. She was taught right from wrong."

"She was taught to see impropriety and dissolution everywhere, even when it didn't exist. She was taught that laughter was offensive, and smiling unladylike, no doubt by you."

"The Lansing line has always been ruled by propriety. So was the Lockridge line until you came along, a bitter disappointment to the parents who gave you life, who depend on you to maintain the family's honor—"

"Stop, Papa. Please." Aurelia came to her feet and glared at her imposing sire. "I'll not allow you to say such things to my husband. I'll not allow you to insult him here in our home."

"I am trying to make him stop insulting *you*, daughter. He's insulting your honor and the honor of our family."

"No," she said, holding up her hands. "You've interfered enough. How could you know he was at Wroxham's masquerade? How many spies are doing your bidding? You cannot continue to monitor his behavior as if he were your child. He's a grown man. You must call off your informants and respect his privacy."

"Don't you want a civil, kind husband?"

Aurelia turned back to Hunter and placed a hand on his shoulder. "I do have a civil, kind husband, and I trust him completely. He has a care for my happiness, which you never did."

Hunter wanted to pull her into his lap and kiss her. He would have, except that it would disprove her claim that he was civilized, and Lansing looked rather on the edge of a major apoplexy.

"Your daughter has the right of it," he said instead. "You must let us make our own way. Perhaps your interference has served some purpose, but I assure you, Your Grace, that it is no longer necessary. I have been reformed of my hellion ways."

"How can you say so?" he said. "I have it on authority that Wroxham's party was the very vilest of routs. Are both of you so mired in depravity that you consider such activities mere country amusements?"

"We are not mired in anything but wedded love," said Hunter. He looked hard at the duke, infusing each word with stern import. "I am deeply in love with your daughter. Her happiness is my entire world. So you may believe I would do nothing to threaten it. Not now, not ever."

"Yes, Papa. So call off your spies," Aurelia added with such heat that Hunter finally cracked a smile.

"There, there, my dear," he chided softly. "He is still your father. You mustn't be disrespectful. He was trying to protect you."

"I don't need his protection any longer."

He leaned closer, so Lansing couldn't hear him. "Naughty Aurelia. Remember that disrespectful girls get spanked."

She gave a little snort of a giggle through her nose, then both of them were laughing like children, muffling their merriment with their hands. The duke stared at them as if they'd taken leave of their senses, which perhaps they had.

"Your mother will be greatly disappointed to learn of these changes in you," he said, wagging a finger at Aurelia.

His wife lifted her chin. "I'll be mother to my own children soon. I'm a married woman, for goodness sake. I think it's high time she let me grow up and be my own person. You too, Papa."

Mother to my own children, she had said. His children.

Their children.

Hunter gazed at his wife with unbridled adoration. She wasn't a mouse anymore, and what a fierce, wonderful mother she'd be.

"My dearest love," he said, taking her in his arms. "You are brilliant." He kissed her hard, caressing her belly where, perhaps, a child already grew. He was so charmed by the idea, he barely noted his father-in-law's outraged gasp. The stodgy old aristocrat struggled to his feet.

"If you must engage in such amorous displays," he growled, "then I will not discommode you by staying for dinner."

"Thank God," Hunter whispered against her lips. Then he straightened and said, "I'm sorry to hear it. But you'll be eager to relay news of our marital contentment to Her Grace, and Lord and Lady Severin, who are very fond of Aurelia."

The duke grumbled that he would certainly do so and then tottered out, clacking his cane against the floor. His valet followed with a dismissive sniff. The carriage was brought round with great alacrity, and after exchanging farewells, they waved the duke on his way.

"Well," said Hunter, gazing down at his spitfire of a wife. "That went well."

She burst into laughter. "It did not go well, but I hardly expected it to."

"It *did* go well," he insisted, scooping her up in his arms. "At long last you put Papa Lansing in his place, and I don't think he'll soon forget it. Nor will I, my ferocious little grasshopper."

She shrieked and held tight to his neck. "Hunter! Put me down before you drop me."

"Drop you? Never. That would be an ungentlemanly thing to do."

She arched a brow. "And you've never been ungentlemanly?"

"Naughty girl," he murmured. "The only place I'll be dropping you is over my lap for a lengthy spanking."

She blushed a very becoming shade of pink. "Another spanking? I've already had one today."

"But we got a bit distracted in the process, didn't we?"

Her hand slid down to rest over his heart. "In the most pleasurable of ways."

He groaned, carrying her through the great front doors and up the stairs. "I believe I still owe you a ride, wife. A neck-or-nothing gallop. We'll make a skilled horsewoman of you yet."

"Of course. It's just a matter of proper training." She clung to his shoulders, her lips curved in a seductive grin. "And you, Lord Townsend, are very good at that."

THE END

A Final Note

Before I got into bondage and BDSM, I was into spanking, which exists in its own intimate, playful, and imaginative corner of the power exchange universe. I owe a great depth of gratitude to the folks at ShadowLane.com. I used to mail-order naughty and wonderful spanking material from them, and I placed my first personal ad (via snail mail!) in a Shadow Lane directory. It's been an amazing pleasure to get back in touch with my spanko side and have some fun writing these naughty heroines and stern heroes. If this is your first spanking romance, I hope you found it warm, wicked, and fun.

I also hope you'll want to read the rest of the Properly Spanked series. There are three more books set in this world: *To Tame A Countess* (Warren's story), *My Naughty Minette* (August's story), and *Under A Duke's Hand* (Arlington's story). Be sure to go to annabeljoseph.com and sign up for my newsletter so you'll be in the loop for upcoming releases. You can also follow me on Twitter (@annabeljoseph) or find me on Facebook and shoot me a friend request.

Many thanks to my trusty beta readers Tasha, Linzy, Janine, Doris, and GC, and my editors, Lina and Audrey. They give the best kind of criticism—the kind that makes my books better. Thanks also to my beloved Annabel's Army, both official and unofficial, and all those readers who review and promote my books. I will never be able to say it enough: you make everything worth it, and I'm more grateful than words can express.

Coming Soon: To Tame A Countess, the second story in the Properly Spanked series

The Earl of Warren never considered himself the heroic type—or the marrying type. Unfortunately, while attempting to save the mysterious Lady Maitland from the clutches of a degenerate fortune hunter, he ends up shackled to her himself.

It was never in the plans, and worse, his bride doesn't want him. Rather than feel grateful, Josephine begs to be released from the marriage so she can accomplish her dearest goal—to be left alone. Troubled by an unconventional childhood, scarred by painful memories, Josephine acts out until Warren has no choice but to begin a disciplinary program to bring her to heel.

Although his spankings are firm, painful, and plentiful, he makes little progress in taming his wild countess. But her wildness pleases him in the bedroom, where they spend hours at uninhibited play, fulfilling licentious and carnal lusts. While Josephine struggles to understand her feelings toward her authoritative husband, Warren must decide if having a tame wife is worth the anguish of damaging her already vulnerable heart.

If you liked Training Lady Townsend, you'll also enjoy Disciplining the Duchess by Annabel Joseph

Over five seasons, Miss Harmony Barrett has managed to repel every gentleman of consequence and engineer a debacle at Almack's so horrifying that her waltzing privileges are revoked. If she's not in the library reading about Mongol hordes, she's embarrassing her family or getting involved in impulsive scrapes.

Enter the Duke of Courtland, a man known for his love of duty and decorum. Through a vexing series of events, he finds himself shackled to Miss Barrett in matrimony. But all is not lost. The duke harbors a not-so-secret affinity for spanking and discipline...and his new wife is ever in need of it. Will the mismatched couple find their way to marital happiness? Or will the duke be forever *Disciplining the Duchess*?

This 85K word erotic romance novel contains domestic discipline themes and both harsh and loving spanking scenes.

Also Available: The Cirque Masters series by Annabel Joseph

Enter a world where performers' jaw-dropping strength, talent, and creativity is matched only by the decadence of their kinky desires. Cirque du Monde is famous for mounting glittering circus productions, but after the Big Top goes dark, you can find its denizens at *Le Citadel*, a fetish club owned by Cirque CEO Michel Lemaitre—where anything goes. This secret world is ruled by dominance and submission, risk and emotion, and a fearless dedication to carnal pleasure in all its forms. Love in the circus can be as perilous as aerial silks or trapeze, and secrets run deep in this intimate society. Run away to the circus, and soar with the Cirque Masters—a delight for the senses, and for the heart.

The Cirque Masters series is:
#1 *Cirque de Minuit* (Theo's story)
#2 *Bound in Blue* (Jason's story)
#3 *Master's Flame* (Lemaitre's story)

The Comfort series by Annabel Joseph

Have you ever wondered what goes on in the bedrooms of Hollywood's biggest heartthrobs? In the case of Jeremy Gray, the reality is far more depraved than anyone realizes. Brutal desires, shocking secrets, and a D/s relationship (with a hired submissive "girlfriend") that's based on a contract rather than love. It's just the beginning of a four-book saga following Jeremy and his Hollywood friends as they seek comfort in fake, manufactured relationships. Born of necessity—and public relations—these attachments come to feel more and more real. What does it take to live day-to-day with an A-list celebrity? Patience, fortitude, and a whole lot of heart. Oh, and a very good pain tolerance for kinky mayhem.

The Comfort series is:
#1 *Comfort Object* (Jeremy's story)
#2 *Caressa's Knees* (Kyle's story)
#3 *Odalisque* (Kai's story)
#4 *Command Performance* (Mason's story)

About the Author

Annabel Joseph is a multi-published BDSM romance author. She writes mainly contemporary romance, although she has been known to dabble in the medieval and Regency eras. She is known for writing emotionally intense BDSM storylines, and strives to create characters that seem real—even flawed—so readers are better able to relate to them. Annabel also writes vanilla (non-BDSM) erotic romance under the pen name Molly Joseph.

Annabel loves to hear from her readers at annabeljosephnovels@gmail.com.

14575587R00114

Printed in Great Britain
by Amazon.co.uk, Ltd.,
Marston Gate.